W9-AAP-693

Praise for *Mary Clay's*
DAFFODILS* Mysteries

(*Divorced And Finally Free Of Deceitful, Insensitive, Licentious Scum)

"Witty and hilarious..."
Midwest Book Review

"Much charm and promise ... a crisp pace
with plenty of humor ..."
Romantic Times BookClub

"*The Ya Ya Sisterhood* meets *The First Wives Club.*
A cleverly done light mystery that's a rare find ..."
The Examiner (Beaumont, Texas)

"The Turtle Mound Murder is a solid first mystery
[that] is light and accentuated with the familiar
mannerisms of Southern women. ... A fun book."
Southern Halifax Magazine

Cole Slaw Wrestling

Sun shining brightly, early afternoon, we were going to cole slaw wrestling. Imagine, women wallowing around in shredded cabbage! I wondered if they used real dressing and if it was any good. I normally bought my slaw because I'd never been able to make a decent sauce. Maybe the Cabbage Patch bottled and sold theirs: *Official Bike Week Cole Slaw Dressing.* Considering my record, I'd give it a try.

The new contestants were unusually vocal and evenly matched, making it impossible not to watch. Coated from head to toe in slaw, they rolled in the mush, clawing for dominance. A roar went up from the crowd as someone's halter was flung aside. A few minutes later, a thong bikini went flying.

It was difficult to tell who was getting the upper hand in that roiling pit of flailing limbs and curses. Even the referee seemed overwhelmed until the pantiless contestant landed a punch to her opponent's stomach. Foul!

The referee waded into the slimy fray and tried to separate the women. Bare Butt was obviously not happy with his decision and took a roundhouse swipe at the referee. He dodged the blow and fell backward onto the other woman. Egged on by whoops and hollers, the Bare Butt Wonder jumped from the pit and went into a primal victory dance. That's when a man wearing a Security shirt appeared. He ushered Bare Butt toward us, while the referee and other contestant struggled to get out of the pit.

Bare Butt continued her wild antics even as she was being hosed off, finally bending forward toward the crowd and ripping off her bra. I gasped. Ruthie yelped. The lady's boobs were tattooed with flowers. It was Red.

That's when things went crazy. "Well, if it isn't Bubble Head and Molly." Red grabbed a towel from someone, which she wrapped around her waist and headed our way. ... She pointed at Penny Sue. "I've got bone to pick with you."

A DAFFODILS* MYSTERY
**Divorced And Finally Free Of Deceitful,
Insensitive, Licentious Scum*

Bike Week Blues

Wishing you smooth roads &
sunny skies

Mary Clay

A DAFFODILS* MYSTERY
*Divorced And Finally Free Of Deceitful,
Insensitive, Licentious Scum

Bike Week Blues

Mary Clay

An if Mystery
An Imprint of Inspirational Fiction
New Smyrna Beach, Florida

All Rights Reserved. No part of this book may be reproduced or transmitted in any form or by any means, graphic, electronic, or mechanical, including photocopying, recording, taping or by any information storage or retrieval system, without permission in writing from the publisher.

Published by Inspirational Fiction

P. O. Box 2509

New Smyrna Beach, FL 32170-2509

www.inspirationalfiction.com

Cover Design: Peri Poloni, www.knockoutbooks.com

Quotations from *The Book of Answers* by Carol Bolt
reprinted by permission of Hyperion. Copyright 1999 Carol Bolt

This is a work of fiction. All places, names, characters and incidents are either invented or used fictitiously. The events described are purely imaginary.

Copyright © 2004 Linda Tuck-Jenkins

ISBN: 0-9710429-7-7

Library of Congress Control Number: 2003116959

Printed in the United States of America

For Joe Tuck and Mildred & Harry Jenkins

Like most authors, I benefited from the suggestions and knowledge of generous friends and colleagues. Kelly Armstrong, Donna Austin, Cathy Edwards, Beverly Poitier-Henderson, Chris Jenkins, Donna Lavallee, Deborah Mallard, Chris Miller, Anna Marini, and Carolena, Frances, and John Saccone—thank you!

A deep bow, also, to Kathryn Ptacek, a wonderful writer and editor.

Hats off to the fine establishments of New Smyrna Beach that were so supportive in the writing of this story: Chris' Place, Gilly's Pub 44, J.B.'s Fish Camp, Marine Discovery Center, Norwoods, and The Riverview Hotel, Restaurant & Spa. A very special thanks to Sheri Smith as well as the entire staff of New Smyrna Harley-Davidson for infinite patience and good humor, particularly Guy Gallegos, Paul Klingele, Lowell Penning, Randy Russell, and Steve Shay.

Finally, to the ladies who contributed sayings used in the book—Sherry Brinkley and Shirley White—you're a credit to the Southern tradition!

The absurdity of reality is comical.

Humor interprets life in such a way you can handle it without reverting to the lower levels of grief, fear, anger, and pride.

David R. Hawkins, M.D., Ph.D.

Chapter 1

"Duck—a bombing run!"

Penny Sue's screech pierced me like a dagger. I yelped and bolted from my chair, sloshing coffee down the front of my robe.

"Cover your drink!"

I turned slowly to face Penny Sue, my terry cloth robe steaming in the cool morning air. She stood in the doorway of the beachfront condo, staring up at a V-formation of pelicans flying south from their feeding grounds at Ponce Inlet. Locals dubbed the birds B-52s for their annoying habit of gorging on fish parts at northern marinas, then lazily sailing down the coast ... relieving themselves willy-nilly. No doubt, the birds were the inspiration for the Predator drones the CIA used to hone in on terrorists with missiles and smart bombs. Nothing was safe from the pelicans' foul, fishy projectiles. Penny Sue discovered as much back in college. A group from the sorority was on the deck, where I now stood dripping coffee, when pelicans passed overhead. Bamm! A big splat on Penny

Sue's head that slopped into her wine; hence, the dictum: "Cover your drink!"

Dabbing at the Colombian droplet on my chin, I stared at Penny Sue. "Cover my drink?" I motioned to the stain on my robe. "It's a little late for that. Geez, Penny Sue, I was meditating. You scared me to death."

She pursed her lips. "I know that. You had your head tilted back and your eyes closed. Why do you think I said something? If I hadn't been here, you might have gotten a nasty load right in the face."

"What in the world is going on?" Ruthie, wearing nothing but a bath towel and a look of fright, appeared in the doorway.

"A bombing run," Penny Sue replied over her shoulder. "If I hadn't said something, Leigh would have gotten it right in the kisser." She brushed past Ruthie to the kitchen and returned with a roll of paper towels. She handed me a wad and ripped off a long strip that she dropped on the deck and patted with her toes. "You didn't burn yourself, did you?" she asked sheepishly.

My ire dissolved. It was hard to stay mad at a slightly chubby, middle-aged woman dressed in a pink silk kimono, whose hair looked like it had been chewed by a dog. "No harm done; the robe will wash. You startled me—that's all."

Besides, the condo belonged to Penny Sue's father, Judge Warren Parker, who'd graciously allowed me to use it after my house in Roswell, Georgia sold as a part of my divorce settlement. I'd been in Florida for a little over four months, gathering my wits and will to start life anew. New Smyrna Beach had turned out to be the perfect prescription for a trampled ego and broken heart. Of course, the stay got off to a rousing start when Penny Sue, Ruthie, and I were stalked, threatened, and kidnapped by an assortment of undesirables. Something like that puts your life in perspective. A two-timing husband seems trivial when you're stumbling over dead bodies.

Though I'd made new friends and found a part time job at the Marine Conservation Center, I was delighted to see my sorority sisters again. There's a certain comfort in being with old friends. You don't have to explain, sugar coat, or make excuses because you've been through most of the bad times together and love each other in spite of warts and blemishes. Not that any of us had real warts—a few zits, maybe, but certainly no crusty, virus laden skin eruptions.

Like the old joke about *men*struation and *men*opause, most of our troubles over the years involved men. Besides being college sorority sisters, Penny Sue Parker, Ruthie Nichols, and I—Rebecca Leigh Stratton—had one thing in common— we were all divorced. I was the newest member of our small, but growing, group called the DAFFODILS (Divorced And Finally Free Of Deceitful, Insensitive, Licentious Scum).

Ruthie's split came early—her ex was a two-timing, heartless cardiologist. Penny Sue'd been around the altar three times. Her first husband, Andy, was the well built, but dumb, captain of the football team. Her second, Sydney, was rich, artistic, and bisexual. The bisexual part didn't sit well with Judge Parker, who took that divorce very personally. Penny Sue is quite wealthy today as a result of the huge settlement she got from that parting. Her last, Winston, was the judge's choice. Daddy orchestrated that pairing, convinced Penny Sue didn't know a good man when she saw one. Apparently, Judge Daddy didn't, either. It was the judge himself who caught Winston in a compromising position with a legal assistant. Winston doesn't practice law in Georgia any more.

Despite her dismal track record, Penny Sue was always on the prowl for her *soul mate*, one of the reasons my friends had driven down from Atlanta two days earlier. Though Ruthie was in town to celebrate her birthday as well as attend a conference on Ayurveda, an ancient healing system from India, Penny Sue's motives, aside from the birthday, were romantic. Her newest love, Richard Wheeler, was a motorcycle enthusiast who'd come for Bike Week. He was staying at the Riverview Hotel, an ironic twist—and long story—considering our last visit. Naturally, Penny Sue had recommended the Riverview to Rich because it was close to our condo. After our last visit, she could also drive there blindfolded.

I had to say that this man looked promising. Recently widowed—his wife passed from cancer—Rich was a good-looking, gentle guy who seemed to genuinely care about Penny Sue. He also appeared fairly normal, in stark contrast to Penny Sue's prior loves, which is why I gave this relationship a chance. Though Penny Sue usually equated normal to average, emphatically insisting, *"I am not normal!"* (God's truth), an ordinary person was actually what she needed. According to Ruthie, our metaphysical expert, Penny Sue's Leo penchant for drama and the limelight meant stormy relationships with men whose egos were similarly inclined— the exact type she usually went after. A challenge thing, I suppose. But, this romance did, indeed, appear to be a match made in heaven. Penny Sue and Rich had been inseparable for the last two days, when she'd left early and come home late with smudged lipstick and a smile so wide her gums showed.

"Let me buy you another cup of coffee," Penny Sue said, a clear peace offering. Grinning, she nudged me with her elbow. "Watch this." She squinched her toes and lifted the paper towels she'd used to blot up the coffee spill. "Prehensile toes," she said smugly.

Like a monkey, I thought wryly. "I'll bet your blood is Rh positive."

Penny Sue wadded the paper into a ball. "Yeah. What does that have to do with anything?"

I motioned to her toes. "Rh stands for rhesus monkey."

Still standing in the doorway half-naked, Ruthie choked down a chortle.

Penny Sue curled her lip at me and huffed inside, stopping abruptly when she reached our friend. "What in the world is that smell?" She looked Ruthie up and down.

Ruthie backed away, pulling her bath towel tighter. "Sesame seed oil. Massaging with sesame oil is one of the best ways to balance the humors—you know, Pita, Vatta, and Kapha."

Penny Sue leaned forward and took another whiff. "Honey, I think your pita patta's outa whack-a."

"Not pita patta. Pita, Vatta. Come on, Penny Sue, this is serious. Ayurveda is an ancient science that dates back over 6000 years. Almost everyone would benefit from a sesame oil massage. The modern lifestyle, with fast travel, television, junk food, and computers all tend to cause a Vatta imbalance."

Penny Sue made a face. "If everyone smelled like that, we'd all have bad humors." She dashed behind the kitchen counter to avoid a swipe from Ruthie.

"You wash it off, silly. Which, I would have done, if you hadn't caused such a ruckus. I almost had a heart attack. The last time I heard Leigh scream like that, she'd tripped over a body."

Penny Sue hung her head with mock contrition. "You're right; I'd forgotten about that. Anyway, I was only kidding. Deepak Chopra recommends sesame oil massages, and you know how much I like him. Take your shower, and I'll make bagels with cream cheese and Jalapeño jelly. How's that?" A devilish grin stretched her lips. "Or, I could squeegee you off and do a stir fry."

It took everything I had to keep a straight face.

Ruthie shook her finger at Penny Sue. "You're awful. See if I help when you get sick. I won't lift a finger." She turned on her heel and headed for the shower.

I went to the bedroom to change out of my soggy robe. When I returned, I found a steaming cup of coffee and bagel waiting for me on the kitchen counter. I hopped on the stool and sipped the brew, watching Penny Sue smear cream cheese on more bagels. "What time did you get in?" I asked casually.

"Late," she said without looking up. I couldn't help but notice her chest heave in a satisfied sigh.

"I take it that things are going well with Rich?"

Penny Sue stopped what she was doing and smiled broadly. "He's the one, Leigh." Ruthie joined us at that moment. Penny Sue gave her a cup of coffee and set the plate of bagels on the counter. "Three husbands, lots of boyfriends, yet I've never met a man quite like Rich. He's kind and gentle and strong, but vulnerable."

Vulnerable. Penny Sue'd always had a weak spot for the underdog. In college she was constantly bringing stray cats, injured dogs, and troubled men back to the sorority house.

"How did you meet him?" I asked.

"Ruthie was with me the first time. We were having dinner at that new restaurant on Roswell Square. Rich was sitting alone at a table by the wall. He seemed so troubled, I couldn't take my eyes off him."

The fact that Rich was handsome in a rugged way, no doubt helped. He was about six feet tall, brown hair, with very green eyes. I'm sure Penny Sue's radar locked on him instantly.

She canted her head at Ruthie. "Our waitress told us he'd recently lost his wife and ate there a lot, always alone." She tittered. "Naturally, I started having dinner there more often. We eventually struck up a conversation and a friendship developed. Rich really loved his wife. Her death was quite a blow."

"How long has it been?" Ruthie asked.

"Over a year, I gather."

"What does he do for a living?"

"I'm not sure. He may have been with law enforcement or the courts in some fashion. He doesn't talk much about his past. Too painful, I suppose. I know he quit his job to take care of his wife. She went through a living hell of surgeries and chemotherapy. The experience tore him up— she was in a lot of pain. Even with painkillers, she suffered tremendously." Penny Sue shuddered. "Gives me the creeps to think about it. Anyway, he's come into some money— maybe from his wife's life insurance—and is looking to start a new life. He wants to invest in a motorcycle dealership in Georgia. He's down here to talk to people and do market research."

"Is that what y'all have been doing to the wee hours of the morning?"

"Basically, we've been sitting on the deck at the Riverview Hotel, rocking, and talking."

"About ..."

"Our childhoods, my husbands, philosophy, Harley-Davidsons—which reminds me, my new bike is going to be delivered today."

"Your what?" Ruthie and I said in unison.

"My new Harley." She lifted her chin regally. "It's being delivered to the New Smyrna dealership. It came in yesterday, but they had to prep it. I bought one of the Centennial bikes, a white pearl Fat Boy."

I gritted my teeth for control. A white pearl *Fat Boy!* Though we'd packed on a few pounds over the years (all except Ruthie, who was still disgustingly slim), Penny Sue had gained the most, much of it in her posterior. In college, she'd been a buxom beauty with slim hips; now she was buxom with hips to match—an hour glass figure with a slightly larger bottom than top, which made the thought of her riding a Fat Boy ironic or—to be kind—synchronistic, as Ruthie might say. "Penny Sue, motorcycles are dangerous. Do you know how to ride one?"

She rolled her eyes. "Please, give me and Harley-Davidson some credit. They have a rider education course. I took it at the dealership in Marietta." She sipped her coffee with a smirk. "I finished at the top of my class."

I should have guessed. The last time we were together at New Smyrna Beach, Ruthie and I discovered that Penny Sue had taken a terrorist avoidance driving course. We also learned she carried a gun and could shoot the wings off a fly (her words). So, why did a motorcycle surprise me? Especially since Penny Sue had money to burn and her new soul mate was a Harley devotee.

"I bought some really cool biker clothes. Want to see them?"

Ruthie and I nodded tentatively. "Can our hearts take it?"

"Of course. Don't be silly."

We followed Penny Sue into her bedroom where she pulled one of her largest Hartmann suitcases from the closet. Who knew what the thing cost—had to be over a thousand— it was big enough to hold a body.

"I was going to spring this on y'all later, after I got the bike. But ..." Penny Sue swung the suitcase onto the queen-sized bed.

Though I'd lived in the condo for over four months and been instructed to "use it like it was my own," I'd never had the nerve to move into the master bedroom. I'd chosen the second bedroom, with twin beds, the one that Ruthie and I shared on our first visit, and shared now. Somehow, the master suite had Penny Sue's name all over it. Not to mention, she was such a sloppy, disorganized person, no one—especially Ruthie—could stand sharing a room with her.

"Now, turn your heads," Penny Sue instructed before opening the suitcase, a sure sign something sexy or devilish was about to appear.

Ruthie and I did as instructed. We could hear her rustling stuff in the background. A minute passed—geez, how much was there?—then two.

Finally, Penny Sue sang, "Ta da!"

Ruthie and I turned around and gasped. White leather covered the bed. At the bottom, closest to us, lay a pair of white, leather, thong underwear. (I shuddered at the thought of a slim leather strap bisecting my butt. These biker people must be a lot tougher than me.) Directly above it was a white, strapless bustier—a throwback to saloons in the Wild West—complete with lacing up the front. A pair of fingerless gloves, a white leather jacket, and a red, white, and blue leather vest with Harley-Davidson emblazoned on the chest. Centered above it all was a black and silver open face helmet with a Harley emblem on the front.

Awestruck by all the white, Ruthie and I couldn't speak.

"What do you think?" Penny Sue finally asked.

"There are no slacks or shorts," I observed.

"It's all white," Ruthie said incredulously. "You're going to wear white before Memorial Day?"

Penny Sue folded her arms defiantly. "That tradition is strictly passé. The old stuff about wearing dark clothes in the winter and light clothes in the summer made sense in the olden days. People needed dark clothes to absorb sunlight in order to stay warm in the winter, and light clothes to reflect the heat in summer. But, this is Florida. It's warm year round, so light clothes work any time."

My jaw sagged. That this lecture passed through the lips of Penelope Sue Parker, a fourth generation Georgian who'd been *presented* by The Atlanta Debutante Club, was beyond belief. This was the woman who'd endlessly chided me for wearing patent leather shoes after five, carrying a straw purse in the fall, wearing white after Labor Day, and on and on *ad nauseam.*

In fact, the whole spiel didn't make sense—the answer was too pat. Though an intelligent woman, there was no way Penny Sue would spout off about the reflection and absorption of light. She'd obviously given this matter a lot of thought.

"Come on, what's with the white, really?" I asked.

She pulled her shoulder length hair to the side and began twirling it with her finger, a nervous gesture I'd seen before. "I want to be different. I figure all the other women will be wearing black. In white, I'll stand out from the crowd."

The twirling intensified. There was something else. "And?"

Penny Sue twittered, her finger hopelessly tangled in her hair. "It's from the wedding collection."

Ruthie and I did a double take. "Wedding collection?"

Penny Sue reared back. "An affirmation. Rich is the one, I know it. Like you say, Ruthie, 'You have to own it before you can have it.'"

The phrase was one of Ruthie's favorite New Age adages, and Penny Sue was using it to justify what she already intended to do.

"The wedding collection. You truly believe Rich is number four?"

Penny Sue stood up straight with a serious expression, and said, "I do." It came out the way one might say at a wedding ceremony. At that moment, I decided to help her with Rich—not get, like a possession, but facilitate their relationship. Penny Sue was outrageous and full of herself, but a nicer, kinder person one would never find. Although, I'd only met Rich briefly at dinner the other night, he struck me the same way. For once, it seemed like Penny Sue had found a soul mate, and I would do anything to help her in the quest. DAFFODILS, notwithstanding.

The doorbell rang before I could voice my support. Penny Sue, anxious to escape from our questioning, ran to the door and threw it open expectantly. There was an audible gasp, then an uncharacteristically weak, "Leigh, it's for you."

Chapter 2

As I entered the hall, Penny Sue whispered, "It's a monster!"

I scoffed at the dramatics and brushed by her to the front door. One glance and I broke out laughing. It *was* a monster, of sorts. "Come on in." I pushed the screen door, its rusty spring stretched with a loud twang.

A hulking man entered. He had flowing black hair attached to a ridged prosthesis with bushy eyebrows that covered his forehead. He wore black padded pants, knee high boots with spikes on the toes, and a metallic sash draped across his chest. A large squirt gun-like weapon hung from his shoulder. He was also holding a manila folder.

Speechless for once, Penny Sue peered from the bedroom doorway, her eyes and mouth in the shape of big O's.

"Ruthie, Penny Sue, meet Carl, Fran's son. He's a Klingon."

The big man struck his chest with his fist and growled, "tlhIngan jIH!"

Penny Sue drew back, her face twisted with confusion. "Huh?"

"I said, I am Klingon." Carl grinned mischievously and extended his hand. She gingerly took it.

"Sorry, I don't speak Klingon." She looked at me. "I thought you said your friend, Fran, was Italian."

"Carlo Annina by birth; Klag, son of K'tal, defender of the Klingon Empire by choice," Carl boomed.

Penny Sue's brow furrowed with confusion. "Klingon? Is that one of those former Soviet republics?"

We all howled. "*Star Trek*, Penny Sue." Ruthie said. "You must have heard of *Star Trek*."

Clearly piqued, she squared her shoulders. "Of course, the space show." Penny Sue waved expansively. "I just didn't recognize this particular alien. I was always partial to Mork, the spaceman played by Robin Williams."

Ruthie twittered. "Mork? You're thinking of *Mork and Mindy*; that's old as the hills and a completely different program."

"Old as the hills" got her. Leos pride themselves for being on the cutting edge. To even hint that a Leo may be out of the loop, or God forbid, wrong, is sure to draw a leonine roar.

"Well, which show is it?" Penny Sue demanded tersely.

"The one with Captain Jean Luc Picard."

"Jean Luc. The sexy, bald guy?"

I nodded.

"I remember now." She turned to Carl, smiling smugly. "You're pretending to be Woof."

"Worf," I corrected.

She cut me a look. "Whatever. So, you're on your way to a masquerade party?"

"In a manner of speaking. My buddies and I do role-playing games down at the Canaveral Seashore and Merritt Island Refuge. Today we're fighting the Romulans. This time we're going to win the Battle of Khitomer. We've devised a brilliant battle plan. We're going to surprise them by going in from the water. Kayaks. In a hundred simulations, we triumphed every time."

"Carl is an expert in computers," I explained.

Penny Sue stared past him to the black Harley motorcycle he'd arrived on. "Kayak? Where's you boat?"

"I'm meeting the team at the shopping center."

"Oh," she said, still suspicious of Carl and his getup. "Is that a stun gun?" She pointed to the contraption hanging from his shoulder.

"Paintball. Harmless, washes off." Carl handed me the manila folder. "Mom asked me to drop this off. She has a doctor's appointment and won't get to the center until this afternoon. She said you needed these receipts for the monthly reports." He clicked his heels together. "Got to run—the battle starts at nine. We like to fight before it gets hot." He struck his fist to his chest again. "Qaplá! See you around."

"I hope not," Penny Sue muttered as she closed the door. "That guy is weird. I sure wouldn't want to meet him in a dark alley." She ran her fingers through her hair. "I need a Bloody Mary. He scared me half to death."

"Wait," I said. "Aren't you picking up your new Harley today?"

"Right, I'd better stick to coffee. I have to stay sharp."

Penny Sue compromised with a Virgin Mary, swearing her nerves were fried after all the commotion. Actually, my nerves were pretty frayed, too. I was used to living alone. Though I loved seeing my friends, I found Penny Sue's histrionics were already wearing thin. I actually thought of having a real Bloody Mary, but didn't want to be responsible for getting Penny Sue started. Penny Sue on a bike was a scary thought when she was cold sober—regardless of her claim that she'd passed the Harley rider's course. As far as I could tell, she had a good helmet, gloves, jacket, but no slacks! Lord knows what a real Bloody Mary would bring out in that situation.

Penny Sue nibbled on a bagel. "Isn't Carl a little old for such foolishness? What does his mother think? If my child went around dressed like that, I'd have him committed."

I sighed with exasperation. "He doesn't dress like that all the time, for goshsakes. He's a renowned software engineer. Carl had a hand in the development of global positioning systems—you know, GPS—that they put in cars. It's a game, Penny Sue. A lot of kids, especially science fiction fans, do role playing."

"That big guy's hardly a kid. How old is he, anyway?"

"I believe he just turned thirty."

"Thirty? I'd been married and divorced twice by then."

"Imagine how much heartache you'd have avoided if you had pretended to be a Klingon." I took a bite of my bagel. Ruthie swallowed hard and buried her face in the newspaper.

Penny Sue regarded me with narrowed eyes. I glared back, chewing.

Carl was a nice young man, and I wasn't about to let her make fun of him. Over the last few months, when I'd been in Florida alone, he and Fran had helped me more times than I could count. Whenever there was something heavy to carry or furniture to move, Fran and Carl were there. Never a complaint or expectation of anything in return. They were good people.

Penny Sue—with no children—simply didn't realize that the new generation was different. They didn't feel the pressure to be paired off and get married by the time they were out of high school or college. In fact, they were almost androgynous by olden standards. They pursued other interests and took their time in making commitments. A lot healthier, if you ask me.

Which made me think of my own children. Ann, my younger, was an intern at the American Embassy in London. As far as I could tell, marriage was the farthest thing from her mind. Zack, Jr. was in Vail trying to figure out what to do with a degree in philosophy. Though his girlfriend from Vanderbilt had recently moved in with him, neither seemed in a hurry to tie the knot.

I wondered if a similar attitude would have been better for Penny Sue. Then again, she wouldn't be such a wealthy woman today. One thing for sure, rehashing the past was a road to nowhere. "There are no accidents," as Ruthie always said.

I finished the bagel and winked at Penny Sue, who was still giving me the evil eye. She stuck out her tongue, but eventually softened enough to resume eating.

"You referred to Carl's mother as Fran," Penny Sue said suddenly. "I thought her name was Frannie May."

"It is, Frances May Annina. Her mother gave each daughter a middle name that's a month. There's an April, May, and a June."

"No December, I hope. Or August. Wouldn't that be terrible? People would call you Auggie. Isn't that a type of bull?"

Ruthie looked up from her newspaper. "You're thinking of Aggie, slang for an agricultural school. Texas A & M's football team is called the Aggies."

"Same thing," Penny Sue ran on without missing a beat. "Do people call her Fran or Frannie May?"

"Both. The Frannie May thing began as a joke. When I first started at the Marine Conservation Center, some of the volunteers kidded me about my Southern accent. Then, you called that time before Christmas and left a message for Becky Leigh to call Penny Sue. That really got the gang going. They kidded me unmercifully until the next day when Fran came in. At the first snicker, Fran reared back, announced her name was Frannie May, that she came from the South, and would anyone like to make something of it? That shut them up. I never heard another snicker. Since then, she's called herself Frannie May at work.

"Fran isn't very tall, but has a formidable presence. If you get her riled, she gives you this absolutely frigid stare." I shuddered. "Whew, I've seen her cower big men with the *look*."

"My grandfather had a look like that. Where's she from?" Penny Sue asked.

"South Boston."

"Virginia? That's pretty country."

"No, the South Shore of Boston, Massachusetts."

Penny Sue chuckled. "That's a twist." She raised her glass. "To Frannie May, defender of Southern honor."

"And her son, Klag, champion of the Klingon Empire."

We didn't linger over breakfast. Ruthie was attending the final session of her Ayurveda seminar, Penny Sue was scheduled to pick up her motorcycle, and I had to go to work. Since Ruthie was using Penny Sue's Mercedes and running late, I offered to take Penny Sue to the Harley dealership on my way to work.

A good thing, too. If Ruthie had waited for Penny Sue, she'd have missed most of the morning lecture. I'd been dressed for close to forty minutes before Her Highness emerged from her boudoir. Thank goodness she had on some slacks! While the outfit was outrageous by Atlanta standards, it was fairly conservative for Bike Week. She wore white jeans, white boots, and the strapless leather bustier. Her leather jacket was artfully draped over one shoulder, while a white leather rucksack hung from the other. She carried the silver helmet.

She twirled around so I could get the full effect. "What do you think?" she asked breathlessly.

"Pulling out all the stops, eh? Since you're wearing the wedding ensemble, I assume you're going to drop in on Rich after you pick up your bike."

She giggled. "Naturally. Bike Week officially starts tomorrow. I intend to make my impression before the competition arrives. In less that twenty-four hours, the whole area will be crawling with hot babes on hot bikes. I plan to have Rich's full attention before then."

The comment stunned me. Under normal circumstances, Ms. Flirt of the South would be itching to mingle with the hot men on hot bikes. Engagements and marriages hadn't stopped her in the past. While she was completely faithful to all of her husbands, she naturally slipped into a Scarlett O'Hara persona whenever a good-looking man came into view. I'd thought it was an inborn trait, something she couldn't control like flat feet or schizophrenia. Now, it seemed I'd been wrong. Her need to be the center of attention could be satisfied by the right man. Perhaps Rich *was* her soul mate.

We piled—wedged, in Penny Sue's case—into my new, yellow VW Beetle convertible. For years I'd driven a four-door BMW, obligatory before SUVs for wives of up-and-coming executives and lawyers. Considered a symbol of wealth, stature, and good taste, I traded my Beemer in on my yellow toy the minute I arrived in Florida. I even got some money back on the deal.

"Lord, this thing is tiny," Penny Sue groused as she struggled to arrange the rucksack, helmet, and jacket in her lap. "Put the top down," she ordered, fanning herself. "I'm either having a hot flash or panic attack."

"It's a hot flash," I said, thinking it was actually asphyxiation. The new leather odor combined with her heavy-handed application of Joy cologne was overwhelming. I flipped the lock and pressed the button to lower the roof. Thankfully, a fish-scented sea breeze blew through—a welcome relief from the perfumed, wet dog smell.

"What's your schedule today?" I asked as we started the eight-mile drive from Sea Dunes to the dealership.

"I'm picking up the bike, then taking it by to show Rich. From there, who knows ..." her voice trailed off into an impish grin. "Don't expect me for dinner. What about you— any plans?"

"Ted offered to take Ruthie and me to dinner. You, too, if you want to come. He'll be working double time for the next ten days."

"Ted?!" She gave me a saucy wink. "As in *Deputy* Ted Moore? I've been here two whole days, and this is the first I've heard of it?"

"You haven't, exactly, been around."

"This is important! I'd have made time for this story. What gives?"

Ted Moore, a deputy with the Volusia County sheriff's office, was one of the few sympathetic policemen we'd encountered on our last visit. Though the ink was barely dry on my divorce decree then, I was drawn to him in a platonic way. As it turned out, Ted was recently separated, too, and not interested in anything more than a friend and occasional meal companion, which suited me fine. "There's not much to tell. He's divorced, and we've had lunch and dinner a few times. We're friends; that's it."

Penny Sue traced the outline of the Harley emblem on the helmet with her index finger. "Try to stay open and give him a chance."

I stopped at the light on Mission Road. The dealership was in the next block. "Look—friendship is all he wants. His life is complicated; he has two teenaged sons."

Penny Sue shrugged. "They'll grow up eventually. Never say never."

Bike Week preparations were in high gear at the dealership. A temporary chain link fence had been erected around the parking lot for the dealership and Pub. Vendors' orange tents were already in place and a crowd of people were unloading merchandise and stocking the booths' shelves. As far as I could tell, most of it was leather, Harley paraphernalia, and hoagie fixings.

I pulled into an empty space directly in front of the dealership. A young woman—probably mid-twenties—straddled a Harley Sportster in the next space. Penny Sue and I both gaped. She had on short-shorts that barely covered her butt and thigh high boots. Her shirt stopped shy of covering her boobs, which had obviously been enhanced, judging by their incredible size and upswept pertness.

"Hmph," Penny Sue muttered, scrutinizing her competition. "That's an old bike," she said dryly.

"I doubt people will notice her bike."

Penny Sue ignored my comment. "Look!" She pointed at a gleaming white Fat Boy parked in front of the dealership's entrance.

"Isn't it pretty," Penny Sue gushed, juggling her belongings. "Help me—I'm stuck," she said suddenly. Clutching her prodigious load of stuff, she pushed the door open with her foot. I cringed—footprints on my brand new car. "This damn thing is too low. Gawd, how do you get out?" she griped.

I reached in, grabbed her folded forearms and pulled. She made it halfway up, but fell back. The hot honey next to us in the thigh-high boots snickered and rode away. I braced myself for another try. This time Penny Sue made it. "I guess

I should have gotten an ejector seat for the passenger side, too," I said, puffing.

"Your side has one of those lift chairs like you see on television? The ones that hoist up old people? Neat-o."

I shut the door. "I was joking."

"Very funny."

Fortunately, a tall man strode out of the dealership at that moment. Penny Sue inclined her head toward the white bike. "I think that's mine."

"It is if you're Penelope Sue Parker."

"The same."

"I have some papers for you to sign."

Penny Sue handed me her helmet and jacket. "Would you hold this, Leigh? I'll only be a minute."

I hoped so—I was already late for work. I put her things on the passenger seat, pulled out my cell phone, and called the office, informing them—as if they hadn't already noticed—that I would be late. Sandra, the director, answered and assured me there was no problem as long as the billing was completed by the end of the day. Compared to the workload at my last job, a car dealership, the center's books were a snap and the people a lot more fun. There was also the satisfaction of working for a worthy cause.

The Marine Conservation Center was a nonprofit organization dedicated to education and the preservation of the Indian River Lagoon, North America's most diverse estuary. I have to admit that I didn't have a clue what estuary meant when I started work, but soon learned the word referred to the part of a river where it met the ocean, which in New Smyrna's case was the inland waterway. Initially, I visited the center because of an interest in sea turtles developed on our earlier visit. Fortunately for me, a part-time job opening was posted on the very day I arrived to take a tour. My inner voice said, "Grab it," and I did. Except for the kidding episode, I'd never had a doubt about the decision. It's hard to complain about living in paradise and working at the perfect job. A year ago, I was in the pits of depression over my divorce. Although I was not completely over it, things had turned out better than I'd ever imagined.

Ruthie said that stresses like divorces are the times for the greatest spiritual advancement. "Unfortunately, we all get set in our ways. Sometimes it takes a big jolt to catapult us to the next level."

I'd been catapulted, all right. Shot from a cannon, or so it felt. But, four months after October and the Big Split, I had to admit that I was a lot better off. I'd come to realize it was the fear of change that plagued me all those months. I'd become comfortable with my BMW, big house, social standing, and perfect kids (okay, they weren't completely perfect; but damn good by most standards.) Truth be told, I *had* stopped growing or evolving as Ruthie would say. I was in a comfortable rut to nowhere—a bored stupor of luxurious existence. A darn shame it took a skinny stripper with silicon breasts to blow me out of the rut.

Penny Sue emerged from the dealership with the salesman.

"Remember," the dealer said as he handed her the key, "don't go over sixty for the break-in period. And, be sure to alternate your speeds."

Penny Sue nodded obediently.

"Check the maintenance schedule in the owner's manual."

She nodded again.

"I know you took the riding course, so you can handle the bike. Is there anything you'd like to ask?"

"Yes," she said with a glint in her eye. "You've been very nice. Are you married? I have some single friends."

If he hadn't been standing there, I would have kicked her. The nerve!

He glanced at me and chuckled. "I appreciate the compliment, but I'm taken. Four kids."

Penny Sue gave him the up and down. "Too bad," she said, straddling the white and chrome bike. I retrieved her helmet and jacket from my car. An instant later, the bike came to life with a deep rumble.

I waved as she maneuvered the Harley into the parking lot and headed for Route 44. I couldn't help but notice that all heads turned as she roared by. Decked out in white leather, riding a slick new bike, Penny Sue was not as slim as the woman in the skimpy outfit, but she was still a traffic stopper. I glanced down at my cotton capri set and suddenly felt very frumpy. I got in my car and started the cute little Beetle. Next to the roar of Penny Sue's Fat Boy, my car sounded like the little bug it was.

Darn, I was totally out of sync with bikers and Bike Week. There wasn't anything I could do about the car, but I could at least buy some biker-friendly garb. I resolved to swing by the shops on Flagler after work to look for some cool duds. In any event, The Wicker Basket had received a shipment of swimsuits that I wanted to check out before they were picked over.

The Wildlife Nature Cruise had left by the time I arrived at the center, which meant I had a good two hours of uninterrupted work. As part-time bookkeeper, my primary duty was to tally and reconcile receipts from donors and the various cruises. I had all but finished the weekly reports when Bobby Barnes, our pontoon boat captain, ambled in. A retired Navy Seal with bulging biceps, he was the perfect person to lead the cruises. While most of our patrons were responsible adults and families, sometimes a vacationer arrived who'd had one Mimosa over the line. Bobby's commanding presence at the helm inevitably kept them in line. A light-hearted comment about one of his Navy adventures was all it usually took to keep the sobriety-challenged patron seated and quiet.

"Sandra said you stopped by the Harley shop on your way to work. Did you spring for a Harley Sportster?"

"No, your old Seal buddy, Saul's mopeds are more my speed. But, Penny Sue bought a Fat Boy."

Bobby let out a low whistle. "Not bad. Good for Penny Sue. Are you and your friends going to hit the biker hot spots this weekend?"

"Penny Sue definitely is. She has her eye on a biker for husband number four. I don't know if Ruthie and I will go. I'm not sure we'd fit in."

Bobby sat on the edge of the desk. "At least, you have to go to the Pub. Half the people there aren't real bikers. They drive their cars and park across the street at the shopping center. It's fun, a big party. There are bands, lots of food, and a hoard of geezers like us pretending they're young.

It's an experience—something you'll talk about for years. You shouldn't miss it."

I'd had that thought. Next to stock car racing, Bike Week was the area's main claim to fame. A Daytona Beach tradition dating back to 1937, it started small with a handful of bikers racing a three-mile route, half of which was on the beach. Since then, Bike Week festivities had spread out to the adjacent communities like New Smyrna Beach and evolved into a ten-day festival of bikes, beer, and scantily clad babes. People attended from all over the world, so shouldn't I at least sample the experience since it was right in my backyard?

An image of Penny Sue and her white leather getup popped into my mind. "What do people wear?"

Bobby frowned at my beige capri set. "Jeans and a tee shirt, preferably one with Harley-Davidson on it. You could have picked one up at the dealership or Pub 44 next door."

Easy enough. Maybe Ruthie and I should go after all. I'd run it by her at dinner.

Bobby chatted for a few more minutes, then left for lunch. I buried my nose in the books, determined to finish early so I could do my shopping before Ruthie got home at three. I'd entered the last number into the computer when Frannie May arrived. "Go," she insisted. "I'll hold down the fort."

She didn't have to offer twice. First, I went to the Pub and picked up two black tee shirts for Ruthie and me. Tight fitting, sexy jobs with a zipper down the front, I chuckled at Ruthie's anticipated reaction. She was a conservative dresser, to say the least, and the shirt had to be a first for her. Actually, it was a first for me, since I usually bought my clothes from beach boutiques or Dillard's Better Sportswear department.

Shirts in hand, I drove back across the North Causeway drawbridge to Flagler Avenue, the beachside commercial district. Luckily, tourists were still on the beach or taking a siesta, so I didn't have to fight a crowd at The Wicker Basket. With the proprietor's help, I'd tried on four swimsuits, made my decision, and was headed back to the condo by 2:50 p.m.

Not bad, even for a person who hated shopping, having acquired a bad attitude about retailing from selling children's shoes during college.

I took a left onto the unpaved, sand driveway for Sea Dunes and rounded the corner to our oceanfront unit. I expected to see Penny Sue's yellow Mercedes. Instead, I found the new, white Harley with her expensive leather jacket hanging from the handlebar. I pulled into a space on the far side of the bike and quickly gathered my packages. Something was wrong, very wrong.

Chapter 3

The one and only time I could remember seeing Penny Sue cry was when her mother passed away—that is, until now. She sat on the loveseat in the living room, dressed in her kimono, swigging wine. Her eyes were red and puffy with mascara streaked down her cheeks. Half-hearted attempts to brush away the tears had only succeeded in smearing her makeup. I dropped my purse, package, and her jacket on a stool at the kitchen counter and rushed to her side.

"Are you all right, honey?" I asked, wedging beside her on the loveseat and putting my arm around her shoulder. "You didn't hurt yourself, did you?" I held her at arm's length to check for blood and bruises.

"No, no," she said, sniffling. "Rich dumped me." She stared into the wineglass.

"Dumped you?" I repeated stupidly, as if she needed a reminder.

Tears sprouted like a sprinkler system. "He said things were going too fast, and we shouldn't see each other for a while."

He must have recognized the white leather wedding ensemble! I'd worried about that, but Penny Sue was an all or nothing type of person. She wouldn't have listened if I'd voiced my concern.

"Hi, y'all. What a beautiful bike!" Ruthie called as she emerged from the hall into the open expanse of the living, dining, and kitchen area. "Are you going to take us for a—" One look at Penny Sue, and Ruthie clamped her mouth shut.

Penny Sue's bottom lip quivered, and she took a drink to cover it.

Ruthie shoved her books onto the kitchen counter. "What's wrong?" She sank into the sofa beside the loveseat.

Penny Sue's eyes brimmed. "Rich dumped me. He doesn't want to see me anymore." She waved her empty glass and headed for the refrigerator.

Ruthie glanced my way, eyes pleading for an answer. I shrugged.

Penny Sue turned to face us, holding her glass in one hand and a bottle of Chardonnay in the other. "Come on, girls, I've got a bad case of the blues. Don't make me drink alone." She poured some wine and raised the glass to her lips.

"Wait," Ruthie shouted. She dashed to the counter, pulled a small vial from her purse and squirted several drops into Penny Sue's wine. "Rescue Remedy," Ruthie explained, taking the wine bottle from Penny Sue and pouring short glasses for each of us.

Penny Sue toasted the air. "To Rich. It was great while it lasted."

"Start at the beginning. What, exactly, happened? You went to the Riverview to show Rich your bike, and he just piped up with 'See you around?'"

"Close. I called his room from the house phone. Instead of inviting me up, Rich said he'd meet me on the front porch.

"I showed him the bike, and he made over it a little. That's when I noticed that two guys had come out of his room and were watching from the balcony. I called 'Hi' to them and asked Rich to introduce me to his friends. He pulled me around the side of the building like he was embarrassed to be seen with me." Penny Sue took a big swallow of vino. "Rich said the guys were old friends, and he'd been doing some thinking. He wasn't ready for a relationship and needed space. He thought we shouldn't see each other for a while."

She slumped onto a stool at the end of the counter and rested her forehead on her folded arms. "I should never have worn that outfit," she said mournfully.

"Yeah, he must have recognized it," I said.

She looked sidelong. "Recognized? What are you talking about?"

I sure didn't want to broach the subject of the wedding ensemble if she hadn't already considered it. "What are you talking about?"

"White before Memorial Day is bad taste—before Easter it's downright bad luck."

Ruthie leaned across the counter and stroked Penny Sue's shoulder. "Don't blame yourself. If those were old friends, Rich had probably been talking about old times, which brought up memories of his wife."

Penny Sue sighed heavily and raised up to her elbows. "You're right, of course." She smiled weakly and took another sip of her drink. "My wise, spiritual friend. A kick in the butt is what I need."

"Try this." Ruthie balled her right hand into a fist and started beating her breastbone, at the point above her boobs. With each blow she emitted a breathy HA. HA, HA, HA. She did it three times, then dissolved in a wave of giggles.

Penny Sue curled her lip at the maneuver. "That's an interesting chant. What happened to OM-M?"

"It's not a chant; it's the thymus thump. I learned this at the seminar. Whenever you're out of sorts, this will realign your energy centers."

"You expect me to beat myself up and laugh about it? What kind of masochistic philosophy is that?"

"At least say HA, HA, HA."

Penny Sue rolled her eyes. "Ruthie, you're really getting weird."

"Come on, do the HA, HA part. I'll bet you can't do it without laughing. You'll try it, won't you, Leigh?"

Why not? As long as I didn't have to pound my chest like a Neanderthal, I'd give it a whirl. I sat up straight and started in, "HA, HA ..." After about the fifth repetition, I started to laugh. Damn, it worked! Whether the giggles came from the HA's or simply because I felt like a fool, I can't say. Of course, it didn't matter, laughter was laughter.

"See?" Ruthie said to Penny Sue. "Try it once—that's all. One time."

Penny Sue let out a half-hearted HA, HA.

Ruthie snapped her fingers. "Pick up the pace."

"HA, HA, HA, HA ..." It took six or seven throaty attempts, but Penny Sue finally started laughing. The mood was contagious. We all joined in, giggling like ninnies until tears streamed down our cheeks. Penny Sue wiped her eyes as she reached for her glass.

I nodded at the wine. "Alcohol is a depressant, Penny Sue. You probably shouldn't drink, it will make you feel worse."

She cut me an *I know that* look. The sass was back—a positive sign.

"That's why I hit the wine in the first place. I wanted my body to feel as bad as my heart. At the very least, I hoped it would put me to sleep. Better still, a massive headache that I could blame on Rich."

"I see your point," I said, reaching for the bottle. "Want some more?"

Penny Sue put the glass down. "No, I'm over it."

Good, she was back to her spunky self. Crying in her beer was not Penny Sue's style. In the old days, she'd have walked away from Rich and never given him a second thought. A new soul mate would have manifested within hours. It was uncanny how she drew men, absolutely like ants to honey. Yet, her crying jag told me that, either Rich was indeed special or Penny Sue's hormones were seriously out of kilter.

The H word was something I tried to ignore since, at forty-seven, I'd reached the age where the old juices started a downhill slide. I'd never given the issue a thought until our last trip. Penny Sue had harped on it continuously, warning

Ruthie—who absolutely could not pass a bathroom without going in—that peeing all the time was not normal and one of the first signs of plummeting estrogen. Foggy-brained, weight gain, unstable emotions—Penny Sue's warnings went on and on. I'd have dismissed it all as her normal chatter had it not been for the fact that she started waving a gun around.

In the months since then I'd noticed one or two of the symptoms in myself. With time on my hands, I decided to do some research. I wish I hadn't, the darn books read like horror novels. First, there was perimenopause, the stage where the hormones became unstable. Up and down, up and down, a roller coaster that somehow involved the pituitary gland. The bottom line of all of this being that many women experienced depression and wild mood swings—PMS run wild that could last as long as ten years!

There was the story of a lady who walked down the aisle of the supermarket, looked at the corn flakes, and burst into tears. Two minutes later, a clerk gave her a sidelong glance and the woman took the poor girl's head off (figuratively, I assume, unless she packed a weapon like Penny Sue.) There were other terrifying tales about memory loss. Misplacing the car keys was nothing, many women suddenly forgot their names and addresses. As if that weren't enough, the anecdotes ran on to encompass wrinkles and osteoporosis and sagging breasts and fat stomachs. Horrible, truly horrible, especially the stuff about memory loss, because I'd experienced some of that myself.

I tried to write it off as being preoccupied, which was part of the problem, but I'd had trouble remembering my name and address on more than one occasion. I didn't think there was a family history of Alzheimer's; still, the episodes were so unnerving, I'd called Ruthie for advice.

"That's great," she'd said.

Great? Did she hear me right? "Ruthie, I said I'm losing my memory. I can hardly recall what I did this morning and I've actually forgotten my address and phone number a couple of times. It's like a brain cramp."

"*The past is gone, it can touch me not.*"

"What?"

Ruthie had slid right through hormones and health into spirituality. "Come on, Ruthie, I'm serious. Do you think I could be getting Alzheimer's?"

"No, of course not."

"Do you think I should look into hormone replacement therapy?"

"Couldn't hurt, if it's bothering you."

Well, I didn't check into it, because all the latest studies yielded wildly conflicting results that confused me more. So, I decided to muddle through until my symptoms got worse. If push came to shove, I could have my clothes monogrammed to jog my memory or start wearing my driver's license hanging from my neck like people did in airports nowadays.

But, Penny Sue was another matter. She was on HRT, she'd mentioned having a hot flash that morning, and now the depression and crying episode which were totally out of character. Perhaps her prescription needed to be adjusted. Then, I wondered if she still carried a .38 in her pocketbook. I wasn't sure I could take another vacation with a flighty Penny Sue wielding a revolver.

"By the way," I said as casually as I could, "I ran into Woody the other day. Did you ever get your gun back?"

"Heck no, I had to buy another one," she said, eyeing me suspiciously. "Why do you ask?"

"Just wondered." I took a good slug of my own Chardonnay.

Ruthie came to my rescue. "Depression is a sure sign of a Vatta imbalance. How about a warm sesame oil massage?" she said brightly. "Nothing better to realign your *humors*."

"You want to *patta* my *vatta*?" Penny Sue quipped.

She was coming around.

Ruthie shook her head peevishly. "Yes, Ms. Smarty Pants. Go put on your swimsuit, and I'll warm the oil."

The laughing and sesame massage lifted Penny Sue's spirits considerably, but it was Deputy Ted Moore's arrival for dinner that really fine-tuned her *humors*. Simply, testosterone worked on Penny Sue like Prozac.

When Ted arrived, I met him at the door and explained the situation. "Let me see what I can do."

Well, the boy's good. A few superlatives about her new motorcycle and, next thing I knew, Penny Sue was hugging his waist and they were riding off into the sunset. I have to admit that I felt a tinge of jealousy. I'd never hugged Ted's waist. We'd both been so adamant about merely being friends, we went through an awkward avoidance rite whenever we found ourselves within two feet of each other.

Ruthie read my mind. "You know, Penny Sue's just the touchy, feely type." She nodded in the direction they'd gone. "It doesn't mean anything. Besides, it might be time for you to loosen up a little."

"What do you mean, loosen up?"

"Just a thought," she said, heading down the hall to the great room. "Me thinks ye doth protest too much about Deputy Ted."

"You, of all people, know I'm not ready for a relationship, and neither is he. We're buddies and we both like it that way."

"Whatever you say. Come on, let's catch the news."

The hour-long show was almost over before Penny Sue and Ted returned. As time drew on, the tinge of jealously I'd felt before grew to a trickle.

Penny Sue bounced down the hall grinning from ear to ear. "Look what I have," she exclaimed, waving a video-cassette with huge red lips on the cover. *"Rocky Horror!* Ted and I thought—"

Ted and I. The trickle expanded to a good-sized stream.

"—we could get take-out from the steakhouse and watch the movie. Won't that be fun?" She put her hands on her hips and started hopping around, mimicking the Time Warp dance number from the movie. A few hours ago she was in the pits of depression, and I felt fine. Now, she was back to her old self, and I felt like hell. A strange turn of events, if you ask me.

My eyes must have shot darts, because Penny Sue abruptly stopped the antics. "Ted, take Leigh for a ride on my bike." She handed me her helmet. "Come on, it's fun. We'll order dinner while you're gone."

"The bike handles like a dream, and it's a beautiful night." Ted flashed his movie star smile.

My jealousy evaporated. "Okay," I said, strangely excited
by the prospect of clinching his waist.

"Wait, what do you want to eat?" Penny Sue was back
in charge. All was well.

I opted for chicken and shrimp, while Ted ordered
prime rib.

"And dessert, we must have dessert," Penny Sue decreed.

"Chocolate's good for depression," Ruthie commented.

Penny Sue winked at me. "And, an aphrodisiac," she
said under her breath. "What's that super, duper chocolate
thing?"

"Chocolate Avalanche," Ruthie replied, nearly swooning.

"Right," Penny Sue said, adding that to the list with a
big star. "We'll get a couple of them."

* * *

This was the first time I'd ever ridden on a motorcycle.
Until that night, I'd viewed bikes as loud, dangerous, and
borderline uncouth. My opinion changed immediately. First,
there was something positively sexual about the low rumble
and rhythmic vibration of the motorcycle. (Better than having a
vibrating cell phone in your pocket!) Add to that the musty
scent of Ted's cologne, the muscular warmth of his back, and
the feeling of oneness as we leaned into the curves, and I
was close to heaven. But, the icing on the cake was the feeling
of elation and freedom I got from the wind in my face—the
same sensation I felt as a kid, when I coasted my bike down
the long, winding hill in front of my parent's house. I snuggled
closer to Ted as we took the swooping curve where A1A
paralleled the beach. Maybe Ruthie was right; I should
relax a little.

The food was waiting when we returned to the condo. No time was wasted since our dinners were cooling fast and re-warming steak seldom worked. As we caught our breath before tackling dessert, Ted asked, "What are your plans for the week? I assume you'll hit some of the bike events."

"Do you think it's safe for the three of us to attend without a male escort?" Ruthie asked nervously.

"Some of the places in Daytona can get a little rough, but you'll be fine if you stick to the beaten path."

"Bobby Barnes suggested we go to the Pub," I said.

Ted nodded. "Gilly's Pub 44, J.B.'s, the restaurants on Flagler, even Main Street in Daytona—you'll be fine at any of them. In fact, I'll probably be doing traffic duty at Pub 44 most of the week."

The Pub it is, I thought. I turned to Ruthie. "Bike Week is world famous. We really should go to a few events."

Ruthie didn't look particularly excited, but didn't get a chance to argue. Penny Sue started the tape for *The Rocky Horror Picture Show* and began passing around the desserts. The rest of the evening was a blur of food and frivolity, which did everyone, especially Penny Sue, a world of good.

Chapter 4

I awoke to the smell of coffee which summoned a memory so old, I'd never have guessed it was there. I thought of Zack. When we were first married, before the kids, Zack would make the morning coffee. An ambitious young lawyer in Parker, Hanson, and Swindal, one of the most prestigious law firms in Atlanta, he got up at five so he could beat his colleagues to work. In those days there was intense competition between the associates, each vying to rack up the most billable hours to insure they'd receive a coveted partnership. Everyone tried to be the first to arrive and the last to leave, which meant no one left while a single partner was on the floor, after which, they still played a silly cat and mouse game to see who could outlast whom. Thankfully, by the third year, Zack and his close colleagues came to an unspoken agreement that they'd all leave together. A darn good thing, otherwise I'd never have seen my husband, and we certainly wouldn't have had children.

I rolled onto my back and stared at the ceiling. All of that happened twenty-five years ago. Twenty-five years, a quarter of a century. I suddenly felt very old.

Old. Hey, today was Ruthie's birthday. Finally, we were all the same age.

I snatched a cotton robe from the closet and followed the scent of Colombian roast. Ruthie sat at the kitchen counter reading the newspaper. The television, tuned to CNN, played in the background. An insatiable news junkie, Ruthie was never out of touch with world events. Which struck me as ironic, considering her metaphysical leanings. As far as I could tell, most of the woo-woo people avoided the media claiming, at best, it fostered fear and wanton materialism. At worst, it was nothing but a mouthpiece for a vast right wing— or left, depending on one's political philosophy—conspiracy.

I snuck up behind Ruthie and started to sing softly. "Happy Birthday to you, Happy Birthday to you—"

A thunderous warble came from the hall. "HAPPY BIRTHDAY, DEAR RUTHIE," Penny Sue skipped into the great room, "HAPPY BIRTHDAY TO YOU-U-U. And man-n-ny mo-ore." She was wearing the red silk robe with a dragon embroidered on the back, holding her cell phone, and grinning like a stereotypical Cheshire cat. For a person who'd been in the pits of depression less than twenty-four hours earlier, she'd made a remarkable recovery, I thought.

"Thank you, thank you." Ruthie ducked her head modestly. "All good wishes are gratefully accepted."

"You're getting much more than wishes," Penny Sue said enthusiastically as she rounded the counter and poured a cup of coffee. She smiled above the rim of her mug. "You're going to get the royal treatment." She grinned at me. "In fact, we're all getting the royal treatment."

"You sure are chipper this morning," I observed, filling my own mug.

"Of course, I'm here with my best friends." She motioned at the sun streaming through the sliding glass doors that faced the ocean. "It's a beautiful day," she paused dramatically ...

"And?" I prodded. I knew something was up.

Penny Sue held up her cell phone, giggling like a teenager. She punched in a few digits and a message began to play. A man's voice sounded, low and slow as if he were whispering. "Penny Sue, I'm sorry I was so abrupt yesterday. I do care about you and didn't mean to hurt you. So much is going on. I need some time. I'm going away for a few days; I'll call when I get back. You're very special to me, Bun—" Her thumb hit the off button.

"Wait," Ruthie said. "What was that last part? I couldn't quite make it out."

I nudged Penny Sue with my elbow. "Yeah, let's hear that again."

Penny Sue pursed her lips huffishly. "It's just a nickname."

Ruthie arched a brow. "Did he say, butt? He calls you Butt?"

That got her. Penny Sue drew up to her full five-foot-eight stature. "Not butt—Bunny," she said smugly. "As in Honey Bunny."

I gave a low whistle. "Honey Bunny? That is serious."

Ruthie nodded. "Like I said, it was all a misunderstanding. Rich was probably acting tough in front of his friends. You know how men are—have to play Mr. Macho all the time. Besides, you don't know who the guys were. He said they were friends, but one of them could have been his wife's brother or cousin or something."

It was good to see Penny Sue back to her sassy self. I clicked my mug to hers. "I know you're relieved. I'm happy for you."

"Yeah. Yesterday was completely out of character for the Rich I know. It threw me for a loop. He's not the chest beating, macho type. Yet, all's well that ends well." She opened the refrigerator. "Y'all want a bagel or some cereal?"

"Raisin bran," I said quickly, still feeling stuffed from the decadent chocolate desserts we'd eaten the night before. Even miming the *Rocky Horror Picture Show's* dance numbers did little to work off the heavy dinners.

"What's in the news today, Ruthie?" Penny Sue asked as she poured three bowls of cereal.

"Weather for Bike Week is supposed to be perfect. Record crowds are expected."

"That's good," I said. "Last year was rained out—a real bust."

Ruthie flipped to the front page and scanned the headlines. "An Atlas V rocket is scheduled to go next week. They haven't announced the launch time, because of the terrorist threat. It's taking up a military communications satellite." She looked up from the newspaper as Penny Sue slid Ruthie's cereal onto the counter. "Do you think we'll be able to see it from here?"

"Sure, a perfect view from the beach," Penny Sue said between bites of cereal. "As the crow flies, Cape Canaveral is only about 30 miles. I hope it's a night launch. When the shuttle goes at night, it's like the sun coming up. You can't believe how it lights up the sky."

"When will they announce the launch time?"

"Twenty-four hours in advance."

Penny Sue shook her head. "This terrorism stuff is a real bummer. I hate to fly any more, it's such a hassle."

"Better safe than sorry," I said.

Ruthie nodded. "A shipment of missiles and ammunition was hijacked in North Carolina yesterday. The police have no clues and speculate it could be anyone from Mafioso arms dealers to American extremists to Al-Qaeda."

"There are a lot of kooks in this world. That's why I carry a .38," Penny Sue declared.

Yes, and you're one of them, I thought bleakly. Her last .38 got us in a passel of trouble, all because a guy called her a bitch. I hoped she kept the darned gun in her purse during this visit.

"Do you still have the Taser?" Ruthie asked me.

"Oh, yeah, it's in the linen closet." A cutting-edge prototype that Ruthie's father sent us for protection, the liquid Taser looked like a child's super soaker squirt gun. Only this booger was no beach toy. Unlike the models used by police which shot barbed probes on wires, this gun used an electrified saline solution capable of delivering a shock that knocked manly men on their behinds. Simply put, this Taser had multiple shots, a range of 25 feet, and could stun more than one person. And, the good news, it was a completely defensive weapon that wouldn't seriously injure anyone unless, perhaps, they had a pacemaker. "I received a shipment of electrolyte solution before you arrived. Your dad obviously wanted to make sure you'd be safe."

"Is the battery charged?" Penny Sue asked.

"Yes, I charge it once a week. Even with the new alarm system, I like having it around. It gives me a sense of security. Ted thinks it's a good idea, too."

"Ted thinks—"

I cut Penny Sue off. "What else is in the news, Ruthie?"

"There's a feature article on Dolly Parton's theater in Orlando. You eat dinner while watching a rodeo."

I grimaced. "That sounds a little stinky to me. I mean, horses aren't usually potty trained, are they?"

Penny Sue waved dismissively. "I'm sure they've worked around that—deodorized dirt or something. Besides, I like Dolly Parton. Her hair's a little extreme, but I admire her guts—she's not afraid to be who she is."

Ruthie chuckled. "You'll love this, then. The article quotes Dolly as saying, 'It takes a lot of money to look this cheap.'"

Penny Sue hooted. "I can relate. My biker get-up cost a fortune. Maybe we should go to the show. Is Dolly in town?"

An image of Dolly Parton and Penny Sue, both riding Harleys and decked out in the white leather wedding ensemble, popped into my mind. What a pair they'd be. They'd either hate each other or love each other—no middle ground. That was one meeting I'd love to witness. "I'm game."

Ruthie scanned the article again. "It doesn't say whether she's here."

"Well, if the week gets boring, we'll give it a whirl." Penny Sue rinsed her cereal bowl and put it in the dishwasher.

"Leigh, do you mind making another pot of coffee? I'm going to get something, and y'all must promise not to peek."

"Is this part of the royal treatment?" I asked, feigning fear. For Penny Sue, the royal treatment could encompass a lot.

"Yes, I promise you'll love it. Don't look—this may take a minute."

Ruthie rolled her eyes. I made the coffee. Who knew what would appear? A male stripper might come streaking through. Cute puppies, handpicked men for each of us, dozens of roses, biker outfits—heck, bikes!—anything was possible with Penny Sue.

I'd chided her for her extravagance, especially recently, when I couldn't afford to reciprocate. She blew me off like a pesky fly. "Forget it, this is Harold's money. I get a HUGE THRILL out of spending it!" Harold was the rich, second husband who'd had an affair with his male assistant. For all her bluster, Penny Sue'd never gotten over that slight. As heartbreaking as any divorce was, there's an extra kick when a person like Penny Sue gets dumped for a man.

Ruthie and I didn't have to wait long. The coffee had just started to drip when noises came from the hallway. *"Whoops!"* a mechanical voice, reminiscent of Ruthie and Penny Sue's Furbies (a long story) said. Another second, and *"Whoops!"* again. I came around the L-shaped bar, while Ruthie leaned back in her chair.

It was classic Penny Sue. A robot about two feet tall, looking like R2D2 from *Star Wars*, rolled erratically down the hall, exclaiming *"Whoops!"* every time it hit the baseboard. Penny Sue stood by the front door with a remote control that she'd obviously not mastered. The mechanical man's right arm was raised to balance a tray with an envelope on top.

Ruthie giggled with glee and hopped down from her stool.

The robot, sensing her presence, stopped and said, *"Hello, hello, hello."*

"What's his name?" Ruthie called to Penny Sue.

Penny Sue strode down the corridor. "Not him, her. This is Lu Nee 2."

Even I had to laugh at that one. Lu Nee 1 was Penny Sue's Furby that had met an untimely end.

"What else does Lu Nee do?" I asked.

"She's our new maid and bodyguard."

"Maid?" Ruthie said.

"Sure, we can use her to serve drinks and snacks."

I took the remote from Penny Sue. "Assuming we can master this thing." I studied the control panel's three-inch color display surrounded by a slew of buttons and dials. "We need a ten-year-old to show us how it works."

Penny Sue leaned over my shoulder and pointed to the screen. "It transmits everything Lu Nee sees and hears."

"Great, we can use it to spy on each other." I said flippantly, giving back the control.

"Not on each other, intruders." Penny Sue pointed to a button on the right of the unit. "See, it has a Sentry mode that detects motion and issues an alert." She pushed the button, Lu Nee 2 swiveled slightly, then demanded, "Halt! Who goes there?"

"Cool," Ruthie exclaimed.

"Well, don't stand there, take the letter," Penny Sue ordered.

Ruthie snatched the envelope and angled it so I could see. It had Riverview Hotel embossed in the upper left corner.

Riverview Hotel! The name unleashed a flood of memories about my divorce and our vacation in October. From Ruthie's hesitation, I could tell it affected her the same way. Lu Nee 2 lurched forward. *"Watch out!"* Darn, the robotic beast had Penny Sue's personality. Ruthie and I both jumped backward.

I nudged Ruthie with my elbow. "Open the envelope before we get killed."

"Right." She ripped it open, making no effort to be neat. Inside were three gift certificates for the Royal Treatment at the new Riverview Spa.

Penny Sue smiled broadly. "No argument. I've made all the arrangements. First, we're getting the Royal Treatment at the spa, then we're having a gourmet dinner at the Riverview Restaurant. The three of us, on the deck. Just like old times.

I said a silent prayer to the spirits that Ruthie claimed watched over us all: *Please guys, cut us some slack. Let this not be like old times!*

Sadly, Penny Sue's desires must have carried more weight than mine.

Chapter 5

The Royal Treatment was a misnomer—the proper term was heavenly. Three and a half hours of saunas, whirlpools, massage, facials, and paraffined feet left us warm, glowing, and as limp as overdone pasta. We made it to the car, then just sat, too relaxed to move.

"Wouldn't you like to stretch out and go to sleep?" Ruthie asked.

"Yeah, I feel like a side of Kobe beef," Penny Sue said, forehead resting on the steering wheel.

I bit my lip. She said it, I didn't! Kobe beef came from Japanese cattle raised on beer and massaged with sake. Its claim to fame was the sweet taste and extensive *fat marbling.* That she'd call herself sweet was no surprise, to admit to being fat marbled was another matter.

Penny Sue finally mustered enough strength to drive the four miles to the condo where we tumbled into bed. Three hours later, refreshed and dressed for dinner, we gathered in the living room. I brought out my presents for Ruthie to open.

Penny Sue poured wine into plastic cups that she placed on
Lu Nee 2's upraised arm and tray. Unfortunately, she still
hadn't mastered the robot's controls. It bumped into a stool,
exclaimed, *"Whoops. Where did that come from?"* and all
three cups went tumbling. "Darn, that Chardonnay cost thirty
bucks a bottle."

Considering we were down to one glass apiece of the
expensive stuff and running short on time, we convinced
Penny Sue that she should work with Lu Nee later. With
wine in stemmed glasses that we fetched ourselves, the three
of us toasted Ruthie's birthday. Though my presents, price-
wise, paled next to Penny Sue's gifts, Ruthie seemed to like
them. Her eyes went wide at the black, stretch biker shirt
with the zipper down the front.

Penny Sue took the top and held it up against Ruthie.
"This and your Moschino jeans are perfect for Bike Week."

Anything's perfect with two hundred dollar jeans, I
thought. Even the paper gown the gyno gave you would look
good with Moschinos. I handed her the next present, a copy
of *The Book of Answers* which I'd picked up at Chris' Place,
a New Age shop on Flagler Avenue. The book was basically
a super-duper rendition of the old eight ball oracle—you
asked a question and opened the book at random for the
answer. Ruthie immediately closed her eyes, stroked the book's
cover, and snapped it apart. The page read, *IT WILL BRING
GOOD LUCK*. Ruthie giggled. "I asked what the next year
held for me."

"May I try it?" Penny Sue asked, already taking the
book from Ruthie's hand. She closed her eyes and stroked
the volume as Ruthie had done. Her lips moved slightly, then

she peeled the pages apart dramatically. Ruthie and I leaned forward to see. *CIRCUMSTANCES WILL CHANGE VERY QUICKLY*. Penny Sue smiled smugly. "I asked what would happen to my relationship with Rich. This must mean we'll get back together soon."

Ruthie nodded tentatively. An intuitive Pisces, something clearly bothered her about the answer. Penny Sue must have picked up on the feeling, too.

"I think I'll ask for clarification." Penny Sue massaged the book like Kobe beef. *YOU'LL NEED TO TAKE THE INITIATIVE*, the page read. Penny Sue pouted. "Now I'm confused. Do you think this means I should call Rich?"

"Ask again," Ruthie said.

Penny Sue's squinched her eyes shut with intense concentration. *MOVE ON*, came the response.

I snatched the book from her. "No doubt about that— it's time to eat. Come on, our reservation is at seven, and with all the bikers, it'll take twice as long to get there." Penny Sue followed reluctantly, glancing back at the book as she picked up her purse and car keys.

* * *

A round, linen-draped table had been set up on the deck next to the railing. A peach-colored napkin folded in the shape of a bird graced each plate that was flanked by an assortment of silverware and stemmed glasses. A wine bucket cradled an ice packed bottle of Dom Perignon. Our three chairs were placed on one side of the table, providing each of us with a view of the marina. Unfortunately, a huge centerpiece of yellow roses, baby's breath, and ferns surrounding a single, glass daffodil stood between us and the pristine view.

"No boats are docked," Ruthie observed, taking her seat in the middle.

"Yeah," Penny Sue muttered with an edge of disappointment.

I exhaled with relief, silently thanking the spirits. This would not be like the last time when a big yacht and yachtsman caught Penny Sue's eye.

A plethora of champagne, wine, appetizers, salads, and entrees, all topped off by cake and an after dinner drink left us feeling full, fat, and limp again. "Coffee. We need coffee," Penny Sue groaned. She turned, raising her hand for the waiter, then froze, eyes locked on the walkway that led from the deck to the street. "That's Rich," she exclaimed. She tossed her napkin on the table and pushed back her chair.

"What are you going to do?" I asked.

"The oracle said things would change quickly, and I should take the initiative. I'm doing just that."

She barreled across the deck and around the corner like a track star. Okay, slight exaggeration. How about a middle-aged woman with incontinence? Anyway, I was surprised at how fast she could move considering the huge dinner she was hauling. I said before that testosterone affected Penny Sue like Prozac—perhaps Prozac laced with an amphetamine was a more accurate description.

The waiter arrived. Ruthie and I ordered three decafs. "Boy, I hope it goes well with Rich," Ruthie said, stirring her coffee.

"You got bad vibes about *the things will change quickly* prediction. What exactly did you feel?"

"Something dark and sinister. I can't put my finger on it, but it wasn't happy."

I stared out over the water, considering. Though I poked fun at some of Ruthie's metaphysical convictions, I did believe that everyone possessed intuition or an unconscious link with the truth, the Universe, or whatever you wanted to call it. Sure, the ability was more developed in some people, but everyone had it. How else could a person, like myself, walk up to a half-finished jigsaw puzzle, pick a piece seemingly at random, and miraculously put it in place? The act took a mere second or two, not enough time for the logical mind to sort though possibilities. It happened all the time, which was one reason I liked puzzles—for the magical, enchanted rush. No question, the unconscious mind was hooked into a vast store of information. Whether it was spirit guides, as Ruthie said, or Jung's collective consciousness, or psychic abilities I wasn't certain. But, I *knew* things from time-to-time, like a sixth sense, and Ruthie was particularly gifted in that department.

"What's Penny Sue doing now?" I asked Ruthie.

"She's frustrated."

Penny Sue rounded the corner at that exact moment, red faced from exertion.

"No luck?" I asked casually.

Penny Sue poured a dollop of cream in her coffee and stirred vigorously. "I lost him." The stirring increased in intensity. At that rate, the cream might soon turn to butter. "His message said he was going out of town for a few days." Her spoon clanged on the sides of the cup. I reached over and held her hand still. She took the hint and put the spoon down. "He's still registered at the hotel," she said, lips narrowed.

"That doesn't mean a thing. He obviously hasn't left. Besides, this is Bike Week—all of the hotels are booked solid. He'll keep the room while he's gone, knowing he'll never find another when he returns."

She blew her coffee before tasting it. "Why didn't he stop by to say 'Hi?'"

"He probably didn't see us, we have our backs to the room," Ruthie jumped in. "Besides, he was in a hurry."

"I wonder what was so important," Penny Sue said tightly, staring up at the drawbridge and a long convoy of motorcycles. An instant later, her eyes flashed, and she was back to normal. Honestly, it was like the old cartoon where a light bulb went off in Popeye's head. "I think we should look up Pauline."

Pauline was a psychic we'd consulted on our last trip. Her predictions turned out to be right. She was also very strange, bordering on scary. Her house was filled with oils and potions and lord knew what all. She had a mechanical angel named Alice, too.

"It'll be fun." She glanced at Ruthie. "A birthday reading."

Ruthie grinned. "Sure, why not?"

That's all it took. Penny Sue rebounded from the pits of depression, yet again. A few minutes later, Frannie May and Carl (the Klingon) stopped by to offer birthday wishes. They'd spotted us from their inside table overlooking the deck.

"Carl cleaned up good for Momma," Penny Sue observed as the Anninas walked away. "He's actually quite handsome."

I shook my head. "I told you he was only playing a game."

"You have to admit his get-up was pretty wild. Why would such an attractive man want to look so ugly."

"It's a game, Penny Sue, a game."

"Hmph. A game like sickos in Las Vegas play, where twisted twerps shoot nude women with paintballs? There was a TV exposé on it. That isn't a harmless game, if you ask me."

"That was a hoax," Ruthie said. "A guy faked the whole thing to sell videos of the nude hunts on the Internet."

Penny Sue cocked her head skeptically. "You're kidding. I never heard that. Why didn't it make the news?"

"It did, but was buried at the end of the broadcast. I suppose the reporters were embarrassed to admit they'd been duped."

"Proves appearances can be deceiving," I said wryly. "Carl is a nice young man."

"Okay, okay. I'll take your word for it."

It was nearly ten by the time we paid the check and left. The night was pleasantly cool as we strolled up the deserted brick sidewalk. Penny Sue stopped in front of the hotel, presumably to fetch her car keys. While her hand rummaged through her purse, Penny Sue's eyes searched the second floor windows. All the lights were out. The keys miraculously appeared.

"I should have gone to the bathroom before we left," Ruthie said suddenly. "Coffee always goes straight through me."

"Everything goes straight through you," Penny Sue said. "You really should check into that pee urgency pill. Peeing all the time is not normal."

"Don't start that."

"Well, do you want to go back to the restaurant?"

"No, let's hurry. I can wait until we get home."

We double-timed it around the hotel and stopped cold. Blue flashing lights lit up the sky while a siren sounded in the distance.

"Lord!" Penny Sue set off at a jog with us close behind. We rounded the corner of some small shops to the lot next to the spa. "Crap!" Penny Sue stopped dead. Ruthie plowed into her back.

Two police cars were stationed at either end of the lot with a small crowd of people huddled to one side. Siren wailing, an ambulance turned in from Flagler Avenue. A patrolman waved back the crowd, and the EVAC truck pulled to a stop, its headlights illuminating a form on the pavement about twenty feet from Penny Sue's car. Another policeman hunched over the body giving CPR.

"I hope you're wearing a pantiliner," Penny Sue said. "We're not going home any time soon."

"I don't have to go any more," Ruthie said weakly.

I spotted Fran and Carl at the far side of the crowd. "What happened?' I asked, worming in beside them as paramedics rushed to the victim with a stretcher and med kits.

"Gun shot," Carl replied solemnly.

"A mugging?" Penny Sue asked.

"Not likely."

"What do you mean?"

"I've seen that guy around. He's a biker who hangs out with a thug called Vulture who has a reputation for being mean. Some say Vulture's crazy, others claim he's one of those anti-government extremists. Bad news in either case." Carl canted his head at the form the medics were about to shock with a defibrillator. "I'd guess this is some sort of turf battle."

We watched as the EMT applied a shock and checked for a pulse. Another shock. His partner listened with a stethoscope and shook his head. The first medic waved his hands, and everything went into high gear. They lifted the body onto the stretcher and headed for the ambulance. As the gurney rolled past, the victim's head rolled to the side, his lifeless eyes staring straight at us.

Penny Sue gasped and covered her face with both hands. I put my arm around her waist. "Take a deep breath."

She shook her head, hands still covering her eyes. "It won't help," she mumbled. "That's one of Rich's old friends."

"Rich's friend?" I watched as a policeman closed the EVAC's back door. The vehicle inched away, siren blaring.

"He's one of the men I saw on the balcony," she said.

"Uh oh, here comes trouble," Ruthie whispered.

"Penny Sue Parker," a familiar voice said. "I thought I recognized that Mercedes."

I turned toward the voice. *Damn. Double damn.* It was Woody.

Chapter 6

Robert "Woody" Woodhead was the local prosecutor. He was also one of Penny Sue's many jilted college loves. Though Woody was now married and swore he didn't hold a grudge, none of us believed it. Woody made our last vacation pure hell. Needless to say, we weren't thrilled to see him.

Penny Sue set her jaw and glared at him. "We were just passing by."

Woody waved off the remark. "Relax, that was an observation, not an accusation." His lips stretched into a crooked smile. "You have an amazing affinity for men with bullet wounds. This is the first gunshot I've seen since you were in town last October."

"Pure chance," I said.

"It is, indeed." A policeman in uniform approached and whispered something to Woody. His grin grew wider. "I'm afraid we'll need to give you a ride home. It seems the shooter wasn't very accurate. He or she nailed your Mercedes."

"What?" We looked at the yellow Benz, where an officer was prying something from the middle of the first P in the PSP of Penny Sue's University of Georgia vanity plate.

"Yeah, whoever it was shot the center out of Penny," Woody snickered.

"Did they hurt Uga?" she demanded.

A vicious-looking bulldog with a spiked collar, Uga is the Georgia mascot and the only dog to be invited to a Heisman trophy dinner. Actually, there have been a succession of Ugas who are paraded at the beginning of home games in an air-conditioned, fire hydrant doghouse.

Woody stared at the license. "No. A shame. I'm a Gator fan." He chuckled to himself. "We'll have to take your car in to check for prints. You should get it back tomorrow. I'll have one of the officers give you a ride."

"We'll take them home," Fran said forcefully.

I was relieved, to say the least. It had taken some doing after the October debacle, but I'd finally convinced several of the neighbors that we were not homicidal maniacs and hated to queer the relationship by showing up in a police car. The three of us slid into the back seat of Fran's new Jaguar. Spacious with a new leather scent, the luxury car's back seat was a far cry from the rear of my Beetle.

"I don't like that guy," Fran said, starting the Jaguar and cranking up the air conditioner. "Your car was shot, and he laughs about it. And that football comment was totally out of line. I might report him. He's a public employee. Where does he get off with such arrogance?"

He's a lawyer, I thought. Then, two other lawyers—Zack, my ex, and Max Bennett, my worthless divorce counsel—came to mind. They were both snide and overbearing. In truth, virtually all the attorneys I knew, except for the judge, were egomaniacs. Probably a required course in law school, Self-Importance 101.

"He could see how upset Penny Sue was," Fran went on. "His remark was totally thoughtless. I've got a mind to call the mayor."

"No," I blurted. Fran was right, but a run-in with Woody was the last thing we needed. "Woody's not worth your time. Besides, he's one *old acquaintance* we really want to *be forgot.*"

"Well, I'm going to keep an eye out for that guy. Public employees need to show a little respect for taxpayers. After all, we're paying their salaries." Fran reached through the space between the front bucket seats and patted Penny Sue's knee. "Are you feeling better?"

"Much, thank you." She sighed. "I suppose insurance will cover the bullet hole. But, that's the least of my worries. The victim is one of the fellows I saw outside of Rich's room the other day. Rich said he was an old friend."

An old friend that hangs out with a person named Vulture. I also couldn't help but wonder about the coincidence of Rich rushing through the restaurant and the old friend's body being discovered less than a hour later. The look on Ruthie's face said she was thinking the same thing. Surely, it had also occurred to Penny Sue.

"I can hardly believe all of this. Rich seemed so kind and gentle," Penny Sue said.

"He's into motorcycles," Ruthie said quietly. "Some of the motorcycle crowd are pretty rough."

"Yeah, but they're a minority," Penny Sue said defensively. "It's always a few bad apples that give the bunch a bad name. Like Muslim fanatics—everyone from the Middle East isn't a terrorist."

Fran nodded. "All Italians aren't in the Mafia."

"True, but all bikers don't hang out with a Vulture," Ruthie said.

Penny Sue looked at her lap, crestfallen "You're right. I just can't imagine Rich is involved in this. He's such a sweetheart." She glanced up, tears rimming her eyes. "He's my soul mate."

I swallowed. Lordy, I'd heard that line a million times before. Best I could tell, Penny Sue had been in a harem in several past lives, and everyone was her soul mate. Still, the tears threw me. I'd seen more tears from Penny Sue in the last two days than the last twenty-five years.

Penny Sue tugged on Carl's shirtsleeve. "Are you sure *that man* was a friend of Vulture's?"

"Positive. I've seen them together at the Canaveral Park several times and at the Pub, too. It's definitely the same guy."

"What in the world were they doing at the park? Surely not sightseeing."

"Paintball battles."

Penny Sue recoiled. "They're Klingons?"

Carl scowled. "No. Paintball battles are all the craze. Lots of people play them. Corporate team building seminars even use them."

"Yeah, and Muslim terrorists use paintballs to train for jihad." Ruthie, our news junkie, jumped in. "There was a big article about it in the *Washington Post.*"

"I always suspected Vulture and his crowd were training for a conflict. Like I said, some people say he's an anti-government extremist."

"Rich is not an extremist. I'd stake my life on it."

"I'm sure you're right," I said with more conviction than I felt. I hoped Penny Sue's faith was justified. I was beginning to like my new single life and hated to stake it on anything.

*   *   *

The telephone rang at seven o'clock the next morning. I bolted upright, heart pounding, struggling for air. I was right in the middle of the damned dream about Zack. The nightmare I'd had over and over since I discovered his secret life. The wrenching horror that my divorce decree had not silenced.

I was sitting in the garage waiting for my husband. My feet were propped up on a carton of wooden figurines identical to the ones Zack claimed to have carved. I'll never forget the moment I found that box marked *Country Originals* hidden under his workbench. In a flash *I knew* and felt like my heart had been ripped out. It must have been the same sensation suffered by virgins in Aztec sacrifices when the priest savagely severed her heart, and ate it, still beating.

The utter emptiness in my chest was almost more than I could bear, yet it was peanuts compared to the feeling of abandonment I felt when I confronted Zack. He callously brushed me off and categorically refused to give up his girl-friend. I couldn't believe the man I'd slept next to for so many years, the man I'd put first in almost everything, had so little regard for me and our marriage! Dumped for a strip club dancer hardly older than our own daughter.

The shock was more than my system could stand. I started to hyperventilate, from pain, back then. Since the divorce, I heaved from rage. A rage that spurted from my chest like a ballistic missile. A furor so fierce it could destroy Zack, me, and the entire planet.

The shift from pain to rage happened shortly after I moved from Atlanta to New Smyrna Beach. Alone, away from family and friends, it worried me. Should I consult a therapist, I wondered? My track record with psychologists in Atlanta was dismal. Desperate for support, I had called Ruthie who was an aficionado on the newest spiritual and psychological theories.

"That's terrific," she'd said, when I told her my feelings of despair had turned to rage. "You're making great progress. Rage is much farther up the consciousness scale than despair. Don't be concerned unless the nightmares get worse. Otherwise, I think your unconscious is working it out."

Geez, everything was terrific to Ruthie. She said the same thing about my memory loss. Heck, maybe she was right. Perhaps I'd just forget Zack pretty soon.

The phone emitted another electronic jingle. Ruthie stirred in the next twin bed. "Wha—" she mumbled.

I snatched the portable from its cradle and headed for the kitchen. It was all merely a dream, I told myself, trying to clear my head.

I looked at the clock. The only person who would call at that ungodly hour was my daughter, Ann, who still hadn't gotten the hang of the time difference although she'd been in London six weeks.

"Hello."

"Mom, are you all right?"

I cradled the phone on my shoulder and reached for the coffee can. "Sure, I'm fine," I replied, trying to calm my racing heart. You woke me up, that's all. It's seven a.m. here."

"Sorry, I keep forgetting. I just finished lunch."

"That's okay. How about you? Still loving your job?"

"Yes, more than ever."

My antenna went up. *More than ever.* A hidden meaning there. "Another junket to Scotland?" I asked, pouring water into the Mr. Coffee.

"Nothing like that. Mom, I've met someone."

My heart raced again. Ann was a smart, attractive, twenty-two year old who'd had many boy friends over the years. She was pinned to Gregory at one point and hinted at marriage. Yet, even then, she'd never sounded so serious. I took a deep breath to calm myself. "Is your boyfriend an intern?"

"No, Patrick is a career employee. A Deputy Public Affairs Officer."

Career employee. Deputy Public Affairs Officer. That sounded like an important position, not one they'd give to a recent college grad. "Wow, he sounds impressive. How old is Patrick, honey?" I detected a transatlantic gulp.

"He's a little older than I am."

An image of Monica and Clinton flashed through my mind. Then, an image of Zack and his young honey. My blood pressure shot up. "Oh? How much older?"

"He recently turned forty."

"Forty!" Magawd, he was nearly my age. Was this one of those contemptible, cloying Casanovas? A philandering slime bucket who preyed on dewy-eyed interns? "Is he married?" I nearly shouted.

Penny Sue entered the room, eyes wide. "Who is it?" she whispered.

"Ann," I mouthed back.

My friend poured some coffee and perched on a stool to listen.

"He's divorced, Mom. Don't get excited."

I let out a long breath. "I'm sorry. Eighteen years is a big age difference."

Penny Sue's eyebrow shot up.

"Does he have kids? How long has he been divorced?"

"No children from either—"

"Either?"

Penny Sue's other brow arched.

"It's not what you think, Mom. He got married right out of college. Young and stupid, as he said."

Like you!

"That one only lasted a little over a year. His second marriage ended two years ago. His wife didn't like living in England and went back to the states. She came from a big family and never adjusted to being away from her mother."

Being away from her mother. If Ann married this guy, she'd live in England. I'd never see her. Worse, Patrick might be transferred to Zimbabwe or Latvia, or an obscure post that was only accessible by dog sled. Smelly dogs that pooped and peed as they mushed along.

Then what? I'd never see my grandchildren, if Ann had any. She might catch a horrible disease like SARS or be embroiled in a revolution. For godssakes, why did we let her major in European Studies? Darn it, she should have gotten a degree in accounting and gone on to get an MBA. A good ole USA MBA. Maybe I could still talk her into it.

"What's the temperature over there? It's going to be in the upper seventies here. Sunny, not a cloud in the sky."

"Mom, what does that have to do with anything?"

"I was just thinking that England must be awfully cold and dreary. You know, University of Miami has a great MBA program. South Beach is the place to go."

"Momma, Patrick proposed."

I nearly swallowed my tongue. "Did you give him an answer?" I finally managed.

"I told Patrick he had to meet my parents first."

I sighed with relief until the meaning sunk in. "Parents, as in Zack and me?"

Both brows went up as Penny Sue took a pull of her java.

"Well, yeah, you are my parents."

"You mean, us, together?"

Penny Sue's jaw dropped.

"That would be nice."

"I'm not sure your dad will go for it."

Penny Sue nodded emphatically.

"I'll call him," Ann said.

"No." I had to slow this thing down. She barely knew Patrick—how could she consider marriage? "I'll *try* to get your father." I would try, I just wasn't saying how hard.

"That's great. Mom?"

"Yes?"

"Be happy for me."

"I am, baby." I pushed the power button and started to cry. Penny Sue plunked down her mug and rushed around the counter to comfort me. At that instant Ruthie emerged from our bedroom.

"What now?" she moaned. "The *humors* in this place are clearly off. Leigh, do you still have that smudge stick?"

I motioned to the sideboard in the dining area where Ruthie retrieved a Baggie containing the charred remains of what looked like a bundle of broom straw, a feather, and a pack of matches. She wasted no time lighting the mixture of sweetgrass, cedar, and sage and fanning the smoke around the room. An American Indian purification tradition, smudging was supposed to clear negative vibes and invite the presence of good spirits. It hadn't worked all that well the last time. Ruthie said it was because we didn't use enough sage. Who knew? After the weird Zack dream and Ann's call, I was willing to give anything a try, even another smudging.

"Can't you do that somewhere else?" Penny Sue coughed as Ruthie fanned us with the smoke.

"You know it won't work unless I cleanse your auras first." We held our breath as Ruthie smoked us from head to toe.

"Whew," Penny Sue snorted as Ruthie and smudge stick moved into the hallway. "That stuff smells like marijuana, doesn't it?"

"It's the sweetgrass," Ruthie replied. "Grass is grass— it all smells about the same."

"I suppose you're right." Penny Sue turned her attention to me. "Now, what's wrong with Ann? Why in the world are you crying?"

I sniffled from the smoke as much as the tears. "She's in love with some old government employee. He's probably married and leading her on like Clinton did Monica. Ann's going to get hurt and humiliated. These old men preying on young girls, they should be ... be ... have their privates cut off!" Then I thought of Zack and his sweetie, a stripper who was clearly as guilty as he was. "Well, maybe all the licentious old wieners shouldn't be whacked off—"

Penny Sue went into hysterics. "They wish!"

"Mind in the gutter." I shook my head. "You know what I mean!"

"Sorry," she sputtered, clapping her hand over her mouth.

"Darn it, Ann is an innocent and, as far as I'm concerned, this Patrick is a candidate for radical surgery ... without anesthesia!"

"Slow down," Penny Sue said, finally calming herself. "You're jumping to conclusions, like Daddy did with Sydney—" She grinned weakly. Sydney was the bisexual husband. "Okay, a bad example. But, Patrick—that's his name, right?—may be sincere. Ann's a lovable person. She's sensible, too. Don't you suppose your values have rubbed off on her, that your troubles with Zack have made her cautious? Don't prejudge the relationship before you get more details. This could be a match made in heaven."

"He could be her soul mate," Ruthie said, emerging from the hall with the smoldering wand. "Get his birthday and I'll do an astrological comparison. That'll tell us if he's the one."

I wiped my eyes. Yes, we'd check this out. He might be the one, and he might not. I grabbed the phone and held it up for Ruthie to smudge before I dialed. Ann answered. "Before I agree to come, where and when, including the time, was Patrick born?"

"Ruthie's with you, right?" Ann asked flatly. "Is Penny Sue there, too?"

"Yes. We're going to check him out."

"Does Ruthie do this to her daughter?"

To? "Do you do this *for* Jo Ruth?" I asked Ruthie who was running water over the straw in the kitchen sink.

"Of course," she said over her shoulder.

"Of course."

"Okay, if it'll make y'all feel better, I'll find out."

"It will," I said, feeling relieved already.

* * *

My reprieve didn't last long. Literally, the moment I hung up the phone, someone knocked on the front door. I looked at the clock, eight.

"What is this, Grand Central Station?" Penny Sue said, smoothing her hair and hitching her robe tighter. "Who in the world would drop in unannounced at this hour? Honestly, what's become of common courtesy?"

I keyed the alarm code into the panel as Penny Sue stomped to the front door and peered through the peephole. "Damn, it's Woody and another guy, probably a detective."

"The smoke," I exclaimed, thinking how it smelled like marijuana.

Ruthie caught my meaning and ran to the bathroom for air freshener. She only got out a few squirts before another knock, this one louder.

"Don't answer it," I hissed.

"I have to—they've got my car."

Terrific. Why did it have to be Woody? The one person who wanted, more than anything, to get even with Penny Sue for dumping him back in college. The little weasel who'd given us a fit in October.

Another knock. Crap, the smudging hadn't work. Maybe we should have used more sage.

Chapter 7

Penny Sue surveyed the parking lot through the screen door. "Good morning, Woody. I was hoping you were here to return my car. I'd invite you in, but at as you can see," she did a Vanna White/*Wheel of Fortune* hand sweep, "we're not prepared to accept visitors."

Woody flashed a smarmy grin. The detective standing in the background was visibly sniffing the air.

"Sorry to intrude. We tried to call, but your line was busy." Woody inhaled deeply and glanced back at his side-kick. "We'd like to take your fingerprints and ask a few questions. It's important. How about we wait in the car while you get dressed?" He slipped his card through the edge of the screen door. "Call my cell phone when you're ready."

"It could be a long wait," she said under her breath, closing the door.

"What do you think that's about?" Ruthie asked anxiously. "Your car was shot, what could Woody possibly want from us?"

"He's a jerk who intends to badger me whenever possible. Come on, let's get a cup of coffee. I'll be darned if I'm rushing to meet with Woody and his lackey."

"I don't think it's smart to toy with him. He can make things very difficult," I reminded her.

"Woody wouldn't dare." Penny Sue did a hair toss. "I'm the injured party here. We've done nothing wrong, and I refuse to be intimidated."

"That's not a wise move. I think you could be accused of obstructing justice or something." I'd learned that much from my years with Zack. "Let's throw some clothes on and get it over with."

Penny Sue gave me her aristocratic expression. "I will as soon as I have my coffee."

She finally called Woody at quarter after nine, declaring that the proper time to accept visitors. Of course, she could have opened the front door and hollered, the men had been waiting in their car for over an hour. Which told me Woody did, indeed, have something serious to discuss.

When finally summoned, he bristled with anger to the point, I swear, his hair stood on end. He plunked down in the rattan chair by the fireplace. His sidekick, Detective Jones who looked none too happy either, stood like a sentry. While the smudge stench had dissipated considerably, the combination of odors from the herbs and vanilla air freshener was nauseatingly sweet. In any event, Woody was clearly allergic, his eyes teared immediately.

"Did the victim make it?" Penny Sue asked, taking the bull by the horns.

"I'm afraid not," Woody mumbled through his handkerchief.

"I'm sorry. Could you lift any prints from the car?"

"The only clear prints appeared to be women's, probably yours." Woody nodded to Jones who produced a fingerprinting kit. "For comparison purposes, we need your prints so we can rule them out."

We held out our hands. The detective rolled our fingers in black ink and pressed them roughly to fingerprint cards. He was definitely furious at us for keeping him waiting.

Penny Sue looked Woody in the eye as she wiped her hand with ink remover. "Why do you want to talk to us? The killer was a lousy shot who happened to hit my car. We don't know a thing; we were on the deck of the Riverview all night. You can check with the restaurant staff as well as our friends, Fran and Carl Annina—they can vouch for us."

"We're not so sure the killer was a lousy shot."

"What?" we blurted like an out-of-key chorus.

"The chances of the bullet hitting the exact center of the P in your license are virtually nil. The fact that the slug wedged in the plate without penetrating the trunk means the shooter pulled that round from a fair distance and also says he's a crack marksman."

Ruthie went white. "Yes, but it could have been luck, right?"

Woody nodded slowly, still holding the handkerchief to his nose. "The victim was shot at close range. Nailing your car seemed to be an afterthought."

"It's a Mercedes. Maybe it was someone angry about Germany not supporting the U.S. against Saddam Hussein," I said.

"Or class envy," Ruthie speculated.

"Maybe someone who hates the Georgia Bulldogs," Penny Sue added, jumping on the rationalization bandwagon.

"Possible." Woody regarded Penny Sue sternly. "What do you know about Richard Wheeler?"

The blood drained from Penny Sue's face. "He's a friend from home," she replied, doing her best to look nonchalant.

Detective Jones consulted a small notepad. "Did you see him last night?"

Penny Sue drew up haughtily. "Yes, I saw him. We all saw him, but Rich didn't see us. We caught a glimpse of him as he left the restaurant."

"Left, as in run?" Jones said.

"Left, as in hurry," Penny Sue replied stiffly.

Jones consulted his pad again. "You ran after him. Isn't that right?"

"Please, a Southern lady may rush, scoot or hustle, we do not run!"

Jones, clearly from the North, probably New York, was not amused. "Cut the cutesy stuff. You followed him. Why?"

Penny Sue's lips tensed; she was morphing into a Steel Magnolia. "My affairs of the heart are none of your business."

Woody snickered into his handkerchief. Jones glared. "It is when there's a murder and someone apparently has a vendetta for you."

Vendetta! There was no vendetta, certainly from Rich. He'd left the sweet message on Penny Sue's phone.

The Steel Magnolia mutated into a Titanium Oleander—the blood red kind, deadly poisonous. "First, Rich is NOT involved in the murder or attack on my car. He's a good friend, one I cherish. I *followed* him last night because I needed to clarify something. I didn't catch up to him, so checked with the hotel to make sure he was still registered. That's it, *fini,* no more to tell."

"We hear Wheeler was seen with the guy who was murdered. Would you know anything about that?" Jones asked.

Penny Sue's demeanor streaked through Titanium Oleander to Southern Bitch. "I'm not saying another word until I call Daddy and have counsel present."

"Fine," Woody snapped, pocketing his handkerchief. "Call Daddy. And, be sure to tell Daddy that you and your friends are in danger. The murdered man and your *good* friend were known to hang out with a most undesirable fellow, a gang-type who doesn't give a hang about the University of Georgia or Germany supporting the U.S. in Iraq."

"Vulture," Ruthie whispered.

"Ah, you know of him."

"From our friends, the Anninas. Carl's a biker and he's heard rumors about Vulture."

"This Carl recognized the guy on the pavement as Vulture's associate?" Jones shot.

I nodded.

Woody stood. "There you have it. Who did the shooting? I don't know. Yet one thing's for certain—this is not a group to trifle with. And, with a half million bikers in the area for Bike Week, many with conflicting allegiances, this incident could explode into a turf war of monumental proportions if we're not careful. Be sure to mention that to Daddy. My phone numbers are on the card. I'll expect to hear from you by the end of the day."

"What about my car?"

Jones and Woody started down the hall. "I'll give you an update when you call me."

* * *

Penny Sue sat at the counter with her head in her hands. "Bloody Mary. I need a Bloody Mary," she whimpered.

"I'll have one, too," Ruthie said.

I did a double take. Ruthie rarely drank alcohol, except with us, and then nursed a single glass for hours. That she wanted a cocktail before noon was a clear sign that Woody's speech had shaken her. I took the Tabasco Bloody Mary mix from the refrigerator. Heck, I might as well have one myself.

"Let's smudge the place again," Penny Sue said without looking up.

"The bundle's still wet."

"Put it in the oven."

I slid the cocktail in front of Penny Sue as Ruthie put the smudge stick in the toaster oven on low.

"Sage," I said, handing Ruthie her drink as I took a long sip of mine. She went to the cabinet, found a bottle of Spice Islands sage and dumped it in a bowl. Ruthie handed the saucer to Penny Sue to do the honors.

"Wait a second." Penny Sue scooted (barreled was more like it) down the hall and returned with a gold lighter and a pack of cigarettes. "For luck," she said, touching the flame to the spice, then lighting a cigarette.

"I thought you quit smoking," I said.

Penny Sue raised her hand to ward off comment. "Please, don't start on me now. I have an occasional cigarette, that's all.

It calms my nerves. Anyway, what's good for Native Americans is good enough for me. Right, Ruthie?"

Ruthie nodded. "Yes, it was a sacred herb to the Indians. And, new research shows that nicotine is beneficial in Alzheimer's."

My jaw dropped. I could hardly believe this revelation was coming from Ruthie "Holistic Health" Nichols.

She saw my disbelief. "It's true. Nicotine acts like acetylcholine, a crucial brain chemical for memory and attention."

Penny Sue took a long drink of her Bloody Mary and a drag of her cigarette. "I can vouch for that—I haven't been right since I quit smoking."

I looked at her puffing and wondered when she'd quit smoking. I also wondered when Penny Sue'd *ever* been *right*. One thing for sure, needling Woody was the wrong thing to do and the faster she cooperated with the police the better. "Penny Sue, you need to call your father right now. You're on thin ice with Woody. Besides, if you don't cooperate you'll never get your car back."

"He wouldn't dare." She blew a smoke ring.

"In a heartbeat," I countered.

She snuffed her cigarette in the sage, which had gone out, and downed the rest of her drink. "I suppose you're right. No sense putting it off."

As she dialed her father's cell phone, I fished the cigarette butt from the sage and lit it again, fanning the bowl with the feather to keep it smoldering. Although the spice was part of the mint family, the odor was anything but sweet, sort of a cross between charred paper and a compost heap. While I'd never admit it to Penny Sue, I found its smell far worse than tobacco. I truly didn't think the sage would do any good, but the events of the morning with Ann, Woody, Penny Sue, and even the stupid dream about Zack had left me with a sick sense of impending doom. I headed for the living room, fanning the bowl as the judge came on the line with Penny Sue.

She started out in her bubbly mode, gushing about her wonderful Harley, the wonderful weather, and Ruthie's wonderful birthday dinner. Daddy must have sensed something was coming—if everything was so wonderful, why was she calling?—and demanded she get to the point. Her demeanor changed instantly to Betty Businesswoman. With a brevity I'd never guessed possible, Penny Sue outlined the situation, ending with a somewhat plaintive, "I thought, perhaps, I should have counsel present, since I believe the police are trying to frame Rich for the murder. You remember Rich, the man whose wife passed away—"

If the judge remembered Rich, he didn't care and launched into a stern lecture, judging from the slump of Penny Sue's shoulders and downcast eyes. I set the sage on the coffee table and drifted back to the kitchen. Ruthie abandoned the bread she was about to put in the toaster oven to listen.

Eyes fixed on the counter, Penny Sue started, "But, Daddy—" Her lips tensed as the judge forged ahead, ignoring her comment. Finally, "Yes, sir, I understand—"

At which point, the toaster oven erupted into a raging inferno. I ran to the kitchen and pulled the plug from the wall. Ruthie grabbed a potholder and opened the oven door, releasing a thick cloud of acrid smoke. The smudge stick!

"Close it up," I hacked. Ruthie slammed the door shut, but it did no good. The whole smudge stick—not just the tip—was ablaze, forcing sheets of smoke through the outside edge of the door.

"No, Daddy, everything's fine ..." Penny Sue waved frantically, signaling "Do something!" as she hustled down the hall with the portable phone.

Something? What? I grabbed the first thing I saw, Ruthie's Bloody Mary, and threw it into the toaster oven. A hissing, swirling torrent of smoke and steam poured forth, filling the kitchen. The smudge smell was tolerable, the burnt Tabasco/tomato scent too much. Ruthie and I ran like hell to the deck.

We stared at each other, wide-eyed, shell-shocked. We were both covered in a fine spray of tomato juice, which gave us the appearance of a bad case of measles or a streaky application of the old-time, instant tan lotion that always turned people orange instead of brown. As fate would have it, the nosey couple that lived in the two-story condo behind ours was heading down the boardwalk to the beach. The woman—Suzanne? Sarah? Shrewella!—stared at us, sniffing the air. "What in the world is wrong with you? What is that smell?"

Penny Sue stalked onto the deck at that moment. She was hopping mad, primed to unload on anyone that got in her way. Shrewella was in her way. "They have a rash, what does it look like? Probably the West Nile Virus. We found a mosquito in the condo, so we're fumigating. The newest treatment is to burn sage and cayenne red pepper. I'm amazed you haven't heard, since it's been all over TV."

Sarah/Shrewella started to back away. "I'm sorry. Is West Nile Virus contagious?"

"Only from mosquitoes or, sometimes, pets that have been bitten by mosquitoes." I knew she had a big black cat that slept on the deck most of the time.

"Mosquitoes at this time of year?"

"It's been unusually warm, and we saw one. So, you should probably fumigate as soon as possible. Can't be too careful with something like this."

"Sage and cayenne red pepper? You mean the regular spices?"

Penny Sue nodded. "Dump it in a bowl and set it on fire. Be sure to smoke your place really well, especially the closets and your clothes."

Shrewella cut her eyes at her husband, trying to gauge our sincerity. Whether we really convinced them or they were too anal to take a chance, we'll never know. They hoisted their beach chairs and shuffled back home.

"Cayenne pepper?" I said, steering Penny Sue and Ruthie back into the condo. "They may choke to death."

"No they won't—that old lady's too mean to die," Penny Sue snickered. "I hope the cayenne singes her nose hairs. Serve her right. She's the one who called the police on me the last time. I'm doing her a favor, anyway—her nose hairs need trimming."

For the second time that day, we cranked down the air conditioner, turned on the exhaust fans, and opened the windows. Ruthie and I were dying to hear the details of Penny Sue's conversation with the judge, but B.O. won out over curiosity. We showered and changed in record time. When we finished, Penny Sue was peeking through the front door, laughing hysterically. She motioned for us to come see. Mr. and Mrs. Shrewella were hanging over the side of their balcony, wheezing and wiping their eyes.

I shot a look at Penny Sue. "You've got a bad streak, you know that?"

She tossed her hair and strutted away, wiggling her fanny. "Not bad, sugar, bold."

"Well, Your Boldness, what did Daddy say?"

She deflated like a punctured balloon. "I should call Woody and answer all of his questions, ASAP. It seems that a citizen who's not under suspicion has no rights. A person can only refuse to answer questions if it's self-incriminating. Since I haven't done anything, I'm technically not entitled to a lawyer. Bottom line, if I—we—don't cooperate, we're subject to subpoenas, court orders, and even obstruction of justice charges."

I wanted to say 'I told you so,' but didn't. I reached for the phone. "What's Woody's cell number?"

Chapter 8

Woody agreed to see us at one o'clock, and, rather than meet us at the office on Canal Street, as he'd done before, he wanted us to come to the main station—a sure sign he was really angry.

"Daddy says we should dress conservatively, it helps our credibility," Penny Sue instructed.

The comment was unnecessary for Ruthie, who always dressed that way. I already knew as much, having watched a lot of *Perry Mason* with my grandmother as a kid, not to mention the twenty-plus years with Zack who had an entire wardrobe of expensive Canali and Zegna suits, required attire for court-room credibility. But, good for Daddy, he knew his daughter well. Penny Sue was the one who might show up in a short, red dress with a neckline that plunged to her navel—no doubt an expensive, designer job like Versace, but risqué nonethe-less. (As Dolly Parton said, "It costs a lot of money to look this cheap.")

We all dressed in black dresses or slack outfits so, for once, we actually looked like members of the same sorority—albeit a drab, boring, business or academic group.

When we arrived at the station, Penny Sue was ushered to a room with Woody and Detective Jones, while Ruthie and I were led to separate offices for questioning by female officers. Separate interrogations to compare stories and look for discrepancies—standard police procedure, if one believed *Law and Order*.

My officer, a sergeant, proved very nice and I held nothing back. Rich was pleasant enough, but I didn't know him, having only met him once at dinner. Though I knew Penny Sue had complete confidence in Rich, I also knew her judgment was hormone-impaired on occasion. So, I freely relayed the story of Penny Sue and Rich's break-up, as well as the apology he left on her cell phone. I hoped it proved that Rich was not out to get us, for Penny Sue's sake, but left it to the police to sort things out. I absolutely was not interested in getting involved in this mess. I had learned my lesson the last time.

Finishing first, Ruthie and I waited in the lobby for Penny Sue. About fifteen minutes later she showed up, looking flustered.

"Woody's having my car brought around." She tried the front door, it was locked. The receptionist on the other side of bullet-resistant glass looked up from his computer. The door buzzed open. We nodded "thank-you" and squeezed through the entrance en masse.

"I'll ride with you," Ruthie said immediately. I nodded agreement. We'd come in my car, a tight fit, especially for Ruthie who was relegated to the backseat.

"Let's go to Norwood's. There was a sign out front advertising a Bike Week special," Penny Sue said. "The condo stinks. We need to talk and decide what to do."

Do? I wasn't hot on doing anything. I'd just come through a devastating divorce, my daughter was in the clutches of a lecher, and I was still having nightmares. How much could Penny Sue expect? Every time she came around, things went to hell in a handbasket. But, the condo did smell awful and Norwood's was a safe bet—I didn't expect to find Vulture bellied up to a bar that boasted 1,400 varieties of wine. "Okay, I'll go ahead and get us a table."

I found a table in the elevated area next to the bar, ordered water all around, and three glasses of an Australian Chardonnay. I knew Penny Sue and Ruthie wouldn't care about the vineyard or vintage after our ordeal. The drinks arrived at the same time they did. A good thing, because Penny Sue was fit to be tied.

She gulped her wine. "They scratched Uga! There's a gash right between his eyes. I know it wasn't there last night. One of those Florida Gators did it on purpose—probably Woody. Remember how he said it was a shame Uga hadn't been shot? That weasel. He is low, you know that, low. I've got a mind to file a complaint. Gators!" she said loudly. Several nearby customers stared.

I surveyed the crowd. A handful of people were dressed in biker garb, while the majority of patrons wore regular clothes. A bald man at the end of the bar had on a University of Florida golf shirt. "Calm down, Penny Sue. This is Gator territory, and we need to be discreet," I muttered through clenched teeth. "Besides, we can't be sure it wasn't done by the shooter. It was dark. Let it go. We'll put a Band-aid on the scratch when we get home."

She drained her water. "A Band-aid? No way."

"I'll bet we can fix it with white fingernail polish. I learned the trick from one of our cleaning ladies. She used it to fill nicks on sinks, tile, just about anything." Ruthie chuckled. "She eventually got married and moved away. The white globs drove our next cleaning lady crazy. The poor thing spent untold hours scrubbing and scraping them all off. Bless her heart."

Penny Sue shrugged. "I guess it's worth a try. Better than leaving him injured and defaced."

I hurried to change the subject. "My interview was not bad. Sergeant Hooks seemed nice."

"Mine wasn't tough, either. Lieutenant Gunter moved here from Valdosta."

"Well, mine was the pits." Penny Sue spat the words, still furious over Uga. "They're after Rich. It's guilt by association. I've got to warn him!"

"Penny Sue, this is not our business," I said.

"Would you stand by and watch while someone was mugged?"

"Of course not."

"This is the same thing. Woody is convinced that Rich is the killer. I know with every fiber of my being it's not true. I have to find Rich and warn him. Convince him to go in for questioning on his own. I don't want him getting caught in the middle of a shootout between Vulture and the police. Whether or not y'all help me is your decision."

Help me—I wish she hadn't said that. Penny Sue had come to my aid more times than I could count. Heck, I was living in her father's condo free of charge. How could I refuse her plea—even if I thought it was stupid? "What do you have in mind?"

Her brow furrowed with concentration as she sipped her wine.

"Did you try calling his room? We could leave a message for him at the front desk of the Riverview," Ruthie suggested.

"Too obvious. I'm sure the police have his room under surveillance. Heck, they've probably instructed the staff to notify them when Rich returns."

"Why don't you call his cell phone? Or page him. Does his phone have a pager?"

"Yes, but that would leave a paper trail. Warning Rich might be misconstrued as obstructing justice, even though we're trying to do the exact opposite."

I hadn't thought of that angle. Neither had Ruthie, judging from the expression on her face.

"A shame we couldn't get Lu Nee 2 in his room. It does surveillance, you know," Penny Sue said. "There's a way to hook it into your computer so you can see and hear everything at a remote site. Problem is, the instructions for connecting the computer are complicated."

"What about Carl?" Ruthie asked. "I'll bet he could do it."

"I'm sure he could, but I don't want to get him involved. Besides, how would we get that big robot into Rich's room?"

Penny Sue dug into her cosmetic pouch and came up with a key. "I have a key to his room. He locked himself out the second night and got another key from the desk. I was supposed to return this when I left." She smirked. "I forgot."

"Sure, I believe that," I said, rolling my eyes.

"No, really, I was preoccupied."

I thought of the nights that she'd come home late with no lipstick and a grin. I supposed she might be telling the truth. "Penny Sue, even if we have a key, we can't take Lu Nee in there. Spying is illegal. Besides, the cleaning crew would surely notice it."

"Put it in the closet?" Penny Sue suggested.

"Closet? Lu Nee 2 wouldn't see anything."

"She could hear." Penny Sue stared at her wine as if trying to divine the future. A bust, since the Australian was crystal clear, no grape flakes or residue to swirl into patterns or portents. "Okay, we'll forget Lu Nee and concentrate on finding him in person. Rich came to survey Harley dealers. I'm sure he's already visited the local shops. My guess is that he's scoping out the major bike events now."

"Do you think it's safe for the three of us to go?" Ruthie asked nervously.

"Ted said we'd be fine as long as we stuck to the beaten paths—the Pub, J.B.'s, the bars on Flagler, even Main Street in Daytona," I reminded her. "Why don't we start with the Pub tonight? That way we can check things out and see how everyone is dressed. We want to blend with the crowd." I gave Penny Sue a look that said, "No wedding ensemble." She curled her lip at me. "Anyway, Ted's probably working traffic there tonight—we couldn't be safer."

"Won't we stand out if we pull up to bike bashes in a car?" Ruthie asked.

"My car," Penny Sue insisted immediately. "No offense, Leigh, but your little bug is not fit for adults."

At the police station, I'd had to pull her out of the front seat, again. Size wasn't the only issue here, agility was a factor, too. Penny Sue probably needed to sign up for a yoga class or something. The old joints were stiffening with age. (Gawd, what was I saying? We were the same age!)

"Ted said that most of the people who go to the Pub park at the shopping center across the street. No one will know we arrived in a car," I said. "I do wonder if we should take the Mercedes, since someone has a grudge against it."

"Pooh," Penny Sue said, draining her wine and holding it up for a refill. "It's Woody who has the vendetta—the gun shot was pure chance." Our waitress arrived with glasses of water and another wine for Penny Sue. "Do you go to Bike Week?" Penny Sue asked the petite blonde whose nametag read Angie.

"Sure, it's a lot of fun. The Pub has a slew of great shindigs. Bands, contests, and there's a web site where you can get the schedule."

"Do you go with a man on a motorcycle?" Ruthie asked.

"Sometimes. Sometimes I go with a bunch of girls."

Ruthie was still not convinced. "So, you think it's safe?"

"Oh, yeah. It's a big party, like Mardi Gras."

Penny Sue sipped her wine demurely, wheels turning in her head. Finally, in her best Georgia Peach persona, Penny Sue drawled, "You've lived here a while?"

"All my life."

"Do you know of a man named—he has a funny nick-name—Vulture?"

Angie stiffened instantly. "I've heard of him," she said flatly.

Penny Sue showed surprise. "What have you heard?"

"He's a rough dude—the kind that would kill your mother for a warm Busch beer. If I were you, I'd steer clear of him. I also wouldn't throw his name around." She eyed our conservative black outfits. "People might get the wrong idea."

Ruthie held her hands up. "We don't know this guy; we've only heard about him."

"I don't know what you heard, but he's not a person I'd want to look up." Angie turned on her heel.

"Thanks, we appreciate the advice," I said to the girl's back as she walked away.

Ruthie came unglued. "Don't you ever mention that name to a stranger again!" She wagged her finger at Penny Sue. "We want to find Rich, not Vulture. Otherwise, you can count me out of this whole mess. I'll take the next plane to Atlanta."

Penny Sue tilted her head contritely. "Get a grip, Ruthie." She stared into her drink again. "Woody showed me a picture of Vulture. He's the second man I saw with Rich at the Riverview Hotel the day we broke up."

"For goshsakes," I nearly shouted, "why didn't you tell us before?"

She avoided my eyes. "I didn't want to upset you. Besides, I thought you might not help if you knew about Vulture and Rich."

"Darn right. I'll help search for Rich, but at the first sight of Vulture, I'm out of here with Ruthie."

"Vulture is our only lead for finding Rich, so we have to ask about him. There's a half million bikers in the area, if we don't use the Vulture connection, we're looking for a needle in a haystack."

She was right. The probability of running into Rich was virtually nil. Yet, I feared that asking about Vulture was like spitting in the wind—it might blow back in our faces. If the guy was as nasty as everyone said, he probably wanted to keep a low profile and wouldn't take kindly to someone spreading his name around. Still, without him, we didn't have a chance of locating Rich. "I'll concede that we need to find Vulture, but we're not going to probe everyone we meet. We'll only ask people we know and trust—people who won't tell Vulture we're after him. Lord knows, we don't want him to come after us." I glanced at Ruthie.

She shrugged. "I'll go that far, no farther. If things start looking dangerous, I'm making reservations on the next plane."

"Fair enough," Penny Sue conceded.

We downed our wine, paid the bill, and headed to the condo. On the way, we stopped at Publix for air freshener, the kind that killed odors instead of simply masking them. The vanilla scent we used had made things worse. Vanilla simply did not compliment sage, smudge stick, tobacco, and Bloody Mary mix—the result being a putridly sweet stench of monumental proportions.

We'd purchased three cans of freshener and each of us entered the condo with our can spewing. Within a few minutes we'd expended our ammunition and opened all the windows, for the third time that day. While we waited for the place to air out, Ruthie fixed Uga's wound with white finger-nail polish. Even Penny Sue had to admit that it did the job and said she'd remember that trick for the future. By then, the odor in the condo was finally approaching tolerable, so we sat in the living room, next to the open sliding glass doors.

"Angie said the Pub had a web site. Let's check out today's events." Ruthie fetched her laptop computer from the bedroom and put it on the coffee table.

I watched curiously. "Don't you have to plug it into a telephone socket?"

"No. Poppa gave this to me for Christmas. It has a remote access card and connects to the Internet by satellite."

"Amazing. Pretty soon people will just talk to their computer instead of using keyboards."

"I wish they already had that. We could sure use it for Lu Nee 2," Penny Sue said.

Ruthie nodded as she typed in the commands for a Google search on the Pub. Amazingly, she found it right away. "Tonight is the Blow Out Party. There's also something called the Wall of Death."

"They used to have those at the state fair," Penny Sue said. "You know, a guy rides a motorcycle on the inside wall of a big barrel thing. It's amazing."

"Centrifugal force," I said, recalling college physics.

"Whatever. It would be fun to see again."

I sighed. "You know, we only have a week together, and I really don't want to spend the whole time hunting for Rich. We have to compress this search—go to several places each day. Let's hit J.B.'s and the Pub tonight."

"We'll start at J.B.'s—their seafood is good—then swing by the Pub," Penny Sue suggested. "We won't be conspicuous in my car at either place. Main Street in Daytona is a whole 'nother matter. I don't think we should go there in either the Mercedes or your bug."

"It's a Turbo Beetle."

"Excuse me, I didn't realize you were so touchy. But, even a Turbo Beetle is not a match for a Harley."

"Frannie May's son, Carl, has a motorcycle. Maybe he'd go with us to Main Street," I said.

"I'll ride with Carl," Ruthie blurted. "I prefer an experienced driver."

"Like a Klingon?" Penny Sue asked peevishly.

"Don't make fun of Carl. Do you want to hear snide comments about Rich? There's plenty of material there."

"I wasn't making fun of Carl—well, maybe a little— but Ruthie dissed my driving."

I shook my finger. "I'll ride with you, but you must promise to leave Carl alone."

* * *

We dressed in the hippest, most biker-looking outfits we could manage. Ruthie wore her $200 black Moschino jeans and the biker shirt that I'd given her. I wore the same black tee and Liz denim capris. (No $200 jeans in my wardrobe.) Penny Sue was decked out in the white bustier with black stretch pants, a leather jacket, and Harley boots with red flames on the side. She hadn't shown us the boots before. I shuddered to think what else was stashed in her closet.

We took the Mercedes and arrived at J.B.'s a little before six, thinking we'd beat the dinner crowd. Wrong. One of New Smyrna's oldest fish houses, J.B.'s was known for Southern Cooking with Attitude, a trait that explained Penny Sue's fondness for the place—the food matched her personality. The other reason was a tall, handsome bartender she'd all but swooned over on our first visit.

On normal days J.B.'s was busy, but Bike Week pushed it to a new height. The parking lot was packed with bikes, mostly Harleys, forcing us to park on a side street a block way.

"We'll never get a table," Ruthie said as we tromped along Turtle Mound Road.

"Don't be negative," Penny Sue chided. "You'll jinx us. You said yourself that we create our own reality. Think positively. See a booth open up the minute we walk into the restaurant."

Bikes—three abreast—rumbled by, forcing Ruthie off the pavement. She teetered in her high-heeled boots, and I had to grab her arm to keep her from falling flat on her face. "Hmph. Hard to be positive when I'm about to break my neck," Ruthie complained. "Why I let you talk me into wearing these Prada boots, I'll never know."

"You look fantastic," Penny Sue, in the lead as usual, said over her shoulder.

"I doubt anyone here would know a Prada if it fell on them."

"Honey, Prada stands out in any crowd. Besides, half of these people are pretenders like us. Remember Jonathan McMillan with his fake tattoo?"

Jonathan was president of a Marietta bank. We ran into him and his wife Marie on our last visit. Dressed in leather and holey denim, they looked like average bikers at first glance. Closer inspection revealed perfect manicures, movie star teeth, and an amazing lack of wrinkles or spare baggage for people our age—a clear testament to collagen, Botox, and a terrific plastic surgeon.

"Keep your eyes open, I'll bet you spot some Prada and Gucci, maybe even a Manolo," Penny Sue said.

"Manolo? That's pushing it," Ruthie scoffed.

"You just see."

We wormed our way through a throng of beer-drinking bikers who swayed and danced to a hot country band on a stage set up in the parking lot. A thick fog of steamed shrimp, body heat and beer vapor hung in the air, so strong, I swear, I was tipsy by the time we reached the front door.

Since most people were in the parking lot or on the back deck where another band played, the dining room was full but not crowded. And Penny Sue's positive thinking must have worked. As soon as my eyes adjusted to the darkened room, I spotted a muscular arm waving at us from a six-topper booth at the far end of the room. It was Bobby Barnes, the boat captain from the Marine Center, and his Navy Seal buddy, Saul Hirsch. Both men were dressed in jeans and tank tops that showed off their sculpted, bronzed bodies. Bobby gave Penny Sue the once over, conspicuously zeroing in on the strapless bustier, then stood and motioned us into his side of the booth. Eyes glued to his striated biceps, Penny Sue shoved me into the booth first, ensuring she'd get to sit next to her newest Adonis. Saul rose too and smiled appreciatively at Ruthie. Catching the obvious flirtation, she slid into the booth, color rising in her cheeks.

"Prada?" Saul said to Ruthie.

Her face went blood red. "What?"

"Your boots. Prada, aren't they?"

"Yes ..."

Saul quaffed his beer. "My mother owns a shoe boutique in Dallas. I just got back from a visit. She roped me into helping her take inventory and she has those exact boots in stock."

I felt Penny Sue give Ruthie a *See!* kick under the table.

"Oh-h-h," Ruthie wailed, rubbing her shin.

"I didn't mean to embarrass you," Saul apologized.

Ruthie shot Penny Sue a dirty look. "You didn't. Someone with big feet can't control her Harley boots."

Big feet. I clamped my lips together. Penny Sue's eyes shot daggers.

Bobby came to our rescue. "Bobby Barnes." He tipped his bottle toward his chest and winked at Penny Sue. She winked back. "And, this is my old Navy partner, Saul Hirsch. He owns the scooter store downtown."

"You own all those cute little motorbikes with the Rent Me sign on the back?" Penny Sue chirped in her Scarlett O'Hara voice.

Saul nodded.

"They look like fun. Do you have one outside?"

Saul took a swallow of his beer. "Hardly, I'd be laughed off the lot. I'm a 1947 Indian Chief."

Penny Sue squinched her eyes doubtfully. "Indian? Are you from the Timucuan tribe?"

Saul coughed into his napkin, while Bobby guffawed.

Penny Sue frowned, her eyes shifting from Bobby to Saul. "What did I say? What's wrong?"

Saul wiped his mouth. "I guess I mumbled. My tribe is from Israel, and my bike is an Indian Chief. It's an old brand, a classic. Be happy I'm not an Indian from these parts. The ones down by Canaveral were cannibals." Saul gnashed his teeth.

If there's anything a Leo hates, it's looking silly, and Penny Sue was true to her astrology. She loved poking fun at others, but had a hard time taking it herself. I hoped she didn't flip into one of her snippy personas. I had to work with Bobby and didn't want her to mess up our relationship.

Clearly miffed, Penny Sue leaned back. "I didn't think you looked like an Indian, but one never knows. In this day and age, all the races have become so intertwined, some scientists think racial distinctions should be dropped all together. Real blondes are supposed to become extinct in about two centuries."

Good recovery. I gave her a thumbs-up under the table.

Satisfied with herself, she rattled on. "Of course, a good Buckhead hairdresser," she ran her fingers through her streaked hair, "can overcome genetics any day."

"Amen," a platinum blond waitress said, her pen poised for action.

Announcing, "When in Rome—" Penny Sue passed up her usual Chardonnay for a long neck beer and hot wings. I followed her lead, but Ruthie, whose heart—in spite of Saul—was not into Bike Week or finding Rich, ordered a cola and a plain hamburger. The guys went for another round of brew.

Through our meal, we stuck to non-controversial topics. Who'd been raised where, been where when, married to whom where and when, finally ending with Saul's visiting Bobby in New Smyrna, falling in love with the beach, and opening the moped store.

"How fast can those little boogers go, anyway?" Penny Sue asked.

"Depends on whether you're talking about the gas or electric models. I have both. The new electric models can almost hit forty miles an hour. Since they're virtually silent, they're perfect for tourists who want a leisurely ride with occasional conversation."

"That explains it," I said. "I took a walk a couple of weeks ago and a scooter passed me from behind before I knew what happened. It scared the fool out of me, I never heard it coming. It must have been one of your electric models."

"Probably. Older folks, especially the ones with hearing problems, prefer them. No buzz to interfere with their hearing aids."

"They do look like fun," Ruthie finally said something. "That's one bike I think I could enjoy."

Saul smiled. "Come by any time and I'll set you up. Escort you myself. Riverside is a beautiful drive. The speed limit is only about thirty, so there are no impatient drivers riding on your bumper."

Ruthie blushed and studied her fingernails. "I will. I'd really like that."

Saul handed her his card. "Call. I'm available any time."

Penny Sue poked my thigh. Ruthie agreed to a date! That made two firsts in one day. First, she wore a sexy, biker tee shirt. Second, she'd all but agreed to a date. Would wonders never cease? The planets must be in a special alignment, I thought with a faint smile. Who knew what else was in store?

Saying they were scheduled to meet some old service buddies on Main Street in Daytona, Bobby called for the check. I'd been biding my time, looking for a chance to ask him about Vulture. One thing I was certain of, Bobby could be trusted.

I took a deep breath and dove in. I told him about Rich, Penny Sue, and the murder. Penny Sue jumped in with Woody's decidedly weasel characteristics, his desire to get even with her, and his attempt to frame Rich.

The check came. Instead of whipping out a credit card, the men ordered another beer. The drinks arrived as I breathlessly added the tidbit about the P being shot out on Penny Sue's vanity plate.

Bobby and Saul gaped at each other, took a big swig of brew, then looked us over like we'd dropped in from Mars. "Boy, Leigh, you saved the best for last. We've worked together for four months, and you've never talked about anything other than facts and figures. Now, I could believe this story coming from Frannie May, but from you—a total shock."

"Frannie May was with us when we found the body."

Bobby took another swallow of ale. "Figures."

Fingers steepled in front of his chest, Saul glanced at Ruthie. "One thing's for sure, steer clear of Vulture. He's twisted. Rumor has it he's a former Special Ops who flipped out in Vietnam or something. Dishonorable discharge for beating the crap out of his commanding officer. Definitely not nice. Definitely not someone you want to meet, much less mess with."

Bobby fixed his gaze on Penny Sue. It was hard to tell if he was looking at her cleavage or chin. "I know you consider Rich a friend, but if he's mixed up with Vulture and his crew—none of whom are in the running for the Good Housekeeping Seal of Approval—I don't think you really know or need Rich. Vulture and his friends are nuts." Bobby put his elbow on the table and tilted the beer bottle into his mouth. His biceps popped out like a large melon. "I'd think twice before I'd provoke Vulture. I damn sure know you women shouldn't trifle with him. He's got a weird band of followers who treat him like a god. Almost a cult thing. Stay away. Rich is a big boy—let him take care of himself."

Penny Sue set her jaw, and her face twisted into the defiant, Annie Oakley expression. She hated being told what to do, even if it was a muscular hunk doing the telling. Crap, I thought. All of this advice was going in one ear and out the other. She was going to pursue the original plan, come hell or high water. Annie, here, was going to drag Ruthie and me along with her—I could see it coming. Damn. And, the set of her jaw said there was no way to convince her otherwise.

Chapter 9

No one knows exactly what to call the shopping center across from the Pub. The sign reads NSB Regional Center, but store addresses and ads label it everything from the Wal-Mart Center to the New Smyrna Mall. It took me a couple of months to realize that all the names referred to the same place—the L-shaped shopping center across the street from the Frozen Gold, New Smyrna Harley-Davidson and the Pub. The road it skirted was just as bad. In the course of ten miles the highway changed names six times—from Turtle Mound Road to S. Atlantic to Third Avenue to the South Causeway to Lytle Avenue, finally ending up as Rt. 44. I'd encountered only one street crazier in my lifetime, and that was in Charlotte, NC. There's a street in Myers Park that doesn't have a simple succession of appellations, the name changes in one block, reverts to the original in the next, and then changes to something completely different a little while later.

Whatever one called New Smyrna's largest shopping center, all the spaces close to the highway were taken, forcing us to park between a big pick-up truck and a custom-painted van in front of Publix Supermarket. A long line of denim and leather streamed from the store pushing carts filled with beer, snacks, hoagies, and an occasional head of lettuce. Sushi might have been buried at the bottom of some carts, but it wasn't something a true biker would advertise. As Joe, a visitor from Montana, informed us at J.B.'s, real bikers don't eat sissy food like sushi and quiche.

Saul had asked him if he's ever tried wasabi. "No," Joe said.

"Eat a big tablespoon of that, straight. It's the test of a true man."

"Yeah? What is it?" Joe'd asked.

"A sushi condiment. Sort of like spicy guacamole."

Joe hadn't been convinced, but his buddies were anxious to take the challenge. They'd left immediately for Publix to buy wabasi.

Penny Sue popped the trunk as she got out of the car. "I'm leaving my purse, don't want to look like a rookie." Ruthie and I stuffed cash and a tube of lipstick into our jeans and dropped our pocketbooks into the trunk. Penny Sue paused to examine the hole in her license plate, then hunched into the trunk, working intently at something.

"What in the world are you doing?" I asked, peeking over her should. I caught her as she slipped a holstered .38 into a black pouch belt.

"You're not taking that, are you? Come on, Penny Sue, guns have a way of getting you in trouble."

"Just a little insurance. After all, Daddy may have locked up a biker over there who'd like to get even. That's why I carry it."

I knew, we'd been through all of that before. Still, I didn't like the idea of her packing a weapon. It had been nothing but trouble before. "Why don't you carry mace?"

"Doesn't make the same impression," she said, slamming the trunk and frowning at the license plate again. "I guess I should call my insurance agent tomorrow." She twisted her belt so the pouch was hidden under her coat. "Come on, sooner we find Rich, the sooner we can relax and have fun."

"Wait," Ruthie said weakly.

"Don't tell me," Penny Sue said. "You need to shake the dew off the lily?"

"Shake the dew off the lily?" I repeated.

"The bathroom. That's what my great Aunt Eve used to call it. She grew up in Richmond. Well, if ya gotta, ya gotta. Let's go in Publix. They have nice restrooms and I need some mint breath strips. You go to the girls' room, and I'll get the strips."

Dodging carts of beer and chips, we wiggled our way into the store. Ruthie went her way and I went with Penny Sue. As I stood in the checkout line, I studied the portrait of George Jenkins, Publix' founder. The clerks at the beachside store claimed George kept his eyes on everything and that his gaze followed you no matter where you went. I glanced sidelong at George, his eyes did seem fixed on me. I walked down the aisle to the right. The eyes followed. I met Ruthie and Penny Sue at the front door; George was still watching.

"Let's go," I said, a stupid comment since Penny Sue was already well ahead of us.

Ruthie and I hurried to catch Penny Sue, who stomped—no matter what she said about Southern belles, she was stomping, not sauntering, walking or gliding—toward the Pub. It was all Ruthie and I could do to keep up. Saul and Bobby's warnings had, indeed, gone in one ear and out the other. Ms. Leo knew best, as usual. They were too timid, she'd said.

Yeah, Navy Seals are timid. Right. The lady had brain damage. Or, maybe it was Ruthie and I who were mentally impaired. After all, we were the fools following her around.

We reached the crosswalk to the Pub and found Ted directing traffic. He took my arm as I drew near. "I need to talk to you." His tone was urgent. He must have heard about the murder.

"Sure, do you get a break?"

He checked his watch. "Meet me at the inside, front bar at ten-thirty."

I nodded, suspecting we were in for another lecture. Bobby's was enough for me, it was Penny Sue who needed convincing.

If you can imagine, the Pub was even more crowded than J.B.'s. Motorcycles—row after row of sparkling paint and chrome—were lined up like sardines, leaving only enough space between them for the riders to get on and admirers to pass in review. Ground not taken by bikes teemed with a milling throng of leather, flesh, tattoos, colognes, and body odors. To a seagull circling high overhead—albeit a deaf gull that hadn't been scared off by the hard, driving bass of the rock band, or the piercing whine of the motorcycle in the Wall of Death—the scene would have looked liked a roiling, boiling ant hill.

A shirtless man with a beard to his waist and a gold front tooth bumped me. "Sorry, Babe," he rasped with the worse halitosis I've ever encountered.

I held my breath and nodded, "No problem." Thankfully, he staggered away.

Back to the seagull—correction: a roiling, boiling, *stinky* anthill.

Penny Sue grabbed my forearm and pulled me to a small space beside the front door. "Okay, this is the plan. We're going to weave through this crowd and look for Rich and Vulture. We'll split up so we can cover more territory."

"Unh uh," Ruthie said. "I'm not going it alone."

"I'm with Ruthie—I think we should stay together. With this crowd, we'd have a hard time finding each other if we got separated. Besides, Ted wants us to meet him at the front bar at ten-thirty."

"You're not going to tell him about Vulture, are you?" Penny Sue asked.

"I have a sneaking suspicion he already knows. Besides, it doesn't hurt to have a second opinion."

"But, he's one of them!"

"One of who?" I asked crossly.

"Them. The authorities. The police. Woody. For godssakes, Leigh, we don't want them to know what we're doing. It might be misconstrued, look like we're obstructing justice."

"We'll tell Ted the truth, that we're trying to convince Rich to go to the authorities."

"Will Ted believe us? Suppose he has an obligation to report this to Woody?"

"He doesn't like Woody any more than we do."

"Yeah, but he's probably sworn an oath or something. You know, to uphold the U.S. Constitution, the Florida Constitution, the local constitution. Daddy had to swear to all that."

"Local governments don't have constitutions," Ruthie said dryly, obviously not liking the direction Penny was taking. "I told you I was not going to get involved in any dangerous stuff, especially concerning Vulture. I mean it. I'll be on the next plane."

Penny Sue put her hands on her hips. "I'm not stupid."

She was morphing into someone, though I couldn't tell who. I glanced at the black leather pouch around her waist. Please, not Annie Oakley again!

"I'm not going to fool with Vulture. In fact, I don't want to get near him, since he may recognize me. All I want is for y'all to follow him with the idea he may lead you to Rich."

Ruthie's jaw dropped. "Us follow Vulture?"

"Of course, he doesn't know y'all from Adam or, rather, Eve. To him, you're a pretty face in a very big crowd."

Jessica Fletcher, *Murder She Wrote*. That's who Penny Sue was now. Okay, I'd play along, since Jessica didn't brandish a .38. "So, what do we do if we find Vulture and he leads us to Rich?"

"We'll bide our time—"

"We?" Ruthie shot back.

"Me. I'll bide my time and go to Rich. Explain the situation and tell him he must turn himself in for questioning."

"What if he won't?"

"He will."

If you'd asked me a couple of days ago, after we'd first met, I'd have said, "Yes, Rich will go to the police." Now, after all the talk about Vulture and his twisted, anti-government cult, I wasn't willing to bet on anything. "But, what if he won't?"

"He will," she said defiantly. Then, with a shrug, "If he doesn't, we've done all we can do. The future is in his hands."

Ruthie looked askance. "You'd walk away from him."

She drew up solemnly. "I'd walk away from him."

Ruthie chucked her on the arm. "Okay, let's go."

First, we made our way to the outside Tiki Hut at the rear of the main building. "We need a drink so we don't look conspicuous," Penny Sue pronounced. Unfortunately, the bar, like everything else, was full. We stood to the side, waiting for an opening, when a very tall, black man with dreadlocks backed up to create a sliver of space about eight inches wide. Impossible for Rubenesque Penny Sue, questionable for me, just right for our skinny friend, Ruthie, if she turned side-ways. We pushed her into the space between our benefactor and a short, balding white guy dressed in khakis and a golf shirt. Mr. Preppie was miffed; Dreadlocks wanted to flirt. Ruthie's nervous giggles only endeared her to the big guy, who saw that her order was filled forthwith. We all thanked him profusely and backed away.

"Never hurts to have friends," Penny Sue said as she sipped her beer. She glanced over her shoulder. "Don't look now, but I think Mr. Dreadlocks is following us."

"His name is Sidney," Ruthie said.

"As in Poitier?" Penny Sue asked. "He's good looking enough to be his son."

Ruthie pursed her lips disgustedly. "We didn't exchange resumes or phone numbers. And, he's not following us. Besides, I think Sidney Poitier's children are all girls. His oldest daughter, Beverly, lives in Roswell. I went to her book signing not long ago.

"Well, Sidney may not be a Poitier, but he's rich," Penny Sue said.

"How do you know that?"

"His manicure. Sidney's not your average biker. Maybe a pro ball player. I'll bet the hair's a wig or hair extensions."

"Could be."

Penny Sue dipped her head for another stealthy glimpse. "I see him, but he's walking the other way. Too bad."

"What did you think of Saul?" I asked Ruthie, since we were on the subject of men. "I think he was attracted to you."

"Yeah, and his mother owns a shoe boutique that obviously carries the top of the line. Maybe he could get us discounts," Penny Sue said.

Ruthie pursed her lips. "Aren't you jumping the gun a tad? I've only met him once, for goshsakes." She turned to me. "Yes, I liked him. He seems very sensitive in a macho sort of way."

Two men on the same night. Ruthie's planets must be in good alignment. I hoped mine were doing okay. My conversation with Ann was bothering me, not to mention the whole Rich/Vulture thing. And, what did Ted know? I checked my watch, it was only nine-thirty. I'd have to wait an hour to find out."

"Well, let's get this show on the road. Where should we start?"

"The Wall of Death," Penny Sue said instantly.

Geez, I didn't like the way that sounded.

We paid our money and walked up a ramp to the top of a giant wooden barrel. Inside a brave soul was riding a motorcycle around the wall. It made me queasy just to watch him.

"Now, keep your eyes open," Penny Sue instructed.

"I'm getting dizzy."

"Not on him, silly." She pointed to the rider in the pit. "We're up here to survey the crowd. There's no better vantage point. Turn around—we need to find Rich."

Good thinking. Ruthie and I did as instructed. A biker chick in cutoff jeans and a leather vest looked at me like I was crazy.

"Vertigo," I explained. "I'm starting to feel nauseous."

She gave me a dirty look and inched away. I could almost hear her mentally scream, *Wuss!*

Let her think what she wanted, I'd never see her again. My back to the show, I surveyed the crowd. Short, tall, fat, thin, black, white, yellow—all of humanity was represented in the horde below. And, regardless of physical and ethnic differences, they all shared a love of motorcycles, denim, leather, and tattoos.

A busty woman with spiked red hair caught my eye. Clad in a slinky bandeau top and leather shorts that were scalloped in the back to expose the bottoms of her buns, she swayed sensuously before the lead singer of the band.

I pointed. "Look at that."

"Hmph," Penny Sue said. "A little fanny tuck needed—"

At that moment, the singer dropped to one knee and crooned, "Give it to me. Give it to me." The redhead yanked her bandeau over her head revealing melon-sized breasts painted—or tattooed—with big red flowers around each nipple. The audience went wild with catcalls and shouts of "Give it to me. Give it to me." Grinning like a Cheshire cat, she launched into a series of gyrations worthy of the best tassel twirler. Upstaged, the band segued into a raunchy rendition of *I'm Your Hoochie Coochie Man*, at which the woman started fumbling with the clasp on her shorts. That's when two men—bouncers, I assumed—muscled out of the crowd and hustled her away.

My eyes almost bulged out of my head, while Ruthie's jaw dropped to her chest. I'd heard Bike Week could get bawdy, but I wasn't prepared for a striptease.

Penny Sue shook her head. "Sad. Just sad to have to stoop so low for attention. Must have had a deprived child-hood. A shame. The poor dear needs counseling."

Maybe, but we didn't have time to discuss it. The Wall of Death show had ended, and the spectators where ready for another drink. A surge of bodies pushed us down the ramp and half way to the Tiki Hut before we could break away.

"Now what?"

"We continue to look."

Ruthie shook her head and took the last sip of her beer. "Penny Sue, there's no way we're going to find Rich. First, we can hardly move, much less sneak around searching. Second, the chances of his being here, now, are miniscule. For all we know he's on Main Street, at the Cabbage Patch— heck, he might even be at J.B.'s. This whole exercise is hopeless." She held up her empty beer can and looked around. "We can't find a stationary trash can, much less a person on the move."

"I know this is a long shot, but we've got to try. We've only been at it for a few hours. What did you expect, that we'd waltz right into him? Come on, give it a little more time." She pointed over Ruthie's shoulder. "There's a trash can—" Her eyes went wide. "—and Rich with that redheaded hussy!"

Hussy? What happened to the poor dear? Penny Sue started to push past me, but I held her back. "Wait. That lady looks rough, I'm not sure you should tangle with her."

Penny Sue brushed my hand away. "I want to talk to Rich. What's the big deal?"

I glanced over my shoulder. The redhead was rubbing her once-again-clothed breasts against Rich's chest. "She may not like your horning in on her territory."

"Her territory?" Penny Sue started to bulldoze by us, but Ruthie stopped her.

"Leigh's right. Let's follow them and corner Rich after she leaves. No sense taking unnecessary chances. Besides, Rich is more likely to listen if you catch him alone."

Penny Sue looked at us and then back at the redhead. Rich was gone! She bolted, worming her way through the crowd with Ruthie and me in tow. "We've lost him," she said through gritted teeth.

"It might not have been Rich."

"It was, dammit!"

Next thing I knew she'd strutted up to the redhead who had turned her attention to another man. "Come on." I dragged Ruthie with me.

"Excuse me," Penny Sue said to the woman. "Was that Rich Wheeler you were talking to a minute ago?"

"Maybe. What's it to you?"

"He's an old friend from home. Do you know where he went?"

Redhead gave Penny Sue the once over, no doubt noticing her expensive duds. "I don't give out that kind of information." She turned away and zeroed in on a biker with a shaved head, a spiked dog collar like Uga's, and a long chain connecting his belt and wallet.

"I wanted to say hello. It's been ages—"

"And it's going to be a lot longer," Redhead snarled. "Shove off. I don't have time for people like you."

Uh oh. I could tell from the tension in Penny Sue's jaw that she was about to morph into a Southern Bitch. "People like who?"

"You. Establishment fakes."

"Fakes?!" Penny Sue squared her shoulders. I kept my eyes on her hands to make sure she didn't go for the gun. Under normal circumstances, I didn't think Penny Sue would shoot anyone. But, she'd been acting strangely and Rich was her supposed soul mate. Under those conditions, I wasn't sure how far she would go.

"Yeah, fakes. You're not fooling anyone in your rich girl getup. Go home to your soap operas and," she motioned at Ruthie and me who were standing to the side like deer caught in headlights, "take your bubbleheaded friends with you."

At that second I felt a heavy arm drape across Ruthie and my shoulders. I almost peed in my pants and given Ruthie's dewy lily (as Aunt Eve from Richmond put it), I sincerely hoped she was wearing a pantiliner.

A deep voice said, "I think bubbleheads are kind of cute."

Sweat—er, perspiration—popped out on my forehead as I forced my face upward into a mass of dreadlocks. It was Sidney, the guy from the bar. And, another very tall African-American wearing a kerchief stood behind him. Though Sidney's lips were stretched in a big smile, his eyes had narrowed in a steely, no nonsense expression. He glanced from Redhead to Spike. Redhead met his stare with an expression of pure contempt. Sidney kept smiling.

Spike, who was outclassed by at least four hundred pounds of muscle in comparison to his one-eighty of flab, broke the impasse. "Red, I need a drink." He literally dragged her away.

"A lot of stupid people in the world. A sorry case that has to pump themselves by putting others down," Sidney said. "Hope you don't mind my intervention. I bristle at prejudice. Encountered my share in this lifetime."

Intervention. This lifetime. Sidney was well educated, had a great manicure, nice manners, and might even believe in reincarnation. No run-of-the-mill biker, I thought.

"We really appreciate it," Ruthie said, smiling up at Sidney and his friend.

"Absolutely. Thanks," Penny Sue said, her eyes following Red's form through the crowd. "The nerve of that woman!" She turned to us with outstretched arms. "Soap operas? I haven't seen one since college. Fake! I have a Harley Fat Boy, don't I?" She did the Vanna White hand sweep. "This is an authentic Harley outfit, isn't it?" She raised her foot. "These are Harley boots. See the red flames?"

Sidney and his friend said, "Nice."

"So, who's the fake?" she rattled on. "Me or Ms. Exhibitionist?"

The men started to back away. "We have to meet someone about a bike." Sidney dipped his chin. "You ladies have a nice evening."

The two men could not get away fast enough. "Thanks, again," I called as they left.

Penny Sue! Her self-absorption was downright obnoxious. Ruthie said she couldn't help it, because of a strange aspect as well as being a Leo. "Leo is ruled by the Sun. So, Leo natives think everything revolves around them, like the planets revolve around our Sun."

Well, they need to consider someone else sometimes. Since I was an Aquarius, ruled by Uranus, my ego was on the outer edges of the solar system. And, Ruthie—a Pisces, ruled by Neptune—was even farther out. Which, I guess, explained why we followed Penny Sue like sheep. Most of the time, it was simply too exhausting to oppose her. But this time she'd gone too far.

I put my hands on my hips. "Penny Sue, you were rude to Sidney and his friend. They stuck their necks out to help us, and you hardly thanked them."

"I did so."

"Yeah, a weak thanks followed by a litany of your ego affronts. Really, you need to be more sensitive." There, I'd said it. I hoped her hormones were in sufficient balance that she didn't pull out the .38 and shoot me. Still, I'd had my fill of walking on eggshells and salving her ego. She needed to buck up, act like an adult, and not a spoiled child.

Penny Sue regarded me like I'd slapped her in the face. Then, she put her hands over her eyes and started to cry. "You're right—I've been impossible. I don't know why, but I feel so strange. One minute I'm my old self, the next I'm a bundle of doubts and inhibitions." She looked up, mascara streaming down her cheeks.

I wiped the makeup from her cheek, the same way I'd wiped chocolate from my kids' faces. Heavens, her hormones were definitely in the tank. She needed help, and fast!

Chapter 10

I could see Ted at the far end of the Pub's front bar. We were late. It had taken a lot of wiggling and nudging to get through the restaurant. I waved and caught his eye. He visibly relaxed.

Penny Sue took Ruthie and me both by the shoulder and gave us a serious look. "No mention of Rich, right? This is our secret for now. Promise? Cross your heart and hope to die, stick a needle in your eye?"

Gawd, she didn't have to resort to childish prattle. "Yes, I promise."

"Me, too. For now," Ruthie said.

We paused to plot our course through the room. A circuitous route around the tables seemed the best bet. Several minutes, innumerable jostles, and a bunch of sorry's later we reached Ted. He smiled invitingly as we wedged through the last group of partiers.

"Geez," Penny Sue said, straightening her bustier which was turned half around, exposing a lot of skin even for her.

"Where did these people come from? All of New Smyrna must be here."

Ted flashed an easy grin. "Half a million people from around the world are in the area, and Pub 44 is one of the most popular spots." He held up his mug of cola. "Can I get you something? Water, soda? Sorry, that's the limit of my orders since I'm on duty." Ted inclined his head to a man standing behind the bar. I recognized the guy as the manager who'd waited on us before.

"What'll it be?" the man asked, as he wiped the counter. Penny Sue, still shaky from her encounter with Red, ordered Jack and Coke. Realizing one of us had to drive, Ruthie and I went with diet sodas. The drinks arrived in a matter of seconds.

"That manager is awfully nice. We met him the last time we were here."

Ted regarded me with amusement. "Manager? That's not the manager, he's Gilly, the owner."

Gilly, as in Gilly's Pub 44? My cheeks flamed. I'd made a snide remark to him about a new, young waitress on our last visit. If I'd known he was the owner, I'd kept my big mouth shut. But how was I to know? In a place this big, who expected the owner to wait on customers, other than a few regulars? Hopefully, he didn't recognize me. I turned my back to him and sipped my soft drink.

"What do you think of Bike Week?" Ted asked lightly, though I suspected he was working up to something big.

"Quite a melting pot," Ruthie said.

"Ruthie's being coy. Two good-looking men have already flirted with her."

"Excellent. What about you, Penny Sue?" I noticed he pointedly didn't ask me. Was he afraid of the answer?

Penny Sue gulped her cocktail. "The only thing I've encountered is a rude, redheaded exhibitionist."

"The woman who did the striptease?"

"Yeah, flowers painted on her boobs."

"Tattoos," Ted corrected.

"Well, she's a crude, rude ... person."

"I thought you felt sorry for her deprived childhood," I said.

"I did before she started mouthing off."

Ted appeared surprised. "What did she say?"

"That I was a rich fake in my fancy clothes. The nerve!" She waved her cup expansively. "I ask you, what's wrong with this outfit? It's all Harley. Half the people in this place are wearing Harley duds."

Few people had on so much of it. One or two pieces, maybe, but a whole outfit? I hadn't noticed anyone with a Harley emblem on every item of clothing. As far as I knew, Penny Sue might even be wearing her Harley thong underwear.

"Is that all she said?" Ted asked. His tone was very serious.

"Yeah, what's wrong? Do you know her?"

"Her name's Red, and she hangs out with a rough crowd. A very rough crowd."

The emphasis on *very* was unmistakable. I felt a sinking sensation. Ruthie bit her fingernail.

"I don't know how you and she happened to meet but, for the future, I'd avoid her at all costs. A minor disagreement with her could escalate quickly." He looked at Penny Sue's belt pouch. "Is your gun in there?"

She eyed him defiantly. "It's holstered. Perfectly legal."

He gave her a hard look. "Don't let it give you a false sense of security. There are people here who would laugh at a .38. And, don't you dare touch it if you've been drinking." He frowned at her cup. She put it on the counter as if it had suddenly developed cooties.

A burly guy, worming his way to the bar, knocked me against Ted. He caught my hand to steady my soda. His hand lingered, longer than necessary. *Uh oh.*

"I hear y'all had an unfortunate experience the other night. Something about a dead body next to Penny Sue's car and bullet hole in her license plate."

I nodded meekly.

Ted put on his police face for Penny Sue. "Your boyfriend, Rich, is implicated. He was seen with the dead man and Red's boyfriend the day before."

"Red's hooked up with Vulture?" Ruthie blurted.

"What do you know about Vulture?" Ted shot back.

"Not much, only that he's a bad guy. Rumored to be in a gang or cult of some kind."

"He's not just in a gang, he's the leader of the gang, and Red is one of his girlfriends."

"She was flirting with every man she could find," Penny Sue said.

Ted took a swallow of his cola. "I didn't say she was his only girlfriend, just one of them. He has a whole stable. These gang things tend to be communal. Actually, it's often the women who recruit new members through sexual favors."

I thought of Red's raunchy gyrations and boob-rubbing come-on to Rich. Is that what she was doing, recruiting him for the gang? But Rich told Penny Sue that Vulture and the dead man were old friends. Was Rich already a member of the group? I didn't like this. Too many loose ends. Too many things didn't fit.

Ted checked his watch. "Ladies, I have to go. Break time's over." He put down his mug and regarded us soberly. "I encouraged you to go to Bike Week for the experience, but that was before the murder and Penny Sue's run-in with Red. Under the circumstances, I think you should stay away. Chances are nothing else would happen, yet you seem to be magnets for trouble and dead bodies ..."

Hmm-m, that's what Woody said.

"... I hope you'll reconsider and lay on the beach or go to Disney. Things have taken a bad turn, and I don't want you involved." He winked at me. "Gotta go." He stood, focusing on Penny Sue. "I like you all and would be very upset if anything happened to you." Then he strode away.

I watched his muscular shoulders move through the room. Perhaps it was his uniform or air of confidence, whatever, the crowd parted before him. We'd had to claw, scrape, and squeeze. He simply strode ahead, unimpeded. Was it like that with the rest of his life? Surely not. I knew he had problems with his ex-wife and children. Still, what a joy it must be to walk—march—unopposed, to your own drummer. What did he have that I didn't? Male, sure. It was a male dominated world, even today, although changing fast, according to Ruthie, with the new generation of androgynous kids. No, I think the critical factor was the confidence Ted exuded. Confidence, a deep certainty that your goals would be met not matter what. Geez, it sounded like Ruthie's New Age dictum, "You create your only reality" or Penny Sue's "What

Man can conceive, Man could achieve." I'd have to give all of that a little more thought.

Ruthie reached into her pocket and dropped a twenty on the counter. "I've had enough for one night. Let's go home and think this through. I don't like that stuff about Red. And, if she's really a right wing extremist, Sidney's help—bless his heart—may have added another complication."

Even Penny Sue hadn't thought of that one. We thanked Gilly and headed out the front door. The steady rumble of motorcycles was deafening. We passed Ted in the crosswalk and he was clearly pleased we'd taken his advice. He gave us all an affectionate pat on the shoulder. My pat gave me a chill. I'd have to think about that later, too.

Unlike the hoard streaming out of Publix and into the Pub before, the shopping center was relatively calm. The stores were closed, so the only activity was a trickle of primarily middle-aged, out-of-shape partiers (like us) who'd had enough. We walked in silence to the Mercedes that stood out as the only car in front of the grocery store.

"Maybe one of you should drive," Penny Sue said contritely. Ted's lecture had clearly hit home. She retrieved the keys from her pouch belt and hit the trunk release when we were in sight of the car. We took our purses from the trunk, then Penny handed the keys to me and lowered the lid.

"Ah-h," Ruthie choked out, pointing at the car.

"Shit!" Penny Sue shouted.

My heart did a flip. "What?!"

I followed Ruthie's finger. The center of the second P in the PSP vanity plate was shot out! Suddenly feeling light-headed, I backed away. "How could this happen in the middle of a well-lighted parking lot? For godssakes, police were on the street directing traffic. Wouldn't they have heard something?"

"Well, someone did, and they didn't!" Penny Sue stomped—forget the whole Southern Belle charade, she was hoofing it, big time—back toward the crosswalk and Ted. A convoy of motorcycles rumbled by at that moment. The sound was deafening, which explained how a gunshot could go undetected.

Penny Sue outlined what had happened. Ted listened sympathetically, then shrugged. "This is the city, not my jurisdiction. You need to report it, but no one's going to do anything about simple vandalism tonight. Resources are stretched thin. Go home and I'll come over as soon as my shift ends at midnight."

"Simple vandalism?" Penny Sue snapped. "Someone took a potshot at my Mercedes!"

* * *

The message light on the answering machine was blinking when we got home. What now? The first message was from Ann. "Daddy called. He's coming to Europe on business next month. Isn't that great? That would be the perfect time for y'all to meet Patrick. Think you can make it?" So much for stalling the engagement to give Ann time to come to her senses. Zack! He always managed to screw things up, even when he wasn't trying.

The second call was from Frannie May. Could we make it for dinner tomorrow night? Penny Sue and Ruthie needed to taste real Italian food. I checked my watch, quarter to twelve. Too late to return the call.

"Decaf or diet soda?" Ruthie asked, holding up a coffeepot in one hand and a soft drink in the other.

"Decaf. Make a whole pot. I'm sure Ted will want some, too." I peered around. "Where's Penny Sue?"

"In her room, I think."

I lowered my voice. "Do you think she's acting funny? All this crying and carrying on, she's completely discombobulated. I think we should encourage her to call her doctor in Atlanta."

Ruthie nodded. "She's about as high-strung as a mandolin. Of course, I'm not feeling great myself. All this stuff with Rich and Vulture has made me a nervous wreck. I keep taking deep breaths and repeating my mantra, but it's not working."

An electronic screech and "Halt, who goes there?" nearly sent me through the roof. Damn. I folded my arms on the counter and put my head down, trying to calm my racing heart. I guess I was more than a little tense myself. A moment later, Lu Nee 2 whirred into the room.

"What are you doing, Penny Sue?"

"I'm setting Lu Nee up for guard duty. Somebody's out to get us." She flipped the switch to the spotlights on the deck. "This isn't turtle season, is it?" I shook my head. "Good, then I think we need to keep all the outside lights on and post Lu Nee in here to watch the glass doors."

"Those doors are alarmed like the rest of the place," I reminded her.

"Studies show that a good smash and grab artist is in and out in three minutes. By the time the police arrive, a crook would be long gone and so would we!"

Terrific, so much for the sense of security I'd gotten from the new alarm system. "What's the point of an alarm then?"

"To scare off amateurs." She pushed a vertical blind to the side and peeked out on the deck. "Good, bright as day out there." She turned toward us with her hands on her hips. "Where's the Taser and its charger?"

I motioned to the linen closet. "Do you think professional hit men are after you?"

"Maybe," she said, hauling the Taser, charger, and electrolyte solution to the table in the dining area. "As I said before, Daddy's locked up his share of druggies over the years. That's why I have to be so careful. A lot of them would love to get even with Daddy through me."

Since we were her friends, that put us on the front line, too.

Ruthie poured three mugs of coffee. "I think we should go back to Atlanta tomorrow."

"Run away, and let the scum balls win? No way. We're going to stay here and fight. Stand up for our rights!"

I dumped a big glob of milk into my coffee. Fight—I had no intention of fighting anyone. This wasn't Bunker Hill. There was no high-minded principle at stake, just our personal safety. And, I took my safety very seriously.

The doorbell rang, followed by a loud knock. "Wait," Penny Sue said, taking her revolver from her purse and slipping it out of its holster. "You see who it is, Leigh. I'll keep you covered."

"You're scaring me, Penny Sue," Ruthie said. "Put the gun away. It must be Ted."

"Yes, put it away."

"Look, it's not cocked." She angled it toward the side wall. "It's just ready, in case."

"In case of what?" The doorbell rang again and I started down the hall.

"In case someone followed us home."

I stopped cold.

"Wait," Ruthie called, eyes wide. She scooped up the Taser and slapped in the batteries. Crouching low, she followed me down the hall, the weapon trained at the door. I paused to gather the nerve to look through the peephole, an image of bullets and mortars crashing through the door at the back of my mind. I took a deep breath, closed one eye and peered through the tiny opening. Another loud knock sent me reeling, knocking Ruthie flat on her back. Penny Sue appeared at the end of the hall, her gun cocked. Lu Nee 2 swiveled around crying "Halt! Who goes there? Halt! Who goes there?"

"Leigh, it's me. Ted Moore. Are you all right? Open up!"

"Just a minute," I called, helping Ruthie to her feet. As I opened the door, a screech from the burglar alarm warned it was still armed. Penny Sue lunged for the control panel, bumping Lu Nee 2 in the process. The crazed robot launched into a litany of "Watch out, that hurt. Halt! Where did that come from? Halt! Who goes there?"

Ted shook his head with wonder at the scene. Ruthie and I were standing meekly by the door, our hair and clothes askew, with Ruthie trying to hide the Taser behind her back, which was futile since she was skinny and the darned weapon was the size of a large super soaker water rifle. Penny Sue, revolver in one hand, was crouched over the robot trying to turn it off. She wasn't meeting with much success. Lights flashing, the little demon's head whirred from side-to-side as it babbled and sang, "Hello, hello, hello! Take me to your leader! Help! I've fallen and I can't get up!"

Ted began to laugh—not a chuckle, but a full-fledged belly laugh. "What are you ladies doing?"

"It's her fault," I said, pointing at Penny Sue. "Rambo, here, scared the wits out of Ruthie and me. She said some-one might have followed us home."

"Did you notice anyone behind you?" he asked as he closed the door.

Ruthie and I exchanged glances. "No," I said slowly. "Come to think of it, we even commented on how empty the streets were after we reached the island." I scowled at Penny Sue. "In fact, you said everyone was still at the Pub."

She straightened to face me, having finally silenced the robot. "Someone could have been following with their lights off."

"Hardly," Ruthie said, giving Penny Sue a dirty look, too. "The area around Publix is lit up like a Christmas tree. We would have noticed someone behind us."

"Don't blame me if y'all are hysterics." She tossed her hair and started for the kitchen. "Like a cup of coffee, Ted? Decaf."

"That would be nice." We headed to the living room, Ruthie stopping long enough to deposit the Taser back in the linen closet.

Penny Sue, having now transitioned from Rambo to June Cleaver, passed around mugs of coffee and even produced a plate of sugar cookies. Still grinning, Ted studied us.

"I checked your car on the way in. It's definitely a bullet hole, this one from close range because it went through your plate and made a nice dent in the trunk. I called in a report to the New Smyrna Police on the way over. They'll send someone out in the morning to get your statement."

"What do you think?" Ruthie asked nervously.

Ted took a bite of a cookie as he considered the possibilities. "If it weren't for the murder, I'd say it was an immature prank. Someone with a grudge because you cut them off in traffic or something."

"Penny Sue, maybe it's Shrewella, getting even for your cayenne pepper prank. That was mean," I reminded her.

"Get real. That old lady may have a gun, but haven't you noticed how her hand shakes? There's no way she could shoot the middle out of the P's."

"The lab can't make a positive ID, because of the condition of the slug, though chances are the same gun was used for the first shot and the murder," Ted said.

"Shrewella might shoot you or your car, but she wouldn't shoot a stranger."

Penny Sue raked her fingers through her hair. "Heck, with her shaky hands, maybe the murder was the accident."

"Oh, please."

"Could be, you don't know."

I ignored the comment. "Ted, what do you think we should do?"

"Go home—that's what we should do," Ruthie flared.

"This *is* my home, Ruthie. I have a job; I can't just leave."

"Wait," Ted said, patting the air in a calming manner.

It was a gesture Zack used all the time that I'd really come to detest. It always struck me as condescending, and I hated to think Ted had anything in common with Zack.

"Let's look at this logically," Ted continued.

Boy, he was on thin ice now—the implication being that we weren't capable of logic.

"There's a connection between the murder and vandalism, no doubt. Penny Sue, is there any way Rich could have a grudge against you?"

"Absolutely not."

"Well, do you think he's all there? I mean, could Rich have psychological problems like multiple personalities?"

"No! He's always been a perfect gentleman. I've never seen any indication of instability."

I examined my nails. Was she a good judge of that? Her own behavior had been pretty erratic recently.

"Okay," Ted patted the air again. "I think you should keep your car parked for now. Can you put it in the garage?"

Penny Sue answered. "There is no garage. We partitioned it off for storage and a larger utility room. Bicycles and the Harley take up what little room there is."

"Well, I don't think you should drive the Mercedes until we figure out how all of this fits together."

"I'll rent a car. Leigh's bug is for midgets."

"Sh-h, let him finish," I said.

"I recommend you lay low and stay away from Bike Week events."

Penny Sue's jaw tightened. I knew what was going through her mind. She was still planning to pursue Rich.

"Finally," Ted said, setting his mug on the table, "I strongly suggest you leave your revolver at home."

"What, and run around unprotected? I carry it because I'm in constant danger. Daddy's locked up his share of—"

Ted stood. "I know. It was a suggestion. Like I said before, there are some tough hombres in town for Bike Week. Your little revolver would make them laugh."

"I'll think about it," Penny Sue said in a tone that meant it was already forgotten.

"We really appreciate your help," I added quickly.

Ted nodded. "I'll call tomorrow to check on you. Expect the New Smyrna police sometime in the morning."

Goody, I thought. The police again.

Chapter 11

I slept fitfully, my mind churning with Ann, Zack, Vulture—even Uga, the University of Georgia mascot was part of the mix. Every few minutes, I rolled over and glanced at the clock. At 2:22 a.m. I realized this had been happening more and more—the sleep problems, that is. I dozed, but awoke angry—Uga had pooped in the middle of the living room floor as Lu Nee 2 ran in circles shouting Halt! Halt! I checked the time. Damn, only 2:48.

Was I keyed up from the day, or was this one of the dreaded signs of perimenopause? No, of course not—I was keyed up. After all, I hadn't had night sweats, not really. The condo's thermostat allowed too much variation, that's all. But, Penny Sue was another matter. Crying over Rich was understandable, but the episode at the Pub was completely out of character. She needed to have her prescription checked, I thought. I'd talk to Ruthie first thing in the morning and see if we couldn't come up with a delicate way to broach the subject.

I drifted off again. Ann, Zack, and I were chatting over tea. Ann said she was having hot flashes, was so thrilled that she and Patrick were moving to Outer Mongolia. She'd already purchased a tiger skin snowsuit for the baby. You know, like the tigers in the Siegfried & Roy show. The next moment we were in a car, driving on the wrong side of the road. A rickety double-decker bus was headed straight for us! I awoke with a start. 3:13.

"You all right? You yelped." Ruthie asked from the next bed. She rose up on her elbow and looked at the clock. "Three-thirteen, the witching hour."

"I'm okay. Weird dreams … I've hardly slept a wink."

"Me, either. Why don't we get a cup of hot chocolate? Maybe that will help."

I checked to make sure Penny Sue's door was closed so we wouldn't disturb her, tiptoed into the kitchen and hopped on the stool farthest from the hall. I watched as Ruthie put on the teakettle and dumped packets of cocoa mix into mugs. "You said 3:13 was the witching hour. What does that mean?"

"It's the time of day when things are quietest and the electromagnetic gibberish is at its lowest level, which makes it easy for communication to bleed through from other realms. The time when the veil separating dimensions is thinnest."

I could feel a metaphysical bombshell coming. "Other realms? Like this three-dimensional plane and the astral plane?"

She handed me a cup of cocoa. "There's more to it than that—celestial realms as well as an infinite number of other dimensions."

I blew on my chocolate before taking a sip. "This is the multi-dimensional reality you talk about? The new physics, quantum mechanics, that says there's no linear time and everything is happening simultaneously?"

"Right."

"So, this bleed through happens every night at 3:13?"

"Not at that time exactly, but typically between two and four in the morning. There's nothing to be afraid of—it merely means you're more susceptible to psychic impressions from other realms. And when the info comes in, you're more likely to wake up."

I had to admit that my waking at 3:13 a.m. happened a lot—more frequently than statistics would predict. Statistics was not my best subject in college, but I knew the number of times I'd awakened at that particular time far exceeded normal probabilities. Was someone trying to communicate with me?

Grammy Martin would be my first guess, though I hadn't heard any Bible quotations. A staunch Southern Baptist with a photographic mind, Grammy could, and did, provide Biblical guidance in virtually every situation when I was growing up.

A jewel of gold in a swine's snout, so is a fair woman which is without discretion. From Proverbs, the quote popped in my mind out of the blue. I immediately associated it with Grammy and knew it referred to Penny Sue. I stared at the ceiling. *Grammy, is that you? What are you trying to tell me?*

And, if Grammy was contacting me at 3:13, was there someone else at 2:48? Did my dream about Ann and the bus smashing into the car mean anything? My head suddenly felt full. I took a big draw of the cocoa. *Change the subject*, I told myself.

"Do you think Penny Sue is acting strangely?" I asked. There, shift the blame, get my attention off myself.

"Strange by whose standards? Hers or ours?" Ruthie went to the refrigerator and pulled out a jar of Duke's mayonnaise. "How about a good old tomato sandwich?"

A slice of tomato on trimmed white bread with a little mayonnaise was a Southern tradition that couldn't be beat. I hadn't had one in years. "That would be wonderful."

I watched as she sliced the tomato and cut the crust off the bread.

"She's a lot more weepy than I've ever seen her. I suspect it's because she stopped her hormone therapy." She handed me a sandwich.

"What? I hadn't heard about that! She bragged about how good she felt the last time I saw her."

"All the bad press finally got to her. Even though her doctor said the chances of bad side effects were miniscule, Penny Sue decided to stop. I told her to take black cohosh, but I'm not sure she ever did."

Geez, that explained a lot. ... *a fair woman which is without discretion.* Clearly, Grammy was referring to Penny Sue's emotionally volatile state. Yet, what should we do about it? Or was I jumping to conclusions because I'd read all those menopause books? Everyone feels hot from time to time and gets crabby. It doesn't mean the old juices are drying up, right? Certainly, *my* juices weren't drying up! I clicked the mug down so hard, Ruthie jumped.

"What?" she screeched.

"Sorry, I was thinking about my dream," I fibbed. "Ann. I'm worried about Ann. I hope she hasn't hooked up with a smooth-talking Casanova. Twenty years may not seem like much of an age difference to her now, but what about when she's forty? She'll want to go to rock concerts, and he'll want to watch golf on TV. If there is television, or golf, in Outer Mongolia."

"OUTER MONGOLIA?!" It was Penny Sue. She shuffled into the room with the appearance of a person who'd been fighting demons. Her hair was matted with sweat (er, perspiration—Southern Belles do not sweat), her robe was half tied, and her mascara smudged. "What are y'all doing up?"

"We couldn't sleep," I said. "Witch—"

"Witch!" Penny Sue snapped. "You don't look so good yourself." She tied her robe and ran her fingers through her damp hair.

"I didn't mean you were a witch, I meant this is the witching hour. Two to four a.m. Right, Ruthie? That's when the spirits pierce the veil and wake us up."

"Oh," Penny Sue mumbled, heading for the thermostat. "It's so damned hot in here. That's why I got up." She looked at the digital readout. "73? No way. Something's wrong with this dumb thing." She thumped the thermostat with her finger, then opened the panel and punched the button to lower the setting. "I'm having someone come look at this first thing Monday morning. The temperature has to be off, don't you think?" That's when she noticed our mugs. "Is that hot chocolate?" She fanned herself. "You're drinking something hot in this oven?"

"Yeah, we couldn't sleep and thought it would help. Besides, the British drink hot tea in the heat of summer. Did in India, and it cooled them down."

Penny Sue raked her hair away from her face as sweat beaded on her forehead. She backed up to stand under an air conditioning vent in the ceiling. "Then, please, give me some."

At five-thirty we were still talking and watching the Weather Channel. Ruthie voiced the possibility that Penny Sue was having hot flashes and Penny Sue finally agreed to try black cohosh. I'd told them my dream about Ann, which they concluded was simply a projection of my fears. They, also, urged me to go the extra mile to accommodate the trip with Zack, provided Ann gave me Patrick's birth data, as promised. Regardless of Zack's schedule, that was my condition for going to England.

So, I was feeling very empowered, as they say in the women's seminars, when the phone rang. It was almost six o'clock. My first thought, naturally, was of Ann. Crap, I wasn't ready to deal with it. One little jingle, and my nerve evaporated. We all looked at the phone. Dreading the message, I made no move. Finally, Penny Sue got up and answered it.

"No problem. We were already awake, couldn't sleep." She listened intently, then held the receiver out to me. "It's Frannie May. She couldn't sleep either and has been listening to her police scanner. She wants to speak to you."

Frannie May had a police scanner? I took the phone.

"A policeman's going to be there at eight. Something about another gunshot to Penny Sue's car?" she said eagerly.

"Yes, it happened last night. We parked in the shopping center across from the Pub, and someone nailed the other P in Penny Sue's license plate."

"Did they get the dog?"

"Uga?"

"Whatever, the dog on the plate with the spiked collar."

"No, just the second P."

"Then, this is personal." Frannie May stated emphatically. "Go pack your clothes. The minute you finish with the police, come to my house. I have a three-car garage, so we can hide Penny Sue's Mercedes. I also have four guestrooms, you'll be comfortable. Besides, Carl is downstairs and he has lots of friends. You're not safe there. No argument. Call me as soon as the cops leave."

* * *

They came, they saw, they went. That was the extent of the police's interest in Penny Sue's car. An officer, who looked all of fifteen years old, dug out the slug, took a quick photo, and they were off.

"A lot of help we'll get from them," Penny Sue said as the police drove away.

I shrugged. "It's Bike Week, Penny Sue. Their resources are stretched to the limit. A bullet hole in a license plate isn't exactly high priority."

"I know. In any event, it means that if anything gets done, we'll have to do it ourselves." She turned to us and clapped her hands. "So, let's get going."

Lord, she'd morphed into an elementary school teacher. Ruthie and I bit our tongues as Penny Sue barked orders.

"You'd better call Ted," she said, as we stacked our suitcases in the hall. "He'll worry if we're not here. What about Ann? Maybe you should call her, too."

"I'll call Ted, because he may stop by. As for the rest, it will only worry them. We'll check our messages regularly and no one will be the wiser."

Penny Sue nodded emphatically. "Good idea."

By ten-thirty we'd loaded the car, including the liquid Taser, and were ready to go. Penny Sue picked up *The Book of Answers,* put Lu Nee in sentry mode in the living room, and set the alarm. As Penny Sue locked the front door, I caught a glimpse of Shrewella peeking through the blinds of her second floor window.

"Nosey old biddy," Penny Sue muttered as she started the car.

"Look on the bright side," I said. "We have free, round-the-clock surveillance."

Penny Sue grinned. "Yeah."

Frannie May's house is one of many large homes, on big lots overlooking the Intercoastal Waterway on North Peninsula Drive. A modern day adaptation of an old Florida-style house with a metal roof and wide porches, it was huge. A four story structure, the first floor consisted of a three-car garage and an apartment for Carl. A white-railed staircase reminiscent of something from *Gone With the Wind* led to the second floor porch and main entrance. We'd brought both cars and parked in the driveway. Fran must have been waiting, because she appeared in the front door with a remote control in her hand. She pushed the button, and one of the garage doors rose. "Pull in there, Penny Sue," she called. "Quick, before someone sees your car. Leigh, pull in behind her."

As I've said before, Frannie isn't very tall, but has a commanding presence. So, when she said "Quick," Penny Sue and I did exactly that.

"Good," Fran said, giving us each a hug. "You'll be safe now. Let's get your stuff into the house. See that door

over there," she pointed to an ornate hatch about two feet off
the ground. "That's a dumbwaiter. Load your stuff in it and
push three. The guestrooms are on the third floor."

"This is cool," Penny Sue said admiringly as we stuffed
in the last suitcase. "What a great idea."

"A necessity. You don't think I'm going to lug groceries
up all those stairs, do you? And, the way Carl, Jr. and my
Carlo," she crossed herself, "ate, there were tons of groceries.
We have two pantries, and one was always filled with pasta
and crushed tomatoes. Can't get the good brands down here
so we had them shipped from Boston by the case. Well, come
in. Let me show you around." She hit the remote for the garage
door and ushered us up the front steps. The foyer rose two
stories, with a hardwood stairway to the right that led to a
balcony above. Sunlight streamed through a huge bay window
in a country kitchen directly ahead.

Frannie shut the door and immediately drew our attention to a porcelain umbrella stand next to the entrance. "See
this?"

"Very nice," Ruthie mumbled.

"No, not the stand, this!" Fran plunged her arm into
the container and pulled out an aluminum baseball bat. "This
is for emergencies. If anyone tries to get in, whack 'em in the
crotch."

Penny Sue chuckled. "Great idea. I'll have to get one
for my house in Atlanta."

"This way." Frannie May led us up the staircase to the
guestrooms on the third floor. She opened the door to the
dumbwaiter and pulled out our luggage. "Take your pick."
She motioned to the rooms.

There were four cheery guestrooms, each with a private bath and doorway to the balcony that overlooked the water. Lord, I felt like I'd died and gone to heaven. Penny Sue immediately went for the room with a hibiscus theme, in line with the red flames on her boots, I supposed. Ruthie chose the center room decorated in a delicate yellow with dark, Key West style furniture. I picked the room farthest from Penny Sue—she snored on occasion—which was adorned in pale blue.

Fran pointed to a door at the far end of the hall. "As soon as you're settled, meet me in the cupola." She headed up a narrow staircase to the small windowed room. Our interest aroused, we unpacked in a matter of minutes. When we made it to the cupola, Fran was sitting in an old rocking chair next to a tooled leather trunk.

"I'd forgotten all about this until now. It belonged to Uncle Enrico, my mother's youngest brother. He disappeared a few years ago. Since I was the only living relative, I had to clean out his apartment. I found this in a closet."

"Disappeared?" Ruthie asked. "No clue what happened to him?"

Fran shook her head. "He was a loner. Never married. No one in the family even knew what he did for a living. Actually, we were afraid to ask, if you know what I mean. Anyway, I think this might come in handy, considering your present predicament." She pulled a small key from her pocket and opened the trunk. My jaw sagged. The trunk was packed with weapons! One by one, Fran pulled them out and laid them on the floor.

"Magawd, your uncle had an arsenal," I exclaimed. "What are they?" Of course, the crossbow and arrows needed no explanation. Nor the fact that there were a lot of guns in all sizes.

As calmly as a person might give a tour of a flower garden, Fran identified each weapon. "That little thing is a four shot palm derringer. Cute, isn't it?"

It looked like a toy.

"This one is a Beretta with a silencer, and these," she pointed to two blunt-looking rifles, "are sawed off shotguns." Fran stood, cracked her back, and pointed to the right. "Carl, Jr. says that's a sniper rifle."

Sniper rifle? Geez, I was glad Uncle Enrico was missing.

"That little can holds pepper spray." She waved to the left. "Naturally, that's a crossbow, and the bolt cutters go without saying."

"Bolt cutters?"

"Well, I guess he had a need to cut chains from time to time." She rolled her shoulders. "If things get dicey, we'll be prepared." She winked and snatched the pepper spray. Penny Sue winked back.

Was Fran kidding? I wasn't sure.

"Help me put this stuff up, and we'll get something to eat. I made a big batch of tarragon chicken salad. How does that sound?"

"Terrific," Ruthie said weakly, carefully picking up the Beretta with two fingers and placing it in the trunk.

Not to be outdone, Penny Sue ran to get the Taser from her car as we helped Fran set out the food.

I've always heard that Jewish mothers put out spreads fit for a king and won't take no for an answer when it comes to eating. They have nothing over Italian mothers if Fran was typical. The batch of chicken salad could have fed an army, not to mention huge hunks of Italian bread and a literal vat of gazpacho.

"Fran, you must have cooked all morning," I said, placing a soup tureen on a large oak table set in front of the bay window.

She waved off the remark. "The chicken salad is my own secret recipe. I bought the bread, and the soup came from Beach Buns. Why go to all that trouble when the stuff you can buy is nearly as good as homemade? I used to cook everything from scratch when my Carlo was alive. He loved good food and really appreciated the effort. Now, it's typically just me and Carl, Jr. Cooking doesn't seem worth the effort for two. But on weekends he and his Klingon buddies come for dinner after their match. That's fun, especially if they've won. In fact, the Romulans usually come, too." She smiled wistfully. "There's nothing like cooking for a group of hungry men."

"Has Carlo been gone long?" Ruthie asked.

"Almost five years. Heart attack. He was an investment banker in Boston. A very stressful job. We moved down here to get away from the hustle and bustle of Boston about ten years ago, after his first heart attack. As long as Carlo had a telephone, fax, and an airport, he could work from almost anywhere. Even though the pace here is relaxed, he couldn't slow down. Today they'd probably diagnose him as hyperactive—no one thought of such things back then." She pressed her lips together wistfully "I'm thankful he didn't suffer. He died in my arms on that couch over there." She pointed to the great room adjacent to the kitchen.

Ruthie was such an empathetic Pisces, I thought she might tear up. Thankfully, Penny Sue arrived with the Taser, Carl close on her heels.

Mother and son were both mightily impressed with the weapon. Carl turned it over in his hands and felt the balance. "Multiple shots, longer range—that's quite a break-through. I'm sure police departments will be standing in line to buy this baby."

"I want one," Frannie said, taking the Taser from her son. "Ruthie, do you think your father could get one for me?"

"I'll ask. That's a prototype the company's president sent me as a favor to Poppa. It may be on the market soon; I honestly don't know."

"See what you can do. It sure is better than a gun—not so messy."

Carl surveyed the kitchen. "Smells good in here. Have anything for a starving boy?"

Fran cocked her thumb at the table. "I always do." She grinned at us. "It's amazing how he magically appears when-ever I rattle plates in the kitchen. I sneak a bowl of ice cream in the middle of the night, and Carl's at my elbow before I finish dishing it out."

"Come on, Mom, I'm not that bad," he protested.

"Close. Though, I don't mind."

"How did your battle go the other day?" I asked between bites of chicken salad.

"They skunked us with infrared sensors. But, not tonight. Tonight, we're going to win."

"You play at night?" Penny Sue asked. "How can you see to shoot the paintballs? Besides, isn't the park closed?"

He wiped his mouth. "Canaveral's closed after sunset, so we use the Merritt Island Refuge for night games. We're unveiling our secret weapon tonight, The Bird of Prey. Todd and the others will never know what hit them."

Fran patted her son's shoulder. "Carl and his friends have been working on The Bird for months. You won't believe your eyes—it's really ingenious. We'll take a tour of his apartment and workshop after lunch."

We cleared the table and loaded the dishwasher while Carl went downstairs to tidy up.

"He's got to pick up his dirty underwear from the floor," Fran grumbled. "Thirty years old and still throws his clothes in the floor. He needs a good woman to whip him into line." She sighed. "Unfortunately, he and his buddies don't have time for women. Computers, science, technology, and those *Star Trek* war games are all they think about.

"I suppose I shouldn't complain, he's not out on the street doing drugs like my next door neighbor's son. That kid is twenty-two, flunked out of college, and never worked a day in his life. He's killing his parents with worry. They need to kick him out on his butt.

"At least Carl is a millionaire and pays his own way."

Ruthie, Penny Sue, and I did a double-take. Millionaire! That sweet, young man was a millionaire? Must have made his money on the GPS deal. Now, that's the kind of man Ann needed. Eight years difference isn't much, especially since women mature faster than men.

Fran started the dishwasher and led us into the foyer to an elaborately carved door that fit with the woodwork so well, I hadn't noticed it. She swung the door open to reveal a U-shaped stairwell. "This is the Bat Cave," she quipped.

Star Trek, Batman—hey, millionaires are allowed to be eccentric, I thought with a grin. Instead of a dark, gloomy lair we found a spacious, bright, one-bedroom apartment, complete with an efficiency kitchen that obviously hadn't been used for much more than pizza and popcorn.

"Welcome to my humble abode," Carl said with an expansive wave.

Humble heck. The place had an ultramodern/retro leather sofa and a red upholstered swivel chair shaped like a hand. The palm formed the seat, the little finger and thumb were curved into armrests, with the three middle fingers curving up for the back.

"Try it," he said to Penny Sue.

She eased into the chair, skeptical that it would hold. It did. She leaned back and pivoted the chair from side to side. "Boy, this is really comfortable." She got up. "Try it Ruthie."

Ruthie lifted her feet and twirled in a full circle. "I saw something like this at an art gallery in New York."

"I bought it at a gallery there—don't remember the name off the top of my head. The bedroom's over here." He opened the door to another ultramodern room, complete with metallic sheets and comforter. "I had them made. They're replicas of the ones used on *Star Trek*."

As tacky as it sounds, they were nice and fit the décor perfectly. Not something I would have chosen, but perfect for a single male. At least everything wasn't black like Zack, Jr.'s furniture.

"Now ladies, for the pièce de résistance." He ushered us through the living room and a door at the far end of the apartment.

Another garage—although, this was no ordinary garage. The walls were lined with computers, monitors, and all manner of electronic equipment in addition to regular tools like hammers, wrenches, and an acetylene torch. In the center, mounted on a boat trailer, was something covered in a tarp. He folded the cloth back to reveal a boat that looked suspiciously like the Batmobile.

"The Bird of Prey," Frannie May said proudly.

"What is it?" Penny Sue blurted.

"Victory," Carl gloated. "The Battle of Khitomer is ours."

"Good, but what is it?"

"A stealth runabout."

"Huh?" Ruthie and I said in unison.

Carl lifted a hatch on one side. "A boat that can't be detected. See all the angles and the black coating? It scatters radar. A hybrid engine—gas and electric like the new Honda. The gas engine gets you there fast, while the electric is virtually silent so we can sneak up on the shore." He puffed his chest out with pride. "And, now we've overcome the infrared problem. We've developed a way to scatter the heat signature."

"How?" Penny Sue asked.

"That's confidential. We're applying for a patent." He put his hands on his hips and beamed. "Todd and the Romulans don't have a chance this time."

"I'm surprised they had a chance before. The other team, the Romulans, have something comparable to this?"

"Not exactly, but close."

"They all went to MIT together and, one by one, migrated down here after we moved," Fran explained. "Being so young—they all graduated before they were twenty—they hung out together in college and made up this *Star Trek* game. They've never stopped playing it. Except for Carl's work on the Global Positioning System when he was seventeen— interviewed by *Popular Science* and everything—most of their patents came from trying to outwit each other in the game."

"Most of the Romulans' breakthroughs have been in surveillance. Our forté is countermeasures."

I studied the Bird of Prey, then Carl. He was a handsome man, not to mention smart, rich, kind to his mother. It was time to call Ann. I had to stall that engagement until she could meet this Klingon.

Chapter 12

Fran was scheduled to work at the center that afternoon, having graciously offered to fill in for me so I could spend time with my friends. Free of obligations, we elected to put on our swimsuits and sit by Fran's pool. A large, irregular oval with a three-man Jacuzzi at one end, the enclosure was perfectly positioned to give a panoramic view of the Intercoastal Waterway.

"Doesn't get much better than this," Penny Sue said, dropping a copy of the *Daily Journal's* Bike Week Event Supplement onto her lounge chair and touching her toes a few times.

Clad in a square-necked, black one-piece that contrasted dramatically with her light coloring, Ruthie looked like a fashion model. One of the waif types, not the full-bodied models that I liked so much who were coming into vogue. Ruthie angled her chair toward the sun and sat down with her laptop and a newspaper. "A shame Fran's Carlo didn't get to enjoy all of this. She's a terrific woman and obviously loved her husband very much."

I put my towel and cell phone on a table shaded by an umbrella and plopped down on the side of the pool. The pool was solar-heated and the water was as warm as a bath. "She's been a wonderful friend to me."

"I see that and promise not to make any more snide remarks about Carl," Penny Sue said.

"The revelation that he's a millionaire didn't influence your decision, did it?" I needled.

"That and the fact he's obviously brilliant and not just a nerdy flake. The genius types are always quirky. They say Einstein got lost on the Princeton campus all the time. He'd get so wrapped up in new theory or something, he'd lose his bearings. And, remember the guy in the movie, *A Beautiful Mind?* He taught at MIT, didn't he?"

Ruthie scowled. "John Nash was schizophrenic—that's a far cry from quirky."

Penny Sue pulled her hair back. "All right, he was a nut."

"Schizophrenia is a serious illness. It's nothing to make fun of. You know, Jo Ruth is thinking of going into psychiatry."

Penny Sue chuckled, "Good, we'll have someone to treat us in our old age." She sat down and opened her paper. "Wouldn't y'all love to meet Uncle Enrico? I'll bet he was a character. Had to be in the Mafia, don't you think?"

"Probably, considering Fran said her own family didn't ask him too many questions," Ruthie said.

"I wonder what happened to him? Cement galoshes like they do on the *Sopranos?*" Penny Sue asked.

I leaned forward and splashed water on myself. "Yeah, or maybe he's in the witness protection program. He could be in Palm Beach right now with a new identity."

"Shoot, Enrico could be here at Bike Week. Grow a beard, shave your head, get a few tattoos and piercings—no one would be the wiser. Fran might have passed him in the supermarket a dozen times," Penny Sue said.

"Your imagination's running away."

She pursed her lips and snapped the paper noisily. I dove into the pool and started swimming laps. I began slowly, feeling the tension in my shoulders. It had been a long time since I'd had a good workout. I swam the first two rounds like a klutzy whale, ragged strokes, an irregular kick— it's amazing I make it up and back. By the fourth turn my body was warm and loose and muscle memory kicked it. I poured it on for the several more laps, stopping at the shallow end next to my friends. Panting, I sat on the steps, waist deep in water.

"That was some swimming, girl," Penny Sue exclaimed.

"I was a lifeguard in high school."

"I couldn't do that if my life depended on it. I've never been able to swim. Took lessons as a kid and quit when they insisted I put my face in the water. Pu-leeze, no telling what that chlorine would do to my skin, not to mention that my make-up would run."

Ruthie handed me a towel; I heaved a thanks. "You wore make-up as a child?"

"Not much, only a little blush and mascara. But, I started using moisturizers when I was about six. 'A dewy complexion is a girl's best friend,' Momma always said. Until the end, Momma had the skin of a teenager."

I climbed out of the pool and wrapped the towel around me. "How did you ever get out of college if you couldn't swim? Passing the swimming test was a requirement for graduation."

Penny Sue started twirling her hair. "A dumb require-ment. I went to school to find a husband. What good was swimming for that? After all, I wasn't looking to marry Tarzan and live in a tree. Yachts with life preservers and penthouses are more my style."

I draped the towel over a chair and sat next to my friends. "Come on, how did you get out?"

The hair twirling intensified. "You know how all freshmen were required to take the test and if they didn't pass, they had to sign up for swimming lessons?"

"Yeah."

"I was out sick that day. Lord, I thought I'd made it. Then, a week before graduation, this muscle bound physical education teacher tracked me down and said I couldn't walk down the aisle unless I took the test. I guess they felt sorry for me, seeing how I was on the verge of tears, had already gone an extra semester to get enough credits, and was scheduled to marry Andy in two weeks."

Penny Sue hadn't graduated with us because she refused to take any early morning classes. Consequently, she couldn't get in the core courses and had to go an extra semester, dictating an August wedding instead of the traditional June nuptials.

"Coach Hanson told me if I could get up and back the length of the pool any way, even dog paddle, and tread water for two minutes, she'd pass me. I almost had a panic attack, yet knew I had to do it. Considering the amount of money Daddy had dished out for the wedding, drowning was prefer-able to not graduating."

"You could have still gotten married," Ruthie said.

"No, Daddy knew I would never finish college once I was out from under his thumb, and he was bound and determined that I have a degree from University of Georgia. Not that my degree in anthropology has done a darn bit of good, but he was adamant that I would carry on the family tradition."

She was really twirling her hair now, the mere memory making her nervous.

"So, you passed?" I asked.

She let out a long sigh. "Barely. I dog paddled up and back the length of the pool. The whole time Coach Hanson paced me from the side of the pool with a long pole. I guess if I'd gone under, she'd have speared me like a fish. Anyway, then it came to treading water. I was considerably skinnier in those days, and I swear, if it hadn't been for the buoyancy of my boobs, I'd never have lived through the test. By the end of the two minutes, only my nose was above water." She ran her hands down the front of her torso. "Heckle and Jeckle, here, saved my life—"

Heckle and Jeckle? The talking magpies from the old cartoons. Gawd, I wouldn't touch that with Coach Hanson's ten-foot pole!

"—and the wedding." She sighed and untangled her finger from her hair. "The wedding was great."

Yes, once the wedding started—Penny Sue overslept.

"A shame the marriage only lasted eight months." Penny Sue shook her head ruefully. "It's amazing the difference it makes to live with someone, rather than just date. I had no idea Andy was so dumb. I don't mean to be cruel, but that boy was truly thick."

Duh. Andy played tackle and was captain of the football team. Poor boy had probably become *thick* from butting heads one time too many. Last I heard, he was selling cars in Valdosta.

Penny Sue stared into the distance.

"You're thinking about Rich," Ruthie observed.

"Yeah. I can't believe he's associated with Vulture, and especially Red. She's crude and rude—nothing like his wife, who was the ultimate Southern belle. Soft spoken, never lost her temper, a great cook—from everything Rich told me, his wife was an absolute saint. The exact opposite of Red."

"Red flirted with Rich last night. He didn't reciprocate—he walked away, remember?" Ruthie said.

Penny Sue nodded. "I'm afraid Rich doesn't realize Vulture is the leader of a wacko cult. If Rich does know about Vulture, he's in over his head and doesn't know how to get out." She stared at us, pleadingly. "Don't you see? I've got to help him."

Yes, I did see. Penny Sue, savior of the world, as at it again. Only this time, her good intentions might lead to some very bad results for all of us.

"We should lay low today," Ruthie said. "It's the new moon. Not the time to press our luck."

"You're probably right," she allowed slowly. Penny Sue snapped the Bike Week Supplement open and went back to reading.

I was stunned that Penny Sue gave in so easily and wondered if Ruthie could come up with an astrological excuse to abort the whole silly search. I'd ask at the first opportunity. For now, I was grateful to be off the subject of Rich. I strode to the table at the far end of the pool and retrieved my cellular phone. First, I checked the answering machine at the condo. Thankfully, there were no messages.

Next, to fill Ted in on our new whereabouts. I hesitated before pushing the button. My feelings about him had changed since that motorcycle ride. It was so sensual, and I'd gotten such a warm feeling from hugging his waist. My face suddenly felt warm. Magawd, was I a sex-starved divorcee, or was I falling for him? No, I told myself quickly, we were merely friends. With two boys, his life was too complicated for me, and I still hadn't finished sorting out my own life. I pushed the button and immediately got Ted's answering service. He must be on duty. I left a simple message that we'd decided to take his advice and had moved in with Fran for a few days. If he got a moment, give me a call. Otherwise, we were fine, and had hidden Penny Sue's car in Fran's garage.

Now for Ann. I looked at my watch. Three o'clock here which meant it was eight in the evening in London. Not too late to call. I took a deep breath and dialed.

"Mom, I was hoping it was you."

I could hear a lot of noise in the background. Voices, plates—they must be having dinner. "Is this a bad time? I hear a lot of commotion."

"No, no. We're in a restaurant. Hold on, I'm taking you to the lobby where we can talk." I waited. "Now, this is much quieter. I'm standing by the cloakroom. Can you hear me?"

"I can hear fine. How are you, darling?"

"Terrific. Isn't it great news about Daddy coming next month? I hope you can come then to meet Patrick. He's really looking forward to meeting you both."

Okay, the speech I'd rehearsed. The one I'd stewed over since I heard about Zack going to Europe. "I'm sorry, Ann, but the timing isn't good for me. You know, I have a job and they depend on me. Besides, I'm still sorting through my finances from the divorce. A trip to England would be difficult right now."

"Wouldn't Daddy pay for it?"

I rolled my eyes. Kids. It was like she didn't understand that the divorce was final and our lives were separate now. Heck, her father was living with another woman. I guess, since he was still subsidizing her, Ann assumed nothing had changed on my end. My property settlement would eventually be increased substantially, thanks to Penny Sue's Daddy, but the final accounting was months away.

"Honey, your Dad's not going to pay my way. We're divorced."

I could have come up with the money if I wanted to— I knew Penny Sue or Ruthie would lend it to me. But, I sure as hell didn't want to go with Zack. Besides, I needed to slow down this engagement.

"Don't you think Daddy would give you some of his frequent flyer miles? I'd like Patrick to meet you together. After all, you're my parents, and you'll both be in the wedding."

Oh lord, it was worse than I thought. Formalities aside, Ann was already engaged in her mind and planning the wedding. I stroked my forehead. Penny Sue and Ruthie had both advised me to go the extra mile, no matter how hasty I thought the engagement was. To do otherwise might draw a knee-jerk elopement. "Let me check at work and see how the schedule looks for next month. When exactly will your father be there?"

"April seventeenth through the twenty-fifth."

"What about our agreement? Did you get Patrick's birthday like you promised?"

"Yes. Even though Patrick thought it was crazy, he was a good sport. I have his birth certificate. Hold on, it's here in my purse."

I motioned to Ruthie for a pen. She pulled out her laptop instead. I could hear Ann fumbling in her pocketbook in the background.

"November 19, 1964. Scranton, Pennsylvania. 4:28 a.m."

I repeated the information so Ruthie could take it down. She winked, indicating she was already on the case.

"Ruthie has mine, right?" Ann asked.

"I'm sure she does." Or, maybe Ruthie'd conveniently lost it. Depends on how the astrology went.

"Patrick and I would love to see a copy of the horoscope. Will you send it to me?"

"Of course. Any chance you and Patrick could come to the states for a long weekend? You could stay with me in Florida." And maybe meet Carl. "I'm sure the weather here is a lot better than it is in England."

Penny Sue glanced over the top of her newspaper.

"Mom, that would be tough. I'm an intern—at the bottom of the totem pole. Getting off would be next to impossible."

"I understand," I said weakly.

"Hey, how about if I call Daddy and ask him, as a favor to me, to give you some of his frequent flyer points for a ticket? You'd have separate hotel rooms, of course, but Patrick can probably arrange big discounts, maybe even a comp for you. I have a tiny flat and a roommate, so I don't think you'd be comfortable staying with me."

Free airline ticket. Comp room. Darn, my excuses were dissolving. "Hold off until I check at work. Like you, I'm at the bottom of the totem pole."

Ann paused. "Never thought of that—I guess you are. Mom, Patrick's very special. I love him."

My eyes filled with tears. My darling baby wanted to marry an old man. I thought of her and Zack, Jr.'s precious little handprints that I'd had cut out of the patio in Atlanta before I moved. The new owners where angry, because I'd filled the hole with a decorative tile that said *Home Is Where The Heart Is*. The yuppie twerps didn't like the saying, thought it was old-fashioned. Hmph, I should have gone with my first inclination, that famous Southern saying: *Eat Shit and Die!* They'd gotten a great price on the house, a price that wasn't high enough to include my sweet babies' hands.

Penny Sue noticed my angry scowl and gave me the old finger-across-the-throat motion, indicating I should stop talking. She was right. Stop on a good note. I sniffed. "Ann, all I want is for you to be happy." And, that was the truth.

Ruthie was already punching buttons on her computer. "What's his last name?" she asked.

I didn't know. My daughter was planning a wedding and I didn't even know the man's last name. "I never asked."

"I have to give him a last name, because the program won't work otherwise."

"Call him Old Lecher."

"I thought you were going to give him the benefit of the doubt."

"I said I'd try. I am trying; it's just hard. Ann's already planning the wedding."

"Come on," Ruthie said. "I have to put something."

"How about O'Lech? Goes with Patrick, don't you think?"

"Um-m," Ruthie muttered.

I pulled up a lounge chair and peered at the computer. "What do you see?"

"He's a Scorpio. They tend to be secretive and controlling. His Neptune conjuncts his Sun, which makes him doubly so. Also, makes him very psychic which means he could be a good manipulator."

Ha, I knew it. He was using his psychic abilities to lure Ann into his web. "What else?"

"You have to understand that people are not victims of their astrology. Astrology merely shows traits a person is born with. If a person learns from experience, they can transcend their charts."

"Come on, Ruthie, what are his traits? It's not good, is it?"

"He has a lot of personal magnetism, which makes it easy for him to draw people to him. Unfortunately his emotional life will probably always be a wreck and he's prone to addiction. His love life tends to be a disaster because he doesn't know what he wants. He goes after things for status, then when he gets them, realizes it wasn't what he wanted."

The chicken salad that tasted so good going down suddenly felt like a lump in the pit of my stomach. "Any other good news?"

"He's rash and unpredictable. Could be violent."

"Violent?" That's it. I wasn't completely sold on astrology, still there was no way I'd let Ann marry a potential monster. I had to stop her. How? "What should I do?"

Ruthie closed the laptop. "Don't jump to conclusions. As I said, he may have outgrown all of these tendencies. In childhood, he may have been rash and hasty, yet outgrown it through experience."

Penny Sue put down her paper. "I think it would be wise to delay things if you can. Encourage them to live together. Really let them get to know each other. If Patrick has a dark side, it should come out. If there's one thing I regret about my past is that I was a little hasty."

I looked up at the sky, certain a bolt of lightning would strike me at any moment. Did I hear Penelope Sue Parker, the woman with at least fifty soul mates—that I knew of— admit, for the second time in one day, to being hasty? Mercy.

"I wish I knew Rich's birthday. I can't believe I didn't think of asking. Ruthie, have you checked our forecasts recently?"

Ruthie looked the other way, pretending to watch a large yacht sail past. "Yeah, nothing out of the ordinary."

Uh huh. I didn't buy it.

Penny Sue didn't notice. "Maybe we should try to find that psychic, Pauline. She lives close by, doesn't she? I could go for a reading. How about you, Leigh? You could ask about Ann and Patrick."

"I'd do that." Pauline proved to be amazingly accurate in our last reading, except, we didn't know how to put the pieces together at the time.

Penny Sue got up and headed to the house. "I'm sure the people at Chris' Place will know how to reach Pauline."

As soon as Penny Sue was out of earshot, I turned to Ruthie. "What's in our forecasts?"

"All three of us have some stress—it's one of those aspects that affects everyone at about the same age. Usually, those are no big deal. Only, Penny Sue has two fairly nasty influences right now. One indicates something sudden and the possibility of violence."

Oh boy. "That's already happened, though. The dead body behind her car was sudden and violent."

"Yes, that could be it. Still, I have bad feelings about our trying to find Rich."

"Me, too. Maybe you should tell Penny Sue about her bad aspects. If she knew, she might give up the search."

Ruthie frowned. "I've considered it. But, I firmly believe that people create their own reality. So, if she expects something bad to happen, it probably will. I'm afraid telling her would be a jinx. Besides, it's such a long shot that we'd stumble on Rich again, it may be better to forge ahead. For all we know, the police may have him already."

Ted might know. I snatched my cell and punched in his number. Miraculously, he answered.

"Hi, you caught me on break. I listened to your message a minute ago. I'm relieved you decided to take my advice. That's one less thing I have to worry about."

Hm-m, Ted worried about me. My attitude about our relationship had warmed considerably, did his comment mean that he felt the same way?

"That's the best thing you could do until we find out who has the grudge against Penny Sue's car. Did the police take a statement?"

"Yeah, they dug out the slug and took pictures. That's about it. We aren't high on the list of priorities."

"Don't take it personally—they're as overworked as I am. Luckily, no major disasters so far. A few fights, some wrecks, the usual."

"Right now we're sitting by Frannie May's pool. The weather is perfect. We were wondering if you'd heard anything about the murder? Ruthie's been watching the paper. Nothing's shown up."

"Haven't heard a word, but things are crazy. Everyone's busy directing traffic and taking stolen bike reports, so there's no time for water cooler gossip."

"We suspected as much. We're curious, that's all." Now I felt foolish. There was an awkward silence. "Take care of yourself, Ted. Watch out for all those sexy biker babes."

He chuckled. "I don't have time to notice. I'll be in touch as soon as things calm down. Say hello to everyone for me. And, tell Penny Sue to keep the .38 in her suitcase."

Penny Sue never listened to us, I doubted his opinion would carry any more weight.

"Pauline's out of town," Penny Sue groused as she skipped down the steps from the kitchen. Chris says Pauline leaves town every year during Bike Week. She hates the noise. We could try going to Cassadaga, but Chris says getting a reading this week is a long shot. Apparently, that's a favorite spot for bikers." She plopped down on her chaise. "We could have our own séance." She looked at Ruthie expectantly.

Ruthie held up her hand. "Hey, I'm intuitive, but I don't do readings and I certainly don't do séances."

"I was fooling about the séance part. We could do a group meditation and consult *The Book of Answers,* couldn't we? I wonder if Fran has any incense to set the mood."

"I think Fran is more the potpourri type," I said.

Penny Sue pouted.

"And, we're not burning any more of that darned sage! If you absolutely must have something, I'll take you to Chris' Place. But, no sage and no smudge sticks. Scented candles are as far as I'll go." I looked to Ruthie.

"Sandalwood is good for meditation and spirituality."

"Didn't you tell me it was good for sex, too?" Penny Sue said devilishly. "I have a case of it at home. A shame I didn't think to bring some along."

"I'm surprised that wasn't the first thing in your suit-case," I muttered.

She missed the sarcasm. "With all my new biker duds, I was short on space. As it was, I had to pack some of my stuff in a box. I need another of those big Hartmanns. One isn't enough any more."

One of those suitcases would hold a full-sized adult and was plenty big for anyone other than Penny Sue. Of course, everyone didn't buy a complete wardrobe every time she took a trip or met a new boyfriend. "I'll slip on some shorts and run down to Chris' Place. Sandalwood candles. Anything, else?" I asked, giving Penny Sue a hard look.

"Okay, no smudge sticks. That sage absolutely stank, didn't it?" Penny Sue giggled. "Can you imagine the smell when Shrewella burned it with cayenne pepper?"

"Telling her that was mean," I said.

"You went along with me!"

"I know, and I feel bad about it. Poor old thing might have choked to death."

Penny Sue poked my arm. "Admit it, you don't like her, either."

"She is a little persnickety."

"Persnickety? She's a stuck-up, old prune. She's the one who made all the trouble for me with the police, the last time I was here."

I wanted to remind Penny Sue that she'd done a good job of making trouble for herself by waving her gun around, but didn't. This was one situation when it was best to let sleeping dogs—or Southern belles—lie.

Chapter 13

Ruthie was content to stay by the pool and read the newspaper. With all of the commotion, she was behind on world events and must have felt lost. She was also probably happy to have some peace and quiet. Ruthie was a person who typically meditated twice a day, which was impossible with Penny Sue, Chatterbox of the South, around.

I slipped shorts on over my swimsuit, while Penny Sue put on a lacy, black beach cover-up. Cover-up was something of a misnomer—see-through was more accurate. Oh, well, it's the beach and Bike Week, I thought—anything went.

We piled into my car and headed down Flagler to Chris' Place. It was evident a half million tourists were in the area, I had to circle the block four times to find a parking space. Luckily, my Beetle was small and maneuverable, allowing me to share a space in front of Chris' Place with a Harley. "Your car could never have done this," I gloated.

"Hmph," Penny Sue replied as she struggled to lever herself out of the car. Once again, I had to pull her up. "It's not my fault," she complained. "You parked too close to the sidewalk. This car is for dwarfs. It truly needs an ejector seat. Get one next time, so real people can ride with you."

I ignored her comment and studied the bricks on the sidewalk. Flagler Avenue, like many restored districts, sold commemorative bricks to help finance the street's restoration. While most bricks contained family names and proclamations of undying love for people and New Smyrna Beach, two positioned in front of the shop were standouts. The first proclaimed, *Starpeople Landing Zone!* That's the portent Ruthie interpreted to mean that Chris' Place held answers for us on our last visit. The other was a new one I'd bought, but Penny Sue had never seen. "Look." I pointed to a brick in front of the window.

"The DAFFODILS Were Here," she read aloud. "I'll be darned. When did you do that, Leigh?"

"Christmas. I was feeling lonely and ordered it while I was here buying presents. I thought you'd get a kick out of it."

She gave me a hug. "That is so sweet. In spite of everything, the last trip turned out good, don't you think?"

"Yeah, that's the first and only time I've been on CNN," I said wryly.

We stood to the side as four women in biker garb left the shop. About our age, they all wore pouch belts in lieu of purses. "That seems to be the *in* thing," I observed.

"Those are so good looking. Bigger than mine. Excuse me," Penny Sue called, chasing after them. "I really like your belts."

"The fanny packs?" a slightly graying woman asked.

"I hate that phrase, but, yes. Did you buy them around here?"

The lady chuckled. "I know what you mean. Doesn't make sense, does it? You don't wear the darned thing on your fanny, or at least I wouldn't." She turned to her friends and grinned. "I'm not sure there's one big enough for that. Anyhoo, we bought them at the department store over by Publix."

"Bealls in the beachside shopping center?"

The woman nodded.

"Thanks so much," Penny Sue drawled.

"Where are you from?"

"Roswell, Georgia."

"Thought so. Nice place. I lived there for many years. Well, y'all," she said with special emphasis, "have a nice day."

"You, too," Penny Sue gushed with double the normal drawl. As soon as they were out of earshot, she turned to me and said in a normal voice, "Let's go to Bealls after we get the candles."

Chris' Place was packed, primarily with pseudo-bikers like Penny Sue, judging from the new leather smell and the Rolex on the wrist of a petite woman at the front counter. She was making over a black and red feathery doll with a mirror for a face. "This is the Goddess of Hot Sex," she exclaimed to her friends. They all crowded around her.

Penny Sue almost knocked me over to get to the counter.

"Think I should buy this?" the woman asked playfully.

"Why not?" one of her friends said.

For a moment I thought Penny Sue might snatch the doll from the woman's hands. Instead, she bent over the case, studying the remaining goddess. "Leigh," she hissed. I hurried to her side. "The only one left is for Success." She pointed at a yellow and orange feathered doll with a round bead in the middle of the forehead—the position of the third eye. "This might help us find Rich, don't you think?"

I didn't think the doll would do a thing, one way or another, except lighten her wallet. Still, it was eye-catching and certainly couldn't hurt. If nothing else, it might work like a lucky charm to build her confidence. "It's cute, buy it."

One of the sex goddess' friends moseyed over, eyeing the last doll.

Eyes narrowed, Penny Sue informed her, "That's mine. Chris," Penny Sue called loudly, "I'll take this remaining goddess when you get a chance."

Chris hurried over as soon as she finished with her customer. "Penny Sue, it's been a long time. How have you been?" Chris removed the goddess from the display.

"Pretty good," Penny Sue replied absently, reading the instructions for the doll. "What kind of candles should we burn with this?"

"Yellow," Chris said.

"How about sandalwood?" I asked. "That's what we came for."

"That scent is good to set a meditative mood. Yellow is the color for success—the scent isn't important." Chris led us to a candle display where she picked out a sandalwood candle and a yellow taper.

"That's not enough—give us four of each." Penny Sue turned to me. "I don't want to come up short like we did with the sage."

I suppressed a grin. Penny Sue went whole hog after everything—I was surprised she stopped with only four.

"Anything else?" Chris asked, putting the items on the counter.

"Do you have *The Book of Answers?*"

Chris walked to the bookcase. "Yes, one left."

"I'll take that, too."

We stowed the stuff in the backseat and headed for the Indian River Shopping Center. Wonder of wonders, we found a parking space close to the side door of Bealls. A chalkboard on the sidewalk caught Penny Sue's eye on the way into the clothing store.

"Cornmeal fried oysters with Florida caviar and a spicy sauce. That sounds heavenly. Look, Mojo Marinated Pork Chops." She wiggled her fanny. "Just what I need, to get the ole mojo revved up."

Oh, boy. I wasn't sure Fran was ready for this.

Penny Sue took a step back and checked the neon marquee over the entrance. "Spanish River Grill. Why haven't we been here before? The food sounds terrific."

"I found out about it only a few weeks ago. It's a secret locals hope tourists will never discover."

"Fran's been so nice, let's bring her here for dinner tonight. My treat."

"I'll split it with you."

"No, you won't," she barked. "This whole thing with Rich is my doing; the least I can do is buy dinner for the good friends who are helping me."

I held up my hands signaling no argument. She was getting a little cranky. Besides, she was right.

Bealls had a whole rack of bike belts, as the sales clerk called them.

"That's a much more civilized term. A man must have named them fanny packs—no woman would have been so stupid." Penny Sue picked one up and examined it. "These are nice. Glove leather and two pouches." She turned it over. "Actually, three. Look, there's one on the inside."

"Designed for tourists who want to keep their money and credit cards out of sight. I guess it's a combination money belt and purse," I said.

We bought four at a good price, in case Frannie May liked the inside pouch design.

Penny Sue suddenly fanned herself. Forget the garbage about Southern belles glistening and glowing—she was sweating like a whore in church. "Let's swing by the health food store across the street. I think I'll try that black cohosh.

"Black cohosh, Omega 3, 6, 9, and vitamin E should take care of it," the sales lady advised.

"Does it come in a single pill?"

"This one's pretty close."

Penny Sue mopped her brow. "Give me five bottles."

The clerk did a double take. "Five? Did you notice the price?"

She wiped her top lip. "I don't care, as long it works."

"It's not instantaneous. It takes a while to get in your system."

"Well, let's get on with it!"

Penny Sue bought a bottle of mineral water and took three pills before we got back to the car.

"How do you feel?' I asked.

She took a big swig of water. "Like someone lit a blow torch under me and I'd smack anyone who got in my way."

Honestly, I hoped the pills kicked in fast. Double fast. Maybe even triple fast. I started the car. "Your testosterone—which most people don't realize women have—is out of balance with your estrogen. It's the testosterone that gives so many older women a 'kick ass' attitude. Your body chemistry is essentially the same as an eighteen-year-old male."

She looked straight ahead. "Yeah, but I'm a lot smarter."

Uh oh, not the time to provoke her. "I'm talking general tendencies."

She threw down two more pills and chased them with a long drink of water. "One thing's for sure—Rich is my soul mate, and I'll kick the butt of anyone who stands in my way, including Vulture, and especially Red."

I put the car in gear and checked the rearview mirror. "Look, isn't that Sidney going into the health food store?"

Still swigging water, Penny Sue glanced over her shoulder. "Yes, I believe it is."

* * *

It was after five when we got back to Fran's. Bikers were everywhere—some in convoys a mile long—turning our five mile trip into a thirty minute game of dodge 'em. Fran and Ruthie were sipping Manhattans out by the pool when we finally arrived. "Let me fix you one." Fran went to the outside pool bar, returning a moment later with two plastic glasses graced with palm trees.

I raised my glass. "To Fran, the perfect hostess," I swept my arm wide, "with the most incredible view."

Fran eyed the packages Penny Sue had dropped on table. "A little shopping, eh?"

"Look what we've found." Penny pulled out the bike belts and passed them around. "It has a secret inside pocket. Isn't that neat?" The others agreed and thanked her for the gift. A gust from the inlet blew through, toppling the bag with the feathered goddess so its head popped out.

"Should I ask?" Ruthie said with a big eye roll. "What in the world is that? I assume you're not planning to pluck a chicken for dinner."

Penny Sue took out the doll and handed it to Ruthie. "It's a Magical Goddess of Success."

Ruthie giggled as she examined the yellow and orange feathered moppet with spindly arms and a button in place of a third eye. Her brows drawn together in a straight line, Fran peered over Ruthie's shoulder. Fran took a sip of her cocktail. "I'm Catholic. This isn't voodoo, is it? You're not planning to pray to this pagan idol, are you?"

"Absolutely not," I said, jumping to Penny Sue's defense. "It's merely an amulet, a good luck charm. A way to focus your attention on a positive goal."

Pointing to the label of instructions, Ruthie handed the doll to Fran.

"Hold your hands over the doll and envision the Universe supporting and fulfilling your desire for success," Fran read.

"The success I want is to find Rich before the police do. If he doesn't turn himself in, I'm afraid he'll get caught in the middle of a shoot out," Penny Sue said as she opened the other bag. "See, we burn these candles to set the mood. That's it. Basically, a meditation."

Frannie May took a sniff of the sandalwood. "Smells good. I can go along with this, as long as we're not praying to this thing and there's no pin sticking."

"No pins, I promise."

"Okay."

We stretched out in lounge chairs, enjoying the picturesque scene of the sun dropping into the waterway.

"Anything good in the news today?" I asked Ruthie. While I was not in her league as a news junkie, even I was feeling out of touch with the world. Between the bikers and Klingons, I felt like Alice in Wonderland where everything was topsy-turvy.

"This is the largest Bike Week on record, and accidents and injuries are at an all time low. Officials speculate it's because the bike crowd has gotten old and finally given up their wild ways. Oh, and tomorrow afternoon is cole slaw wrestling. That's supposed to be the high point of the week."

"I've heard of it, but never been. Carl and his buddies go every year," Fran said.

"I think we should go," Penny Sue piped in. "What could go wrong in the daylight? Besides, if it's the big event, Rich may be there. This could be my big chance."

Rich. Penny Sue was like a starving dog who'd latched on to a bone. There's no way she was going to give it up. "Is the rocket still scheduled to go?" I asked, trying to change the subject.

Ruthie nodded. "Day after tomorrow, in the morning. They haven't announced the time yet."

"I'd like to see that." I glanced at Fran. "We could go over to the condo and sit on the deck. As long as we don't take Penny Sue's car, there's probably no danger."

"Depends on the time. If it's dark, we'll ask Carl to go with us."

"The Middle East is the usual mess," Ruthie went on. "Attacks, counterattacks, you'd think the people would get sick of it and call a truce."

"It's gone on so long," Frannie May said sadly, "it's become their way of life. The people over there don't know how to behave differently. Things probably won't change until all the old leaders die off, taking the past and all the grudges with them. Hopefully, that will happen soon."

Ruthie picked up the paper and turned to the second page. "There was another hijacking of military weapons, this time in Georgia, not far from Atlanta. Homeland Security is afraid terrorist groups are planning a big attack."

"How in the world can a military shipment be hijacked? Don't they have guards?" I asked.

Penny Sue shook her head. "You'd think so. Probably an inside job—Al Qaeda sympathizers."

"This terrorist thing is getting very scary. I never realized how good we had it in this country. Now, I feel like I have to look over my shoulder all the time."

Fran chuckled. "If you'd grown up in a big city, you'd be used to looking over your shoulder."

"I guess you're right," Penny Sue said. "By the way, I want to treat everyone to dinner. I've never been to the Spanish River Grill and would like to try it." She glanced at Fran. "You've already done too much cooking. Please, say yes."

"Fine with me—it's a great restaurant. I was going to make an antipasto for the boys to eat when they get back from their battle. I can whip that up in a jiffy and let it chill while we go to dinner."

"Where are the guys?' I asked. "We saw all the cars and bikes parked next to Carl's workshop."

"Long gone. This is it, finally, victory in the Battle of Khitomer," Ruthie said with a twinkle in her eye. "They were so excited—it was really cute to watch. They were like a bunch of kids with a new toy when they rolled out the Bird of Prey. They spit-polished spots and slid it into the water as if it were a baby dolphin. I hope they win. There will be some mighty long faces, otherwise."

Penny Sue's face brightened. "I know," she almost shouted. "We'll do a success meditation for the Klingons. Couldn't hurt, right?"

Fran smiled. "Asking the Universe for help is okay, I think. But, we'd better do it fast, because the battle will start at dusk."

We drained our cocktails and went upstairs to the kitchen. Frannie May began throwing together *a little* antipasto—she'd pulled out a two-gallon salad bowl—while Penny Sue and Ruthie set up our goddess paraphernalia in the middle of the kitchen table. They placed the yellow candles in an arc behind the goddess, aligned four chairs facing the doll, and lit a few of the sandalwood candles around the room to set the mood.

By then the salad was finished and we took our seats.

"Wait," Fran instructed, hustling through the great room off the kitchen to the master suite. She returned wearing a necklace with a heavy gold cross and a large Crucifix which she put in place of a wreath on the wall. "I'm Catholic," was all she said.

"Ruthie, will you do the honors?" Penny Sue asked, passing her the instructions. "Let's affirm the Klingons, first."

"What do we do?" Fran asked with an edge of anxiety.

"I'm going to read this plea that the Universe support Carl and his friends' desire for success in the battle. Then, we stack our hands over the goddess and silently envision the guys being happy, jumping for joy, giving victory calls— you know, whatever they'd normally do if they'd won the battle."

"That's it?" Frannie asked, clearly relieved.

"Yes. Now for Rich," Ruthie went on. "We'll pause first to clear our minds. I'll read the plea again, asking that Penny Sue find and convince Rich to turn himself into the police. Then, we'll imagine that happening like we did before."

"Let's add a smile on Rich's face and the police patting him on the back. You know, like he's cleared and everything is hunky-dory," Penny Sue said.

Frannie sat forward in her chair. "Good."

We went through the script, just as Ruthie described. No bad vibes, no lightning bolts rocked the house, it all went as planned.

"That was nice," Frannie admitted at the end.

"Hold on." Penny Sue rushed to the sideboard and returned with *The Book of Answers.* "Let's double check."

"What's that?" Fran eyed the black book apprehensively.

"*The Book of Answers*—don't worry, it's published by a Disney company."

Fran nodded as if that was impressive enough.

"You ask a question, then open the book at random. It gives you an answer."

"It's like the old Eight Ball toys." I explained.

Fran nodded.

Penny Sue stroked the book vigorously. "I'm going to ask if our wishes will come true." She closed her eyes and her lips moving slightly. Then, she dramatically pulled the pages apart. The page said *IT CANNOT FAIL*. She hopped up and balled her fist in a victory sign. "Fuckin' A! Now, let's go to Spanish River and celebrate."

Fearing her reaction to the profanity, I glanced at Fran. It didn't faze her. I should have known. Fran was from Boston and was no wuss, apparently.

The locals must have been at Biker events, because we didn't have to wait at Spanish River. This was the beach, where no one dressed up, so almost anything was acceptable, provided you had shoes and a shirt—pants went without saying. But, the bikers had not discovered this nook, so we were seated at once.

Penny Sue went all out, ordering both the oysters and the mojo chops. I shuddered to think what this might do to a woman whose hormones were already on the level of an eighteen-year-old male. Interestingly, Ruthie went for the oysters, too.

Now, I don't know if the old wives tale about oysters is true, but it did get my attention, considering Ruthie'd recently gotten the attention of two good looking men. I hesitated, debating the oysters myself. Then my logical, Baptist brain took over, and I opted for conch salad. Oh, well, another time. Maybe when I came with Ted.

The dinner was delicious and was followed by thick wedges of homemade key lime pie. Fat, happy, and sassy as

Penny Sue put it—there must be something to the oyster thing—we headed back to Frannie's house.

Close to ten by then, the Klingons arrived with victory cries and a stack of pizzas.

The boys, still dressed in battle garb, ambled into the kitchen. Carl stopped abruptly, noticing the goddess in the middle of the table. "What's that, Mom?" he asked.

"Did you win?" Fran asked.

"Yes."

"That's your goddess of success!"

Carl regarded his mother as if she's lost her mind. Then he noticed the Crucifix hanging in place of the wreath. But, the other Klingons were oblivious to the nuances. They picked up the doll, held it high, and let out a deafening victory cry that rattled the windows.

Frannie pulled out plates, the antipasto, and a couple of bottles of red wine. The doll was forgotten as the Klingons, famished from battle, descended on the food and drink.

Chapter 14

Carl took the last bite of his breakfast and wiped his mouth. "Mom, I honestly don't think you should go to the cole slaw wrestling at the Cabbage Patch today."

We were sitting around the table nestled in the bay window that overlooked the waterway.

Carl glanced at each of us as if trying to find the right words. "It's, um-m, a little rowdy. I think you'd be offended."

"Rowdy, as in gunfire?" his mother asked, paling a bit.

"Rowdy, as in vulgar. Women will be flashing a lot of skin."

She gave him an *I wasn't born yesterday scowl.* "We know that a lot of bikers wear skimpy clothes. It's no worse than the stuff you see on the beach."

He cleared his throat. "Mom, some of the skimpy clothes slide off during the wrestling. Nudity is a tradition at this event."

She looked down her nose. "So, that's why you go every year."

He studied his plate sheepishly, and I tried not to smile. Boys will be boys—even brilliant Klingons.

"Are they naked or nekkid?" Penny Sue asked impishly.

Carl regarded her curiously. "What's the difference?"

"Naked means you don't have on any clothes; nekkid means you're nude and up to something."

Carl chuckled. "I guess there's a little of both."

"Don't worry, son, we're grown women. There isn't going to be anything there we haven't seen before."

I thought of Red's tattooed breasts and suspected Fran was in for a surprise. Red was a first for me—heavens knew what else might turn up.

"Besides," Penny Sue added, "it's our best chance of finding Rich. Cole slaw wrestling is *the* highlight of Bike Week. Everyone attends, and we're counting on him to go with the flow."

Carl put his elbows on the table and looked Penny Sue in the eye. "The Cabbage Patch is not a place for serious conversation. It's a big, wild party."

"We've thought about that. If we find Rich, we'll follow him to a place where he can talk," Fran said.

"Mom-m, please don't do this. If Rich is involved with Vulture, I don't want you within fifty miles of that group."

"Carl, we're not stupid. If we see Vulture, we'll go the other way."

"You don't know what he looks like!"

"Penny Sue does."

Carl stood up, shaking his head, and reached into his pocket. "I was afraid you'd be stubborn."

Fran shook her finger. "Watch your mouth, Sonny. Your father never stood for backtalk."

"Yes, and Dad would never have allowed you women to stalk Rich."

"Stalk?" Penny Sue said tersely.

Carl leaned across the table and handed her a silver disk about the size of a thick poker chip. "Yes, stalk! If I can't talk you out of going, at least use this. Try to slip it into Rich's pocket, on his bike, something."

"What is it?" Penny Sue asked.

"A GPS transponder. I'd rather track Rich from my computer than have you and my mother chasing all over creation."

Fran patted her son's arm and smiled. "That's my Carl. I don't know why I didn't think of this before."

"Take the new cell phone I gave you," he continued with a sigh. "Some buddies and I are going out there. If you get in trouble, call me. In fact, you should all take your cell phones in case you get separated. The place will be mobbed." Carl glanced at Penny Sue. "You thought the Pub was crowded the other night. You ain't seen nothing yet."

Penny Sue held up her hand like a reticent six-year-old. "The battery in my cell is on the fritz. Won't hold a charge."

Carl glanced up as if praying for absolution, then reached in his pocket and pulled out a square device only slightly larger than the transponder. "Here, take mine. I'll use my old one. Please don't lose it—that thing cost a fortune."

"I'll bet," Penny Sue said, examining the tiny instrument. "This is the smallest one I've ever seen." She passed it over for Ruthie and I to see. "I'll be careful. Promise." She took the phone from me and slipped it in the inside pocket of her bike belt. "It'll be safe here."

Frannie held her hands up to her hulking baby boy. He gave us an embarrassed glance, then bent down and kissed her forehead.

"You're a good boy. Don't worry, I can take care of myself."

Carl glanced at the umbrella stand in the foyer that concealed the baseball bat. "That's what scares me."

* * *

We piled into Carl's beat-up Explorer right after lunch.

"This won't draw attention," Frannie said. She was dressed in black slacks and shirt with her hair tied back in a kerchief. Since it was sunny and unseasonably warm, Penny Sue wore a red print shirt with cutoff jeans and the Harley boots with red flames. As unpretentious as I've ever seen her look, she wore minimal make-up and had her hair platted in a single braid down the back. I wore black capris and a tank top, while Ruthie wore jeans, a V-neck shirt, and a really cool turquoise and silver belt. For once, Ruthie was the glitziest of the group, and I wondered with an impish grin if Ruthie was hoping to meet someone—or, rather two someones—at the match.

"What?" Ruthie asked, noticing my smile.

"Nothing," I said innocently.

We all decided to wear our new bike belts. Unfortunately, Penny Sue packed her .38 and Fran stuffed the pepper spray into their belts. The firepower made me feel nervous, rather than safe. An image of Penny Sue and Frannie May descending on Rich with weapons blazing flitted across my mind. I was pretty sure Fran had more sense, but I wasn't so sure about

Penny Sue. After all, her mojo was revved from last night's dinner, and I doubted the black cohosh had time to take effect. That Fran would go along with Penny Sue was beyond my comprehension. The two had an affinity that I couldn't explain. I'd never checked, but maybe Fran was a Leo. Or, perhaps, it was her Italian roots.

Everyone—at least, in the South—thought Italians took no stuff from anyone, making them all pseudo-Leos. Even rednecks tread lightly around Italians. It was the Mafia mystique. Certainly, all Italians weren't Mafia, no more than all bikers were in gangs or all Southerners were dumb because they spoke slowly. These were superficial stereotypes based on movies and a handful of weirdo, fringe groups. Still, that horse head from *The Godfather* gave me nightmares for weeks, and no doubt lurked at the back of many minds.

Be that as it may, off we went, armed for who knew what. Sun shining brightly, early afternoon, we were going to cole slaw wrestling. Imagine, women wallowing around in shredded cabbage! I wondered if they used real dressing and if it was any good. I normally bought my slaw because I'd never been able to make a decent sauce. Maybe the Cabbage Patch bottled and sold theirs: *Official Bike Week Cole Slaw Dressing.* Considering my record, I'd give it a try.

With a lot of doing, we finally found a parking spot in a wooded field of bikes. Frannie May, who drove like a professional valet, wedged into a spot I'd never thought possible. "Boston," she said, getting out of the Explorer and adjusting the bike belt with the pepper spray. "Up North, you learn to take any advantage."

What a difference! A Southern woman would drive an hour looking for a big space—preferably two, if parallel parking was required. All that maneuvering into a tiny spot was too tense for a Southern belle. You'd break out sweating and ruin your make-up. Considering it had taken thirty to forty-five minutes to put on your *face*, a few loops around the block were nothing.

We locked up and struck out for parts unknown. The first thing that hit me as we walked across the field was the large number of women in swimsuits.

"Contestants," Ruthie stated. She'd looked up the Cabbage Patch web page on the Internet.

We followed the crowd through the field to an area cordoned off by a wire fence where people were packed in three deep. Judging from the hoots and hollers, we knew the wrestling had already started.

"I want to see what's going on," Fran said. "Follow me." Circling the crowd, we searched for a space. We found nothing until a fine spray of water hit us in the face. "There," Fran called, racing for a spot being vacated by two drenched spectators. It only took a second to see why the couple left. Directly ahead, a man was hosing slaw off one of the contestants. Outfitted in a slinky bikini, she turned her back to the crowd, pulled back her panties, and wiggled in the spray.

Another match was already underway in the middle of the fenced enclosure. The ring was a large pit lined with blue plastic and filled with oily, shredded cabbage. The contestants seemed fairly mismatched. One was a hefty girl, as Grammy would say, while the other was a slim-hipped, buxom blonde. Hefty adopted the stance of a sumo wrestler; Blondie pranced in the slush like a ballerina. Hefty lunged, Blondie did a twirling kick, Hefty fell flat on her face, Blondie fell on Hefty and the match was over.

"That was a nice round off kick," Penny Sue said, lowering her hands from shielding her face as the spray stopped.

"Don't tell me," I said. "You've taken karate."

"Tae Kwon Do. Bodan."

"I tried it," Frannie added. "Got up to orange, then threw my shoulder out. My doctor told me to give it up before I really got hurt."

As Blondie and Hefty approached, we turned around, anticipating the shower. "Now what? Ruthie asked.

"We search the crowd."

"How?"

With the high heels on her Harley boots, Penny Sue was close to six feet tall and could see over the top of the crowd.

"You survey the back lot, we'll scan the people around the fence," I said. "If that doesn't work, we'll meander around."

"This is hopeless," Ruthie moaned.

"You said that at the Pub and we found him," Penny Sue reminded her.

"A lot of good that did."

Penny Sue put her hand on her hip. "Come on, Ruthie, you're Ms. Positive Thinking. Besides, *The Book of Answers* said we couldn't fail. Now, you either believe in the spirits or you don't. Which is it?"

Ruthie huffed. "May I at least wait until the spraying stops?"

"Of course, darling. We don't have to be dumb about it."

Ruthie clenched her teeth and didn't say a word. I thought she would bust. But, in a few minutes the spray stopped and we turned toward the ring.

"I'll take the right," Ruthie said. "Fran, you take the middle and Leigh will cover the left. Okay?"

A shame we hadn't brought binoculars. It was hard to distinguish faces when people were packed together like sardines. Of course, women with binoculars at a female wrestling contest might give the wrong impression. Not that I really cared; however, it could present complications we didn't need.

The wrestling was distraction enough. The new contestants were unusually vocal and evenly matched, making it impossible not to watch. Coated from head to toe in slaw, they rolled in the mush, clawing for dominance. A roar went up from the crowd as someone's halter was flung aside. A few minutes later, a thong bikini went flying.

"Are they naked or nekkid?" Fran asked under her breath.

"Darned, if I know," Ruthie said weakly. By now, Penny Sue had abandoned any pretense of surveillance and was watching, too.

It was difficult to tell who was getting the upper hand in that roiling pit of flailing limbs and curses. Even the referee seemed overwhelmed until the pantiless contestant landed a punch to her opponent's stomach. Foul!

The referee waded into the slimy fray and tried to separate the women. Bare Butt was obviously not happy with his decision and took a roundhouse swipe at the referee. He dodged the blow and fell backward onto the other woman.

Egged on by whoops and hollers, the Bare Butt Wonder jumped from the pit and went into a primal victory dance. That's when a man wearing a Security shirt appeared. He ushered Bare Butt toward us, while the referee and other contestant struggled to get out of the pit.

Bare Butt continued her wild antics even as she was being hosed off, finally bending forward toward the crowd and ripping off her bra. I gasped. Ruthie yelped. The lady's boobs were tattooed with flowers. It was Red.

That's when things went crazy. "Well, if it isn't Bubble Head and Molly." Red grabbed a towel from someone, which she wrapped around her waist and headed our way.

I grabbed Frannie's arm. "We need to leave."

"Do you know that person?"

"It's the lady we told you about from the Pub. She's a friend of Vulture's."

"Good. This is the break we need, right?"

"No, we don't want to tangle with her."

Frannie frowned. "What are you afraid of? There's four of us, one of her, and she can't be armed."

Penny Sue had already started to move away. "Leigh's right, Frannie. This isn't the time or place."

Red was wild-eyed, and the crowd parted before her like the sea before Moses. Unfortunately, we had to slog our way through the throng. She caught up to us as we broke out of the thickest part of the mob into a wooded area next to a hot dog stand.

She pointed at Penny Sue. "I've got a bone to pick with you."

Eyes narrowed, Penny Sue backed off. "We have nothing to talk about."

Red stepped forward, looking up into her face. "Not so brave without your tall buddies, are you?"

"Wait one minute," Frannie May said sternly, giving Red the *look*. Sadly, it was lost on this woman who was obviously high on something.

"Stay out of this, Granny, unless you want your ass kicked, too."

"What?" Frannie started fumbling with her bike belt. Lord, she was going for the pepper spray. I shook my head and reached for her hand. She gave me the *look*. I backed off instantly. Fran pulled out her cell phone and started to dial.

"Fake, chicken shit," Red sneered at Penny Sue. "You think you're so smart. Stay away from Rich. Little Dickie's mine."

Penny Sue set her jaw. "That remains to be seen." She turned to leave, and Red slugged her in the jaw. In one smooth move, Penny Sue swung around, leg extended, and swept Red's legs out from under her. The towel went soaring. With the determination of a pit bull, Red jumped to her feet, naked as a jaybird, with fists flying.

Penny Sue backed up and assumed a defensive posture— something from Tae Kwon Do, I supposed.

Fran fumbled in her bike belt. This time I knew she was going for the spray. "Stop that," she shouted. "Stop this minute!"

Red was not in a listening mood. She lunged for Penny Sue, who knocked her back with a kick to the gut. Considering Penny Sue was wearing the Harley boots and Red was nude, it must have hurt like hell. But, she surely had a streak of wild animal, because she came back swinging as if nothing had happened.

"Enough," Fran said with the force of Darth Vader, waving the pepper spray.

A crowd had formed to watch the commotion. My mouth went dry at the sight of Fran's spray, recalling Woody's comment that any small incident could set off a turf war between bikers. I poked Fran on the arm. "Put that up, you could start a riot." Her eyes shifted from side-to-side. Fran stuffed it in her pocket just as Rich plowed through the crowd and stepped between the women.

"No more," he said, holding them at arm's length. A rough-looking dude appeared on his heels and handed the towel to Red.

"Vulture," Penny Sue whispered.

Vulture pushed Red roughly. "What the hell are you doing?"

Red raised her chin defiantly, clutching the towel. "I don't like fake bitches."

Rich frowned and said under his breath, "Get out of here, Penny Sue."

The urgency in his voice was unmistakable. As we backed up and turned to high tail it out of Dodge, Vulture held up his arms and shouted, "Don't move!"

The entire crowd froze like statues. There was no way for us to get away.

Vulture glowered at Rich, then sidled up to Penny Sue, who towered over him in her boots. "Did I hear right? Penny Sue?" he sneered. "This wouldn't be Penny Sue Parker from

Roswell, Georgia? The busybody who drives a yellow Mercedes?"

Our worst fears had materialized. I'd always thought Penny Sue was overly paranoid about running into criminals that her father had locked up, yet it had finally happened. I watched as her hand inched toward her belt. I also noticed that Rich had suddenly developed an itch on his back.

They didn't make it. A nod from Vulture and two huge guys barreled through the crowd and grabbed Rich and Penny Sue. The biggest of the two, a mangy guy with a scraggly beard, patted Rich down and pulled a handgun from the back of his jeans.

"Sig Sauer, probably government issue."

Government issue? A murmur rippled through the crowd.

The second guy plunged his hand into the front of Penny Sue's bike belt and came out with the .38.

Vulture went nose-to-nose first with Rich, then Penny Sue. Actually, in her case, it was more like nose-to-chin, but the effect was the same. "Hm-m, seems my good buddy knows this meddlesome bitch, and they're both packing hardware. Curious," he said to no one in particular. "I think we should have a little conference to see what's going on here." Vulture nodded and his goons shoved Rich and Penny Sue toward the woods.

"Call the police!" Penny Sue shouted. The mangy gang member clamped his hand over her mouth.

As I fumbled for my cell phone, Ruthie implored the people standing next to her to help Penny Sue. They shook their head and backed away. No one, it seems, wanted to tangle with Vulture. But, Fran had spunk. Hand in pocket, no doubt clutching the pepper spray, she crossed herself and started after them. Suddenly, hands came from behind and pulled us back, through the crowd. It was Carl and his buddies.

"No-o-o," Fran screamed as Vulture and his gang disappeared with Rich and Penny Sue. "Son, we've got to help them."

"Mom, we will, but we're going to do it intelligently."

Chapter 15

We left the Explorer parked in the field and rode to Fran's house on the back of the guys' bikes. I rode with Todd, the Romulan. Luckily, he was not in costume and seemed to have bounced back from his defeat at Khitomer. Whatever happened at Khitomer, it was a big deal to the Romulans and Klingons. One day, when this was all behind us, I'd rent some old *Star Trek* videos and find out. Right now, Penny Sue was my only concern. I thought of Grammy Martin. Please, Grammy, call in the angels and spirits to watch over my friend.

I clung to Todd's back like a scared child clutches a teddy bear. We bumped through the woods and finally onto the highway. What to do? What to do first? Call Ted. He would get the local police on the case. And, Judge Parker. He would get state troopers mobilized.

I choked up at the prospect of what might be happening to Penny Sue. Red was a wild woman and everyone said Vulture was worse. And, why did Rich have a government issue gun? Was it stolen? Was he a cop? Penny Sue speculated he'd been associated with the courts before his wife got sick. The drama where he dumped Penny Sue had been strange, to say the least, especially considering the apologetic phone call he made the very next day. Had Rich hustled her away that afternoon because he didn't want Vulture to see her? If so, what was the connection between Vulture and Penny Sue, or Vulture and Rich, for that matter?

We needed answers. If Rich was law enforcement, his superiors should be notified. Besides, they'd probably know where to start looking. Surely, Rich had made progress reports or something, if he really was a cop. Or, like Penny Sue said, he could simply be a guy who stumbled into something beyond his control, I thought sadly.

The drive down Route 44 to Peninsula and the Annina house was one of the longest of my life—not counting the trips to the hospital to give birth. Those rides were longer, although this was close. The guys parked their bikes beside Carl's workshop where the door was already going up. Carl helped his mother off the bike, then raced to a computer at the side of the workshop. He hit a button and the computer started to hum.

"Does she still have that GPS transponder?" Carl asked as he waited for the computer to boot.

The transponder. I'd forgotten all about it and felt a flicker of hope. "Yes, she didn't have time to plant it on Rich."

"Then, we'll find her in a matter of minutes."

"Shouldn't we call the police?" I asked.

"Yep, though we'll find her long before the police do. With Bike Week, we'd be lucky if the police returned our call by tomorrow."

"We have to try," Ruthie said adamantly. She took out her cell phone and went upstairs to make the call.

Carl's fingers flew over the keyboard. "Vulture is a vicious nut, probably even psychotic. If he's got it in for Penny Sue, for whatever reason, there's no time to waste."

"Vulture's goon said Rich's gun was government issue. If that's the case, something bigger is going on. Penny Sue has a key to his room at the Riverview Hotel. I'm sure it's in her purse. We should search the room, don't you think?" I said.

Carl pointed at a map that had appeared on the screen. "There, looks like they're heading for the Canaveral Seashore."

"Why would they go there?" Fran asked.

"We've seen them there. They've cut tunnels through the palmetto scrub off Klondike Beach."

"Tunnels in shrubbery?"

"You can't imagine how thick that stuff is," Todd said. "And, they're definitely up to something important to slash a path through those prickly palms. The stems are like barbed wire; they'd shred a person in normal clothing."

"If they're so well hidden, how did you find them?" I asked.

Todd smirked. "Infrared. We were playing one of our games, and I picked them up. I knew Carl wasn't masochistic enough to hide in palmetto. We went back later and discovered a whole series of tunnels."

Fran slapped her son on the shoulder. "We must go there and get them, now. Vulture may be torturing Penny Sue."

Carl swung around forcefully. "Mom, you're not going." He looked to Todd. "How can we get in there without making any noise."

"Not on the Harleys, that's for sure. Our dirt bikes would be even worse."

"Saul. Saul has electric scooters," I said excitedly.

Todd grimaced. "Scooters?"

"He told us his new electric mopeds go close to forty miles an hour."

The guys exchanged glances. "That would do," Todd allowed.

Fran was already dialing her cell telephone. "Bobby," she screeched.

I assumed she'd called Bobby Barnes.

"Penny Sue's been kidnapped by Vulture. We have to locate Saul Hirsch. We need his electric mopeds." She listened for a second, then covered the mouthpiece and relayed, "Saul's with him. They're at the Pub." She listened again. "We know where they took her—to the Canaveral Seashore. Carl gave Penny Sue a GPS transponder, and we have them on the map. Carl's buddy knows where they're probably hiding out. Okay, they'll be there." She pushed the off button. "Meet them at Saul's shop downtown. They'll be there directly."

As the guys planned the attack, Ruthie appeared looking like a whipped puppy. "First, I called the city, who told me the Cabbage Patch was in the county. So, I called the county, and the officer I spoke with wasn't convinced that Penny Sue had been kidnapped. I told him about the hoodlum dragging her away and putting his hand over her mouth, but the deputy thought it might be a case of mistaken identity that would work itself out. I have to go to the sheriff's office and fill out a report. As soon as I do that, they'll issue a BOLO—be on the lookout. In any event, the deputy made a point of warning me that resources were stretched thin."

"It's up to us, then." Carl nodded to the Klingons. One went to the Bird of Prey and pulled out a square box with a scope, while the others gathered paintball guns and ammunition from the wall. Ruthie flew upstairs as Carl plugged something about the size of a skinny pack of cigarettes into the computer.

"What's that?" I asked.

"A PDA. I'm downloading the transponder signature so the guys can track Penny Sue."

"From that little thing?" I asked, incredulously.

"Yes," Carl said over his shoulder. "This little *thing* has more computing power than one of the first computers, *Whirlwind I,* developed at Lincoln Laboratories."

Why in the world did I question guys who'd graduated from MIT at age twenty? Talk about stupid.

Carl handed the PDA to Todd. "You're in charge, commander," he said. Todd nodded with the look of a Romulan bigwig.

Ruthie huffed into the room, carrying the Taser and two bottles of solution. She quickly told them what it was. Todd's eyes lit with delight. He took the Taser and examined it appreciatively, then lifted the gun into the air with one arm. "Victory," he cried. The Klingons cheered raucously.

"I think you need real weapons," Fran said, handing the pepper spray to Todd. She looked at Carl. "What about Uncle Enrico's sawed-off shotguns? Wouldn't they help? Or, the crossbow and sniper rifle?"

"Mom, we can get these nuts with cunning and technology. There's no need for brute force."

Frannie May scowled. "It wouldn't hurt to have a few tricks up your sleeve."

"We want to rescue Penny Sue, not get locked up for the rest of our lives!" Carl said sternly.

"So, what's your plan?" Fran asked peevishly.

"Todd and the guys will find Penny Sue. Meanwhile, we'll go to the Riverview Hotel to check out Rich's room."

Fran snatched back the pepper spray. "Good plan, son."

*   *   *

Todd and two Klingons went to meet Bobby and Saul armed with the PDA, Taser, and paintball guns. Under other circumstances I would have been worried, considering all the vile stuff we'd heard about Vulture. Though, knowing Bobby Barnes, I suspected he and Saul—old Navy Seal buddies— might be packing something stronger than paintballs. Actually, I was counting on it. Praying for it, considering Vulture's bad press.

As the group left to Klingon battle cries, I tried to call Ted on my cell phone. As Carl predicted, no answer. Doubtlessly, he was up to his ears in a bike brawl or home asleep, his long shift finally over.

Then, I thought of calling the judge. Gracious, Judge Parker was in his seventies, and I hated to upset him unnecessarily. We had Penny Sue on the radar screen, so to speak, and two Navy Seals plus a Romulan and band of Klingons going to rescue her. State troopers weren't better equipped, and it would take a lot longer for them to get there. No, I'd wait. Carl, Todd, and their buddies were about as smart as anyone could be. Add the *real* battle experience that Bobby and Saul possessed to the Trekkies' technological know-how, and you had a team that couldn't be beat. Best not to disturb the judge yet, bless his heart.

Now, for our part. Ruthie took the keys to my car and headed for the Volusia County Sheriff's department to file the report. I ran upstairs and found the key to Rich's room in Penny Sue's pocketbook. When I returned, Fran was stuffing the pepper spray into her belt pouch. Carl gave her a hard stare, which she ignored.

Since the Explorer was out at the Cabbage Patch, we piled into Fran's Jaguar. As I wedged around the car to the backseat, I noticed, for the first time, a bumper sticker that said, "Mean People Suck." How appropriate! Vulture was definitely mean by all accounts and clearly sucked.

The Riverview Hotel was barely over a mile from Fran's house. We pulled into the lot and parked next to the spa. It was four o'clock, still light.

"I don't think we should go through the main lobby," I said. "After the murder, I'll bet they have instructions to report comings and goings to the police. We don't want them to know we're going to Rich's room, considering he's the prime suspect."

Carl turned to me in the backseat and grinned. "No problem. I know the way. Give me the key."

I gave Frannie May a questioning look as I handed the key to him. She shrugged. Carl caught the exchange and answered, "I've had a few girlfriends who stayed there. I know all the angles."

Ah, this millionaire genius did make time for girls! I needed to call Ann, again.

We followed Carl past the valet stand to a door by the pool. "This is usually not locked," he said, clasping the handle. It wasn't. Good ole Carl, sneaking around after women at night and his mother didn't have a clue. I should have guessed, considering he specialized in stealthy operations. We followed him by the pool and up a flight of steps to a balcony.

"Look," I said, pointing at a tall man with dreadlocks walking in front of the hotel. "That's Sidney, the guy who helped us out in our first run-in with Red. We saw him the other day at the health food store. I wonder what he's doing here?"

"Maybe he's staying at the hotel. You thought he was wealthy, right?" Fran said.

Carl shifted impatiently. "We need to get a move on. In another hour, the halls will be crowded with people leaving for dinner. I want to be long gone before then."

"Of course."

We followed Carl, single file, to Rich's room. Luckily, we didn't encounter anyone in the corridor. I immediately went to the closet. Rich was a friend of Penny Sue's—maybe he had a Lu Nee 3 stashed away. Only a couple pairs of slacks, a few shirts and a sport coat. A suitcase sat at the back of the closet. Carl grabbed the satchel and swung it to the bed.

"The best stuff is usually hidden," he said.

The suitcase was empty. So much for that theory.

Carl put it back in the closet and went to the floral-draped bed. "Leigh, help me lift this up. Mom, you look under it." We hoisted the top mattress on the count of three. Pay dirt! In the center, between the mattresses, too far in for a maid to find, was an IBM laptop.

Fran wiggled between the mattresses and snatched the computer. We lowered the mattress, and as Carl fired up the PC, Frannie adjusted the bedspread.

A moment later, Carl mumbled, "Wow, encrypted, high level. This is not an amateur job. We need to take this and get out of here."

"Should we wipe off our fingerprints or something?" Fran asked, fondling the pepper spray in her belt pouch.

"Too late for that, Mom. Besides, none of us have prints on record, ... yet."

I swallowed hard. I did.

"Let's go."

Carl didn't have to say it twice. Fran smoothed one last wrinkle from the bedspread, peeked out the door, and waved us through. As I pulled the door closed, I wiped the handle with the bottom of my shirt.

We went back to Fran's, and Carl immediately went to his workshop with the laptop, which he plugged into his big computer.

"Can we help you?" Fran asked.

"Something to munch on would be nice."

Fran glanced at her watch, almost five-thirty. "It's time for dinner, and I'm sure everyone will be famished. I'll put something on right away."

Anxious to see what he found, I stayed with Carl. I watched as his fingers danced across the keyboard. "What are you doing?" I asked, feeling like the Sword of Damocles was hanging over our heads.

"I'm copying the laptop's data to my hard drive. The G5 has a faster processor. Then, I'll use an algorithm to try to decrypt the data."

"Oh." I didn't know anything about encryption or what an algorithm was. Geez, life had become so complicated. I suddenly felt old, the way my parents probably felt when they talked to me. They couldn't believe I had a cellular phone or even an answering machine.

Carl was light years ahead of us. Heck, he was on the cutting edge—one of the people who made it all happen.

"Okay, now to crack the code. Just so happens I have a great program. I used it a while back when I was working on the Bible code."

"The Bible code?" I echoed.

"Yeah, many people think there are hidden messages in the Hebrew Bible. You know, like, if you pull out every third letter, you get a message or prediction about the future. It was the rage a few years ago, and I took a stab at it."

I'd never heard of it. Of course, I'd come to realize what a sheltered life I'd led. Tattooed boobs, Tae Kwon Do, Ayurveda, a Bible code—I'd missed a lot. "Did you find any messages in the Bible?"

"Some, nothing conclusive. Hundreds of mathematicians are working on it, so I figured I'd let them take the lead. Besides, I got a lucrative consulting gig about that time." He leaned forward, studying a lightening fast scroll of data. "We're closing in," he said excitedly, then pointed at the corner of the screen. "I've got it!"

Fran entered the room and slid a tray with a soft drink and a thick sandwich onto the counter. "What does it say?"

Carl reached for the sandwich and took a bite. "I don't know. I've found the algorithm. It will take a few minutes to translate the files."

"I've put a batch of my frozen lasagna in the oven so the boys will have something to eat when they get back. Gosh, I hope they've found Penny Sue and Rich. This whole thing is making me tense."

That was an understatement. A hard knot had formed in my stomach. If we didn't hear something soon, I feared a major bout of gastric distress. Knowing Ruthie had a similar inclination, it was fortunate that every room had its own bathroom, otherwise a monumental traffic jam was in the offing. Ruthie. Omagosh, I'd forgotten about her. I checked my watch and wondered how long it took to fill out a kidnapping report.

"The boys will call, won't they?" Fran asked. "They took a cell phone with them, right?"

"They'll call," Carl said, chewing slowly, eyes riveted on the computer. He put the sandwich down and rubbed his hands together. "All right, let's see what we have."

We were huddled together, reading over his shoulder when Carl's cell phone played the theme from *Rocky*. My heart nearly stopped. Carl answered, and his forehead knit with concern. My stomach did a belly flop.

"Come back," he said and hung up. Frowning, he looked at us. "Vulture and his guys took them to the tunnels at Klondike, like we thought. But, all the guys found was the transponder, smashed."

Fran crossed herself.

My hand went to my heart as tears erupted. "Oh, God." I said a silent prayer.

Ruthie walked through the door at that moment. "What's wrong?" she asked when she saw my face.

I told her.

She collapsed on a stool and buried her head in her hands. "I'd better call the judge."

"This might kill him," Ruthie squeaked out. "Doesn't Judge Parker have heart trouble?"

"Someone should tell him in person in case he has a spell," Frannie said.

Zack. I'd have to call Zack to go over there. He was the only person I knew how to contact.

Carl swiveled to face us. "Give me a few more minutes."

"We don't have any more time! It's getting dark. We need to get a search going. Helicopters and airplanes and boats." I broke down completely, sobs coming in uncontrollable waves. "We should never have gone along with Penny Sue's silly scheme. I'll never forgive myself if ... I couldn't say the words."

Fran put her arms around me. "It's not your fault. Penny Sue's a strong-minded woman. You couldn't have talked her out of it."

I blew my nose. No, I couldn't. At least, this way we have an inkling of what happened. If she'd gone it alone, Penny Sue would be one of those people who simply disappeared— a picture on milk cartons and telephone poles.

"Leigh," Carl said. "Do what you have to do. I'm going to work on these files and see if I can come up with any clues on where they might be."

I went to my bedroom to gather my thoughts before calling Zack. I wasn't looking forward to the conversation.

First, and foremost, because I hated the news I was about to relay. Secondly, there was still a lot of pain tied up in the sound of his voice. Third, I was not in the mood to discuss Ann and her impending engagement. Finally, what if his hot honey answered?

I heard he'd moved in with her. I wondered if he took her to his office parties? I'm sure those silicon breasts were a big hit with the old partners like Bradford Davis. Bradford represented Zack in our divorce, and I'd come to loathe the man. I could still see his condescending, crooked smile. Bradford was one man, along with my own worthless attorney, that I'd like to backhand in the mouth one day. *Sorry, Grammy.* I know I should turn the other cheek and practice forgiveness— it wasn't in me at the moment. The wounds were too fresh and deep.

I took a breath and steeled myself for the conversation. Call Zack's cell phone, which eliminated the possibility that *she* might answer. Get right to the point. Hit him between the eyes before he had time to make a snide comment.

He answered on the second ring. "Zack, Penny Sue's been kidnapped. You need to go over to the judge's house and tell him in person. He has heart problems, and we're afraid the shock might be too much. Someone needs to be with him."

"Kidnapped? When?"

"A couple of hours ago."

"Who? Have you called the police?"

"A roughneck biker called Vulture. We think, maybe, he's someone the judge locked up. And, yes, Ruthie filed a police report. But, with Bike Week down here, resources are scarce."

"You were there when it happened?"

"Ruthie and I were both there. It was clearly personal." I wasn't going to mention the potshots at Penny Sue's license plate. That would only evoke a long lecture of about what we should have done and didn't. "We're staying with a friend, Fran Annina. Take down her phone number." I heard him punching it into his cell as I gave it out. "I'll call you as soon as I hear anything." Then, I hung up and started to cry.

Chapter 16

Bobby Barnes' distinctive bass voice blasted me out of my stupor. I ran to the bathroom and splashed water on my face. My eyelids were swollen and red. Crying always did that to me. There wasn't a darn thing I could do about it short of ice packs, which I didn't have time for. I hurried downstairs to the kitchen. Bobby and most of the Klingons were sitting around the table eating huge plates of lasagna and sopping Italian bread in spiced olive oil. Carl and Saul were conspicuously missing.

A wave of emotion bubbled up when I saw Bobby.

"We'll find her, Leigh," Bobby said. "We're working on a plan. Carl thinks he's onto something. Rich was working undercover for someone, but it's not clear who. It seems that Vulture and his wacko band of merry men are worse than we thought." Bobby swigged his soda. "Saul's gone home to change and get some stuff. One of our Navy buddies, Roger, is in town. They're going back to Klondike Beach to snake through the tunnels. They're covering the back door."

"And, the front door?" I asked.

"That depends on what Carl finds."

I wasn't sure I liked hearing that.

Fran handed me a plate of lasagna. "Eat something, honey. Starving won't help Penny Sue. You may need the strength. This could be a long night." I nodded and sat at the table next to a crew-cutted blond Klingon named Thomas.

I'd only taken a few bites of pasta when Carl flew up the stairs from the Bat Cave with the laptop under his arm. "Those friggin' mudderfuc—" he caught his mother's stern glare, "—er, fruitcakes are into drugs and arms dealing!"

He set the computer on the kitchen counter and typed in few codes. "Look at this email—it's from Fox to Shorty. There are several messages from Fox—that's Rich's code name I think. He says the Scavenger—Vulture, probably— is dealing drugs and using the profits to stockpile weapons. He's not sure if the arms are for resale or if the Scavenger is planning to use them himself. Fox says Scavenger's friends believe the Feds have embedded chips in drivers' licenses to track Americans. They also think the CIA is conducting mind control experiments from satellites."

"Boy, those guys are sick," Ruthie said.

"Shorty must be Rich's contact. What's the email address? We could send him an email and tell him Rich has been kidnapped," I suggested.

"It's a Hotmail address, the kind anyone can set up from anywhere. I suspect the addresses are rotated and this one is no longer in use."

"It's worth a try, isn't it?"

Carl rubbed the back of his neck as he thought. "Yeah, but then we'd have to explain what we were doing with this computer." He glanced at Bobby. "I have no idea what laws we're breaking."

"Holy shit," Thomas muttered, then glanced at Fran and shrugged a *Sorry.* "These guys think satellites are being used for mind control and a military satellite is going up on the Atlas V. You don't think they're going to try to sabotage the missile, do you?"

"I hope not," Todd said quickly. "The satellite's nuclear powered. If the missile blows up, it'll contaminate the whole East Coast."

"Holy cow!" Fran said. She uncorked a bottle of red wine and poured a few fingers worth into a juice glass. She chugged some, then tilted the bottle toward Ruthie, who declined.

"When is the rocket going up?" I asked.

"They've stopped announcing the times until twelve hours before launch, precisely because of terrorists' threats," Todd said. "I'll check the Canaveral web page to see if they've released it yet."

"We've got to do something!" Fran took another swallow of wine.

"Damn straight," Thomas said. "I have no desire to glow in the dark." The other guys muttered agreement.

"The launch is tomorrow morning, right before sunrise—six-fifteen," Todd called from the stairwell to Carl's apartment.

"Isn't the area secured? How could they possibly get to the rocket?" I asked.

"A Stinger missile would do it," Bobby said.

"How could they get something like that?"

Ruthie's eyes went wide. "A shipment of missiles and ammunition was hijacked last week in North Carolina. And there was another in Georgia yesterday. The stories were in the newspaper. Maybe Vulture's gang was responsible."

"Or, bought some of the hot cargo."

"A Stinger's range is about five miles," Bobby said. "That means they have to get a lot closer than Klondike Beach. The gang must be headed for Playalinda, which borders the Kennedy Space Center. That's about ten miles from the tunnel we found."

"Ten miles? Could they cut a tunnel that far?"

Bobby nodded. "Sure, fanatics are dogged if nothing else. Extremists tunneled from Egypt to Palestine to smuggle weapons. Drug traffickers dig tunnels from Mexico into California. The Feds find one tunnel, the bad guys dig another."

"Vulture probably had to start that far away," Todd added. "Since nine-eleven, the Space Center's tightened security. Playalinda Beach is closed off for shuttle launches. I don't know what kind of precautions they take for military rockets."

"If the Cape has beefed up security, maybe there's no need to do anything. The park rangers will find Vulture and Penny Sue," Ruthie said hopefully.

"I wouldn't count on it," Bobby said. "I suspect Vulture has scoped out the park rangers' routine and taken steps to avoid them. That's apparently why they've burrowed all those tunnels through the brush. Who knows how long they've been working on it? Probably worked at night for months, maybe years."

"Wait, if there is tighter security, how can we get through?" I asked.

"The Bird of Prey could avoid detection. Going in by water, we could save Saul and Roger ten miles of crawling through the tunnels."

"Yes, but how can we find the gang without going through the tunnels? There's a lot of real estate between Playalinda and Klondike."

Carl grinned. "Infrared. I doubt these guys are smart enough to shield their body heat. Even so, they probably didn't plan on having Penny Sue and Rich along. My sensors will find them. All we'd have to do is run parallel to the coast and scan. Yesterday was the new moon, so it will be dark tonight. Vulture's thugs will never see the Bird."

"Is the Bird seaworthy?" Bobby asked Carl.

"Of course, I've taken it out in the ocean many times. And Todd is an expert yachtsman. I'll let him take the helm."

Bobby sopped bread in olive oil and took a bite. "Okay, Ace, I'm counting on you." He flipped open his cell and dialed Saul. "Change of plans. Come here," he said, then gave Saul the address and hung up. "No offense, but paintballs aren't going to make it with this group. I think we should create a distraction and concentrate on rescuing Penny Sue and Rich. Saul and Roger will take the gang down."

Carl frowned. "We don't know how many people Vulture has. How can two men handle a whole gang?"

"Trust me; they can do it." The force of Bobby's voice left no doubt.

"If they're the back door, what's the front?" Ruthie asked. "What are we going to do?"

Bobby regarded her soberly. "You ladies are going to stay here and answer the phone."

"I don't think so!" Fran flew around the counter and gave Bobby the *look*. He drew back. "Don't talk down to me," she warned.

"I may have been hasty in my statement." Bobby glanced sidelong at Carl. "On second thought, you women would be a valuable asset. Penny Sue may be hysterical and need female reassurance."

"Penny Sue's not the hysterical type," Frannie stated flatly. "And, we can contribute a lot more than reassurance."

Bobby shoveled in a forkful of lasagna. " This is excellent, by the way."

"Friggin' A," Fran said.

* * *

Bobby and Saul were solidly built men who'd kept themselves in good shape. My guess was that they worked out at the gym several times a week. Their old buddy Roger was built like a brick sh—well, you get the idea. We're talking prime Arnold Schwarzenegger, including a hint of a Germanic accent. He filled the entire doorway—top to bottom, side to side—when he thundered into the kitchen. Thomas, the Klingon, immediately got up and offered him the seat next to me. Still sitting, I had to look up at his shoulder. No wonder Bobby said Roger and Saul could handle Vulture. One glimpse at this former Navy Seal and Penny Sue might stomp Vulture herself to get at Roger. Even the largely unflappable Frannie May did a double take at the big guy.

Another Klingon who'd finished eating gave up his seat to Saul. Fran and Ruthie immediately appeared with plates of pasta and bread. I noticed that Ruthie made a point of serving Saul. Bobby quickly filled his buddies in on the new developments. For the most part they listened without comment as they scarfed up the pasta and bread. The mention of the Atlas V and Stinger got Roger's attention.

"Man, these guys are *verrucht,* crazy. That's bad. Men like that will do anything."

"Vulture has that reputation," Bobby said. "I think you have to treat this bunch like a cult—loose cannons that might go off at any minute."

Roger shook his head and resumed eating.

His reaction was not reassuring. At some level, I wanted these men to tell me that Vulture and his crew were merely a bunch of blustering fools. But, if Roger—the Incredible Hulk lookalike—thought the situation was bad, it was truly dreadful. My stomach drew up into a hard knot at that realization and I pushed my plate away. No more food for this puppy.

Bobby continued with the briefing, letting Carl explain the capabilities of The Bird of Prey. That, too, got Roger's attention.

"You came up with this yourself?" he asked.

"I had help from my friends." Carl waved at the group standing around the kitchen.

"This boat has stealth capabilities and can scan the coast for heat signatures?"

"Yes."

"And you did this all for a *Star Trek* game?"

"It's not just a game," Carl replied defensively. "It's a role-playing exercise."

Roger laughed—a deep rumble on the order of a 7.5 earthquake. "I like Worf and Kahless."

Every jaw in the room dropped. Roger was a Trekkie! The sparkle in Carl's eye was unmistakable. I could almost hear the wheels whirling in his head, planning how he could recruit Roger for his team. I also noticed Todd's face droop noticeably.

The big man pointed at Frannie's glass of wine and nodded.

"I'm sorry, how rude of me." She hurried to a cabinet, pulled out two stemmed glasses and prepared to pour.

"No sissy glass, please. I'd rather have one like yours."

Ruthie handed Fran a juice glass for Roger. Saul declined the offer in favor of water.

Roger downed the wine in one gulp. Fran hovered at his shoulder and refilled his glass.

Everyone looked at Bobby, the silent question hanging in the air, "Should Roger be drinking?"

With a flick of his thumb, Bobby communicated, "No problem."

Considering Roger's bulk, the glass of wine was probably as intoxicating to him as gargling with Listerine. In any event, this man, who'd never met Penny Sue, was willing to risk his life to save her. That went a long way in my book. I could almost hear Grammy Martin say, "Judge not, least ye be not judged," then a "The Lord works in mysterious ways."

Yes, ma'am. Klingons, Romulans, and Navy Seals— I'd try not to judge it all. On the plus side, I had to admit my narrow, sheltered life had broadened considerably since my divorce.

Bobby went on to explain his two-front assault plan. Todd, Saul, and Roger would do reconnaissance, pinpoint the gang's location with The Bird of Prey, and ultimately do the takedown. Their objective was to stop the Stinger missile. Meanwhile, Bobby and the rest of us would create a distraction and go after Penny Sue and Rich.

There was some discussion on whether Roger would fit into The Bird of Prey. A customized, stealthized skiff, it held three people, tops. Everyone finally agreed the plan would work if Roger sat in the middle at the apex of an angular protrusion, and Todd kept the hatch open while they motored along on gas power. Once in range of Playalinda Beach, where they'd switch to electric, the top would go down, and Roger would have to hunch forward. "No problem," he assured us, draining the second glass of wine.

Now, for the distraction.

"The pontoon boat at the center makes a little over six miles an hour, which means it will take five hours to get to Playalinda." Bobby checked his watch, it was seven-thirty. "Going at night won't slow us down much, I know those waterways like the back of my hand."

Suddenly, I realized what he'd said. "We're going to steal the tour boat from the Marine Center?" I asked.

"Borrow. Otherwise, we might be glowing tomorrow. Us and everyone in this area."

Good point.

Carl spoke up. "I think our old Klingon assault would be the best distraction." He scanned his friends. "We've practiced it a million times and have it down pat. It would scare the hell out of anyone except Todd and his Romulans. Scared them the first few times. Vulture's never seen it!"

"What is the Klingon assault?" Bobby asked.

"We swoop down on dirt bikes, shouting Klingon battle cries with paintballs flying and lasers flashing."

"That might do it," Saul allowed. "But, how do you get dirt bikes to the site?"

Bobby sat thinking. "I believe it could work. The bikes will fit on the pontoon. We'll take the boat down the Inland Waterway while Saul and Roger come in from the ocean side in the Bird of Prey. We barge in with a lot of hoopla, Vulture and his thugs are distracted, then Saul and Roger take out the missile. Meanwhile, we rescue Penny Sue and Rich. Yeah." He glanced at his two old friends, who nodded. Bobby rubbed his hands together. "We have a lot to do. In order to be in place before the launch, we have to shove off on the pontoon no later than midnight. The earlier, the better. I don't want to wait until the last minute. Besides, every second we waste is a stroke against Penny Sue." Bobby turned to Carl. "How soon can you and your buddies get the bikes and stuff together? By the way, if anyone has Kevlar, this is the time to pull it out. Hopefully, we'll surprise Vulture and they won't have time to get off a shot. Still, better safe than sorry."

"We have some Kevlar. We'll wear what we have."

The Klingons left to get their dirt bikes and battle paraphernalia.

Roger went downstairs to help Carl put the Bird into the water, while Saul and Bobby lingered at the table. Fran and Ruthie had finished loading the dishwater when the phone started to ring. The first call was from Ted.

"Ted," I said. Bobby shook his head vigorously, a clear sign that I should not say anything about our plans. I nodded agreement, though I didn't like keeping secrets from Ted. "The worst thing has happened—Vulture's kidnapped Penny Sue."

"What?"

"We went to the cole slaw wrestling; she and Red had words. The next thing we know, she was dragged off by Vulture and his goons." I choked up again, remembering the horrible scene.

"My God. You've reported it, right?"

"We called everyone and Ruthie filed a report with Volusia County."

"I'm working a shift up here in Daytona. I wish there was something I could do."

I stared at my feet. "I know. I guess there's nothing any of us can do, but wait." I hated to deceive him. I also cringed at the fallout when Ted found out about tonight's escapade, which he surely would. If the Space Center security nabbed us, Ted might be visiting me in a Federal prison.

My phone clicked, indicating someone was trying to get through. I checked the display, it was Zack. "I have another call coming in—Zack. I asked him to personally tell Judge Parker about Penny Sue."

"Take the call, I understand. As soon as my shift's over, I'll see what I can find out. Be careful. Don't do anything stupid."

"Okay," I said faintly. Under other circumstances I'd be insulted by his last remark. Unfortunately, he was right. We were about to do something very stupid.

I clicked off, but not in time to catch Zack's call. Fran's phone rang a moment later. She handed it to me, whispering, "Judge Warren Parker." Bobby's head shaking and hand waving went into high gear. I nodded again.

"Judge, I'm so sorry to give you this horrible news. We've contacted city and county authorities."

"How did this happen?" he asked somberly. "Zack said the kidnapper may be someone I've locked up. Is that true? Who is this man?"

I took a deep breath. "A group of us went to a Bike Week event this afternoon—cole slaw wrestling."

"Did I hear you correctly? Cole slaw wrestling?"

"Yes, sir. It's very famous—like mud wrestling, only women wrestle in a pit of cole slaw," I babbled nervously.

"You're kidding."

"No sir. It's the highlight of Bike Week, which is the reason we went." No need to mention Penny Sue being dumped by Rich. "Anyway, we ran into a rough character called Vulture. Penny Sue's name was mentioned, and he flew off the handle, wanting to know if she was Penny Sue Parker from Roswell, Georgia. Penny Sue's always said she had to be careful, that she was a target for criminals you'd convicted. Anyway, this guy and his gang whisked her away."

"You're telling me Penny Sue was kidnapped in broad daylight, and no one did a thing?"

I felt like a dirty dog. No, a dirty dog gave me too much credit. I was low, lower than pond scum. I'd let my friend be kidnapped and didn't do anything but fumble with my cell phone. Fran, who barely knew Penny Sue, showed more gumption that I did. "Judge, I'm so sorry," I started to sniffle.

"Becky Leigh, I don't blame you. I know you and Ruthie couldn't take on a gang of bikers."

Yeah, because we were shit. Chicken shit.

"What can you tell me about this man called Vulture? I'm going to make some phone calls."

I swallowed a sob. "He's well known in this area, even by law enforcement. Rumored to be the head of an anti-government cult. Some people say he's crazy. Sir, that's all I know."

"This man came up to my daughter out of the clear blue?"

"Penny Sue had some words with his girlfriend. But, it wasn't Penny Sue's fault. She was minding her own business when Vulture's girlfriend came up and accosted her."

"Becky Leigh, I've been a judge for a long time and I know when someone isn't telling the whole truth. I need to know everything if we're going to find Penny Sue."

My chest started to heave. He was right, of course. Bobby's plan was half-baked. Maybe the judge could call out the FBI, National Guard, or something. Anything.

I swear, Bobby must have read my thoughts, because he flew into my face, shaking his head. I waved him off. Okay, I wouldn't tell the judge what we were going to do, but I'd tell him the rest of the sordid tale, including the potshots at Penny Sue's car.

I told Judge Parker about Rich's dumping Penny Sue, the body found behind her car, the potshots at her license plate, the run-in with Red at the Pub—all of it. He seemed to take it well, though, he'd probably perfected a deadpan bearing in his years of judging. Gawd, I hoped Zack was still there, in case the judge's calm demeanor was only a front.

"Is Zack with you by any chance? I missed a call from him on my cell phone."

"No, he went home."

"Are you doing all right with this?"

"As well as any man can do when his only daughter's been kidnapped by thugs."

A big tear streaked down my cheek. That shit Zack went home and left you alone. Pond scum. He was pond scum, just like me.

Chapter 17

By eight-thirty everyone had assembled in Fran's drive-way and was ready to go. Todd, Saul, and Roger had already left in the Bird of Prey. Although the Bird was faster than the pontoon boat when using its gas power, it crept along on battery power. It also needed to be in place ahead of us to pinpoint the gang's location.

We decided to take several cars to the Marine Conservation Center to avoid suspicion. Bobby and the Klingons with dirt bikes went ahead to load them onto the pontoon. We were riding with Carl and Thomas, who'd loaded a computer, other sundry electronic devices, along with paintball guns into the trunk of the Jaguar. Fran, Ruthie, and I had settled in the back seat and Carl was backing out of the garage when Ruthie remembered the Taser. She flew from the car to fetch it at the very moment a gray sedan pulled into the driveway.

"It's Woody, the State Prosecutor, and his detective friend," I shrieked.

Fran pushed me out of the car door that Ruthie had left open and dived after me. Before I knew what had happened, she'd slammed the door and was waving to Carl and Thomas. "Bye, boys. Have a good game." She held her thumb up. "Victory, this time, right?"

Carl got the hint. As the gray car stopped, Carl inched by it and backed down the driveway.

Frannie struck her fist to her chest and yelled, "Qaplá!" at the very moment Ruthie raced into the garage with the Taser. Ruthie took one look at Woody, who was now getting out of the car, and stashed the weapon in the dumbwaiter.

"Hello," Fran said, still waving as the Jaguar reached the street and sped off. "That's my son. He's a Klingon. They're fighting the Battle of Khitomer tonight, and this time they're going to win."

Detective Jones eyed the Beach Bike and Scooter truck parked beside Carl's workshop. "Saul Hirsch plays these games?"

"Oh, yes, he's a Romulan." She extended her hand. "I'm Frances Annina, what can I do for you?"

Caught off guard by the unusual exchange, Woody stuttered, "R-robert Woodhead. Detective Jones and I are here about Penny Sue Parker. We understand she's missing."

Fran hugged him fiercely. "We're so happy you've come. We're sick to death about Penny Sue. Have you found her?" Woody tried to disengage himself from Fran's grip, but she held tight. "She was snatched away by a horrid gang right before our eyes. It was terrible, just terrible."

Woody finally managed to push her away. "I'm sure it was. We'll get to the bottom of it."

Fran winked at me. "Yes, there's not a minute to lose. Penny Sue's probably being tortured or ..." she buried her face in her hands, "worse."

"That's why we're here, Mrs. Annina. We've talked with Judge Parker and need to ask you a few questions."

"Come in," she waved them up the front steps and, as their backs were turned, gave Ruthie a hand sign to put the garage doors down. She led them into the kitchen. "Can I get you something?" Fran snapped Rich's laptop shut and casually handed it to me. I stuffed it in a cabinet in the great room.

"That son of mine," Fran ran on without missing a beat. "Thirty years old and still leaves his stuff laying all over the house. Now, what can I get you? Coffee? A soft drink?"

"Water would be fine, ma'am. We only need to ask you a few questions."

I must say that this meeting with Woody and Detective Jones was far more civil than the last. Of course, much of the former hostility was because Penny Sue had kept them waiting for over an hour, declaring it was socially unacceptable for civilized people to call so early in the morning. The fact that Woody had obviously talked with Judge Parker didn't hurt either.

The two men asked the standard questions, we told them the truth, though we were careful to skirt the issue of Bobby and the Atlas V. I wondered about keeping the secret, but quickly decided we should. With the chaos of Bike Week, I put more faith in Carl and Bobby at that moment. I, also, suspected Woody's visit was basically a courtesy call to assuage the judge and Woody's superiors.

Woody and Detective Jones thanked us and left with promises to keep us informed of any development.

Fran closed the door behind them and her polite smile dissolved. "Of all the luck, now we're left on the sidelines." She patted her bike belt. "I was ready, too."

"Maybe we can still help. Let's look through the emails on Rich's laptop—perhaps there are more clues." I fetched the computer. Ruthie, our computer expert, fired it up and started scrolling through the files. She hadn't gone far when the phone rang. It was Judge Parker again.

"Judge, the state prosecutor and detective left minutes ago. They're on the case and taking this very seriously," I told him.

"I'm sure they are." The unspoken fact was that the Florida Attorney General was probably in the loop, now. "Leigh, I need to know what Vulture said to Penny Sue. His real name is Curtis Hall. I've had my clerks check. I've never been involved in any case with a Curtis Hall. It doesn't seem like the kidnapping was a vendetta against me."

If that wasn't it, what was? "Excuse me a moment, sir. Frances Annina and Ruthie are here with me." I put my hand over the mouthpiece on the phone. "Vulture's name is Curtis Hall and has no connection to the judge! What, exactly, did he say to Penny Sue?"

"He called her a meddlesome bitch," Frannie said. "I remember thinking how coarse he was."

Ruthie piped in, "Before that he asked if she was Penny Sue Parker, the busybody from Roswell, Georgia."

"That's the way I remember it." I relayed the information to the judge.

"Hmph, busybody, meddlesome bitch," Judge Parker repeated. "This is personal to Penny Sue. Can you think of any enemies she's made in New Smyrna Beach?"

Aside from Shrewella, the backdoor neighbor, I couldn't think of anyone who had it in for her that wasn't already in jail. Surely, prim and proper Sarah/Shrewella was not connected to Vulture. "I can't think of a soul. Penny Sue is a kind person. She loses her temper on occasion,"—and her hormones are completely out of kilter—"but, she's not one to make enemies."

"Think about it, Becky Leigh. The link to Vulture may be the key to finding her." He hung up.

I frowned and tapped my fingers on the table. "How could Penny Sue possibly be connected to Vulture? He called her a busybody, implying she'd stuck her nose into something that was none of her business. What could that be?"

"He knew she was from Roswell. Rich has to be the connection. Maybe their love affair was interfering with a deal between Vulture and Rich."

I chewed by bottom lip, thinking. "That doesn't seem like enough justification to kidnap someone. Vulture was angry, as if she'd taken something away from him. Something important."

"If the guy is psychotic like Carl suspects, it may all be imagined," Ruthie said. "Like John Nash in the movie, *A Beautiful Mind.* He imagined all that stuff about working for the government." Ruthie went back to searching Rich's emails for key words and phrases like stinger, missile, atlas, shoot, and came up empty handed. Fran and I hovered over her shoulder. "No luck," Ruthie said dejectedly.

"I think you need to be more obscure. Rich wouldn't come right out and say what Vulture was planning to do, even if it was encrypted. How might he refer to a Stinger missile?"

"A bee, wasp, scorpion," Frannie offered.

"Good." Ruthie typed the words into the search engine. "What about Atlas? He was a Greek god, a Titan that held up the world."

"I think of Charles Atlas. He was Italian, you know," Frannie said. "His real name was Angelo Siciliano. He was the ninety-seven pound weakling who became a bodybuilder after a bully kicked sand in his face."

"That's good. Ruthie, put in bodybuilder, strong man, muscle man."

She typed the words in and one by one began searching the documents. She'd gone through about a dozen when a faint chirp sounded. We all went for the cell phones stowed in our bike belts. It was Fran's phone that was ringing.

"Hello?" Her eyes narrowed with intense concentration. "Hello?" She held it out for me to listen. I heard a gurgling sound like someone clearing her throat. I could almost see the light bulb go off in Frannie's head. She snatched it from me and checked the tiny phone's display. Tilting her head back, she finally found the mute button. "This is Carl's new phone number, the one he gave to Penny Sue!" She handed me the cell. "Keep it on mute. We don't want to tip her hand. I'll call Carl."

Fran rushed to the telephone on the kitchen counter and dialed. "Carl, Penny Sue has called on your cell phone.

She must be gagged and can't talk, but we can hear shuffling noises."

"Is she still on the line?" he asked excitedly.

"Yes. We've got it on mute."

"Keep the line open. There's GPS on that phone. I'll call you right back."

Fran put the handset in its cradle and clapped her hands. "We've found her and she's alive! Carl will locate her with GPS and the boys can probably rescue her right away."

My throat seized, and I started to cry, only this time tears of joy. Keeping one ear on the cell, I glanced at Ruthie who was hunched over the computer, oblivious to the news. "Ruthie, didn't you hear? We've found Penny Sue."

Her face ashen, she glanced sidelong. "I've found it, too." She pointed to the screen. "This email was in the draft folder and probably never sent. 'The big guy should expect the delivery of honeybees on Thursday morning.' Vulture really is planning to shoot down the Atlas rocket!"

My hand flew to my throat. "Omagod, if they're successful, it will pollute the East Coast with radioactivity."

The phone rang, we all jumped. It was Carl. "Mom, we've located Penny Sue, but she's not where we thought. It looks like she's close to the entrance of the tunnel on Klondike Beach, not far from where Saul found the smashed transponder. They must have circled back. I'll contact Todd and have them alter their course."

"No, son, you can't." Fran heaved a big sigh. "Ruthie found a draft email on Rich's computer. Vulture truly wants to shoot down the Atlas. The email was probably never sent, so it's up to you. You've got stop them. Penny Sue will have to wait."

"Mom?"

"It has to be this way." Fran motioned to my cell phone. "Take down Leigh's cellular number. Mine is tied up with Penny Sue."

As she gave him the number, I had an idea. I waved and whispered, "Put him on mute."

"Hold on a minute, I think Leigh has more information." She punched the button to block our conversation.

"Get Todd's cell number."

Fran's brow furrowed with confusion. "Why?"

"Saul's truck. Maybe there's something in there that will help us rescue Penny Sue and Rich."

"Us?" Ruthie asked nervously.

"Right," Fran said, her eyes flashing. She hit the mute key. "Carl, I need Todd's cell number."

"Todd's number. Why do you want that?"

"In case we need to call him—what do you think?"

"Mom, what are you going to do?"

"Nothing, son," she said sweetly. "I'd like to have Todd's number in case I can't reach you. Besides, what if we find important information on the computer that he needs to know?" She took down the number. "Be careful, baby." She hit the off button on the receiver and immediately began to dial. "Todd, this is Fran. I need to move Saul's truck. Ask him if he left the keys here." She tapped her pen on the notepad as she listened. "Under the mat?" She dipped her chin with a big grin. "Thanks. Carl told you the news, right?

Good, be careful, now." She clicked off, eyes narrowed in thought. "Hear anything?" she asked me.

"Scraping and crunching noises, like someone moving through brush." I held up my hand for silence as I strained to hear a new sound. "I think I hear snoring."

"The guard must have fallen asleep. That's probably how Penny Sue got to her telephone."

"It's amazing they didn't find it," I said.

Ruthie smirked. "She put the phone in the inside pouch with her credit cards."

"Come on, we don't have time to waste. Let's see what's in Saul's truck."

We found the key ring under the mat and sorted through it until we found the one that unlocked the truck's backdoor. Wielding flashlights, we did a quick scan of the contents. Four mopeds were strapped down next to the door.

"Have you ever ridden one of those things?" Frannie asked.

"No."

"Me either. And, I don't think this is the time to learn."

"Wait, what's that at the very back?" I handed the cell phone to Ruthie and hopped up on the step at the back of the truck. "My flashlight's too dim." Frannie handed me her halogen spotlight. I panned the bright light on the back of the truck. "Praise the lord," I muttered.

"What?"

"Saul has two dune buggies!"

Fran nudged me aside and stepped up to see for herself. She hopped down with a big grin. "Who needs men? We'll save Penny Sue ourselves."

I climbed back into the truck. "We need to get all of these scooters out of the way. Help me, Ruthie, there's a ramp against the wall." While Fran monitored the telephone, Ruthie and I wrestled the ramp into place and rolled the motorbikes out of the truck. Then, we examined our find.

Fran crossed herself and said a silent prayer before turning the halogen on the buggies. She trained her eyes heavenward. "Thank you, we have the keys."

The buggies were four wheelers with headlights and big, bulbous tires. Open except for a roll bar, they were about the size of golf carts, which in fact they may have been in a previous life. There were two seats and enough room behind them for a person to crouch, if necessary.

"I wonder if they're electric?' Ruthie said.

"Only one way to tell." I swung into the cart, turned the key and tapped the accelerator. It lurched forward. "Yep, electric." I checked out the instrumentation. "This is a piece of cake, I used to play golf."

"What's our plan?" Fran asked.

"We take Saul's truck to the Canaveral Park and drive it to the end. Then, we unload the carts, and head down the beach to rescue Penny Sue."

"Wait," Ruthie said. "Can you drive a truck?"

"No, but—"

"Don't worry, I can," Fran said confidently. "I haven't always been wealthy, you know. I grew up on a farm."

I should have known. Frannie May had more tricks up her sleeve than David Copperfield.

"The palmetto scrub is so thick, how can we get the buggies to the beach?" Ruthie asked, still not convinced.

"There are little trails through the scrub blocked off by chains," I said. "That's how the rangers get to the beach."

Ruthie shook her head. "If the paths are blocked ..."

"The whole place is blocked off. But, Enrico has bolt cutters," Fran said with a smirk.

Uncle Enrico, I'd forgotten all about him and his bolt cutters. No telling what he was up to, but his stuff had sure come in handy.

"I've been down to the end of the road at Canaveral and the beach isn't very wide. If it's high tide, we're sunk— literally," Ruthie said.

"Good point. We'd better check the tides."

Ruthie was still doubtful. "I wonder if the batteries on the buggies are charged. We don't want to get out there, rescue Penny Sue, and end up stranded."

"Easy enough." Fran took my phone and dialed Todd's cell. "Todd, it's Mrs. Annina."

Not Fran, I noticed—she was pulling out all of the stops.

"Please ask Saul if the batteries on his beach buggies are fully charged." She held the phone away from her ear. We could hear Todd stuttering. "Todd, it's a simple question. The girls and I thought we'd take them for a spin."

There was a pause. "Yes, ma'am, they have a full charge."

"Have you located Vulture and his gang?"

"Not yet. But, we will."

She clicked off. "Fifty bucks says Carl will call in about two minutes." She checked her watch. The phone chirped. "He's late." She flipped the phone open. "Yes, son?" She listened, rolling her eyes. "Carl, when did you start giving me orders?" She angled the phone so we could listen.

"Mom, don't do it. These people are vicious. They'd kill you in a second."

"Carl, we're monitoring the cell phone you gave Penny Sue. We hear snoring."

Ruthie put the cell phone to her ear and nodded.

"This is going to be a piece of cake," Fran continued. "We'll take the buggies to the tunnels, sneak in, stun them with the Taser, grab Penny Sue and Rich, and get away. What could be simpler? Besides, when you and the guys successfully foil Vulture—which, you will—Penny Sue will be in greater danger. We have to get to her before then."

I hadn't thought of that. Neither, apparently, had Carl. There was a long pause. "I can't talk you out of this?" he said.

"No," she said in a I'm not in the mood for argument tone.

"Mom, Dad would kill me for this if he were alive."

"He'll be very proud if we are successful. I feel him smiling down on me. Your father was a great patriot and certainly no wimp."

I heard a heavy sigh from Carl.

"Keep the line open to Leigh's phone. I'll guide you to the spot with GPS."

"That's my boy, I knew I could count on you."

Chapter 18

Fran drove, Ruthie sat in the middle cradling the bolt cutters between her legs, and I rode shotgun on, probably, the dumbest expedition that had ever been undertaken in the history of Man. Okay, not the absolute dumbest, but close. And worse, the scheme had been my idea! Lord, I'd spent too much time with Penny Sue, she was rubbing off on me.

Fran said she drove a truck on her parents' farm as a youngster. Either trucks were smaller then, technology had changed, or Fran had lost her touch. She sideswiped one of the Klingon's vehicles as she backed Saul's cargo van out of the driveway.

"Don't worry, I have good insurance," she said, completely unconcerned. We reached the street and the truck jerked spastically as Fran struggled to synchronize the clutch and the gear shifting. By the time we arrived at the Flagler intersection she was doing better, though, forgot to put the clutch in when she stopped at the light and the truck stalled. The light turned green. Fran fought to start the vehicle.

"Put in the clutch when you turn the key," I suggested.

In the meantime, an impatient fool in a small car that had turned out of her next door neighbor's driveway, got out of his vehicle and slapped the back of the truck.

Still battling the ignition and clutch, Fran said through clenched teeth, "It must be that spoiled brat next door. I don't recognize the car, but his parents probably gave him a new one. He doesn't work, he flunked out of school, and still his parents treat him like a prince." She finally got the truck moving and crossed Flagler, headed for A1A/South Causeway. The little car followed.

I thanked the spirits, angels, or whomever who watched over us that Fran mastered the clutch/shifting routine by the time we stopped at the South Causeway light.

"Is that twerp still back there?" she asked.

I checked the rearview mirror. "Yes."

She set her jaw, like Penny Sue did when she was about to morph into a Steel Magnolia. I braced myself.

"Watch this." The light changed to green, Fran took a left and floored it. She went through the gears like a race car driver, slowing at 45 mph to match the speed limit. "Did I lose him?"

I glanced back. "Afraid not."

"Brat." She pulled to the right lane and slowed the truck to 35. The car followed suit.

"Johnny must be high. I don't think he's dangerous, just a smart aleck. Ignore him." Fran pressed the accelerator to the speed limit and never looked back. I watched the car from my outside mirror. It stayed with us until we reached the last cross street on Bethune Beach, then hung a left. Good, we were about to commit a few crimes and didn't need witnesses. Fran kept straight to the Canaveral National Seashore, where she ignored the red light at the guardhouse and barreled along until we came to aluminum turnstiles held together by a padlocked chain.

"Cut the chain," Fran said without hesitation.

I took the bolt cutters from Ruthie, which were on the order of long handled pruning shears, except for a small cutting edge. I peered around for witnesses and, seeing none, snapped the cutters on the chain. Nothing happened. It was a thick chain.

Ruthie climbed down from the truck to help. She took one handle, I took the other and on the count of three we pushed. Still no luck.

Frannie popped her head out of the driver's window. "We don't have time for this. Get in." She revved the engine, popped the clutch, and rammed the gate. The force of the impact pulled one turnstile out of the ground. She stopped, backed up, then ran over the barricade.

"I really do have good insurance," she muttered.

We drove to the end of the Canaveral Seashore and circled the last parking area at Apollo Beach.

"We just passed one of the trails to the beach," Fran said as she stopped the truck with a jolt. We all jumped out. Ruthie and I went to cut the chain, while Fran unlocked the back of the van. Thankfully this chain was not in the league of the other one, so Ruthie and I snapped it easily.

Fran was already in the cargo hold pushing the carts to the doorway as Ruthie and I climbed in to pull down the ramp. We drove the dune buggies off the truck, put the ramp back, got the Taser, and locked up.

"Okay, girls," Frannie May said as we stood by the carts. I'll drive one, you and Ruthie take the other. Ruthie's in charge of the Taser."

Ruthie hesitated only a moment. "Yes, ma'am." She stored the extra solution in a dashboard compartment and shouldered the weapon like a pro.

Meanwhile, Fran called Carl on my cell phone. "We're ready to take the carts to the beach. Any change?" She held the phone away from her ear, and we huddled close.

"Todd picked up two sets of heat signatures. The first is small, only three to four people. It's close to the entrance of the tunnels on Klondike Beach. That's probably Penny Sue, Rich, and one or two guards. There's about a dozen down at Playalinda. Todd's in place, we'll be there in less than an hour. Todd, Saul, and Roger are waiting for us." He paused. "Mom, the tide's coming in. I'm not sure you should try this."

"We know that."

Ruthie had gone online and checked the tide schedule before we left. We were midway between high and low tide when we left—a three-hour window that was now down to two. The beaches were steep and narrow on this part of the barrier island. We were cutting it close and knew it. But, the beach buggies were designed to drive up and around bunkers. Sand trap queen that I was, I'd driven carts around steep bunkers many times. The buggies had such a low center of gravity, it was virtually impossible to tip them over. A sloped beach didn't worry me a bit.

"You're bound and determined to do this?"

"Yes," Fran said, "I feel your father watching over me."

"I hope you're right." There was a pause. "Your phone's still connected to Penny Sue?"

Fran looked to Ruthie who'd been monitoring the phone for sounds. "Yes, it's still connected."

A few minutes passed. "I've gotcha."

"What do you mean, you've got me?" Frannie asked.

"Your phone has GPS, too. Why do you think I gave it to you?"

"Keeping tabs on your own mother?"

"Someone has to."

"I can take care of myself."

"Let's argue about that later. I have you on the map. Drive your buggies to the beach and head south."

With Fran leading the way, we bumped through the underbrush, which was barely wide enough for the carts. Thankfully, we'd worn denim jeans, long-sleeved shirts, and windbreakers; otherwise we'd have been shredded by the palmettos that lashed the cart. Even so, we got a few slashes on our hands and faces. I normally had a fairly low threshold of pain, yet my adrenaline was surging, so I hardly noticed the wounds.

The beach was steeper than I remembered, a good thirty-degree angle. Ruthie had to brace her feet against the dash to keep from sliding into me on the bench seat.

We traveled a long way in silence, each thinking our private thoughts. I'd bet Fran was reminiscing about Carlo, Sr. Ruthie was probably thinking of Penny Sue, her father, and Jo Ruth. I stewed over Ann and Penny Sue. While my friend was foremost on my mind, thoughts of Ann kept creeping in. The astrological stuff about Patrick having the potential for violence really troubled me.

"Let them live together," Penny Sue had said. Under normal circumstances, good advice, except when a person might be violent. Darned if I wanted my darling daughter to learn a lesson by being a punching bag! That was not going to happen. I didn't know how I'd prevent it, but bruises were not an option, even if I had to go to London and drag her home. Perhaps I should take Fran and Penny Sue with me.

A few minutes later, Fran held up her hand and stopped. She hurried back to us. "Carl says the tunnel entrance is right over there," she whispered, pointing to the palmetto scrub on our right. With only a sliver of moon to light the night, the tunnel was invisible from were we sat. "Turn your buggy around so we're ready to make a getaway. Park as close to the scrub line as possible, in case the tide rises while we're gone. And, take the key. We want to be sure the carts are here when we get back."

We did as Fran instructed and made a final check of our paraphernalia. I had a flashlight and penlight in one pocket of my windbreaker and a large pair of scissors for cutting ropes. Ruthie stuffed a bottle of electrolyte in one pocket and patted her flashlight in the other. Fran was packing Uncle Enrico's derringer, which she promised not to use unless absolutely necessary, some duct tape, and a halogen light. Depending on what we found, we planned to blind the guards with the halogen, giving Ruthie enough time to stun them with the Taser. Then, Fran and I would tape their hands and feet, while Ruthie freed Penny Sue and Rich.

Crouched low, we walked the dune line looking for the entrance to the tunnel with the penlight. It took two passes before we finally found the opening in the brush. We entered single file, me leading the way with the tiny light. Fran followed with the halogen, while Ruthie and the Taser brought up the rear. For a fleeting moment, I questioned the decision for Ruthie to follow us. Gawd, I hoped she didn't panic and shoot us instead of the bad guys.

We tiptoed through the narrow opening, as quietly as a person can who's blindly trying to navigate a maze only five feet high. Though the evening was cool, sweat streamed from every pore of my body and my pulse pounded in my ears. If I lived through this, I would start going to church, I told myself, and never, ever get sucked into another of Penny Sue's harebrained schemes. I didn't care how many soul mates were at stake, my participation was finished.

Hunched forward, I snaked around a curve and caught the faint glow of a flashlight in the distance. Fran unzipped her bike belt so she could get to the derringer. Ruthie lowered the Taser, ready to shoot. We nodded and picked up the pace, racing toward the faint light. We reached the clearing and I stepped aside so Fran could pass. Halogen aglow, she darted into the clearing and tripped on a root. The light went flying and conked a prostrate Red on the head. Ruthie, following close on her heels, fell over Fran. I leaped over the sprawling mess of arms and legs, grabbed the Taser, and turned slowly, prepared to fire.

Brush rustled and someone—or something—squealed. I swung around and trained the penlight in the direction of the sound. Black boots with red flames came into view.

By now Fran and Ruthie were on their feet. Fran had her gun out, covering Red. Ruthie raced to Penny Sue and pulled a strip of duct tape off her mouth.

"Ouch!" she shrieked, rubbing her lip. "I don't guess I'll need a lip wax anytime soon. Thank God you found me! I knew I'd gotten through, because I heard you say hello. Then the phone went dead. That really scared me."

"We put the phone on mute so we wouldn't tip your hand," Ruthie said.

Penny Sue held up her wrists. I handed the scissors to Ruthie who hacked at the tape binding our friend's hands and feet. "Red's out cold, unless you woke her up with the flashlight. She took some pills that she washed down with vodka. Check Rich." Penny Sue nodded at a heap to the left of the unconscious woman. "They beat him up pretty bad. Then, Red gave him a shot of something. He hasn't moved in a long time. Is he breathing?"

I kneeled down and rolled Rich to his back. His face was swollen almost beyond recognition, but his chest rose and fell slowly. "Gawd, what kind of animals are these people?" I gasped.

Penny Sue was on her feet rubbing her wrists. "Is he all right?"

"He's alive, but in bad shape. He needs medical attention right away."

Gun aimed at Red, Fran handed me the duct tape. "Hurry, let's get out of here."

Penny Sue snatched the tape from me. "I'll do it," she said through clenched teeth. Red was as limp as a rag doll and offered no resistance. Penny Sue bound Red's wrists and was starting on her ankles when a male voice pierced the night.

"Red, you worthless junkie!" The guy from the Pub with the spiked collar burst through the palmettos. He shoved Penny Sue backward and kicked Red hard. She didn't move.

Fran held the gun on him with shaking hands. I fumbled with the Taser, which I'd carelessly hung from my shoulder.

In one swift move, Spike reached in his belt, and a switchblade flashed in his hand. "Anyone moves and the old lady gets it."

Fran, Ruthie and I froze, uncertain what to do.

Spike's beady eyes stared at us unblinking. "I'm good with blades. Granny will have one between the eyes before she gets off a shot. Drop your weapons."

Fran and I exchanged a glance and prepared to drop our hardware. Spike sneered with satisfaction.

And, that's when things went into slow motion. Out of the blue, Penny Sue lurched like a cat, growling, "Eat shit and die!" She caught Spike around the knees and knocked him into a thicket of scrub. She hopped to her feet like a gymnast and delivered a kick to his groin that must have propelled Spike's privates halfway to his throat. But, the old boy was tougher than he looked. As she kicked, I saw his right hand flip back, ready to hurl the knife.

"Duck," I screamed. Penny Sue lunged over Red, tucked her head, and went into a forward roll. I nailed Spike's arm with the Taser and the knife dropped harmlessly to the ground. To be safe, I gave him another shot in the groin for good measure, as Fran stepped over Red and snatched the knife.

Ruthie hurried to help Penny Sue, who'd landed butt up against a big palmetto. Back on her feet, she brushed herself off and said, "Sorry for cussing, Fran, but I haven't had my black cohosh today, and I'm in a really bad mood."

"No problem," Fran said, holding the tape. "Help me bind this varmint."

"My pleasure." Penny Sue stepped over Red and pushed Spike's wrists together while Fran wrapped the tape.

"Move or utter a single sound and you'll get it in the crotch again" I said, waving the Taser.

His eyes narrowed, but Spike didn't move. A hefty kick and a Taser blast to his family jewels seemed enough for one night. They secured his feet, put a strip of tape over his mouth, and finished binding Red's ankles. Penny Sue was about to put tape over her mouth, when Ruthie cried, "No!"

"What?" Penny Sue asked.

"Red hasn't moved though all of this commotion. She's really out of it and not a threat. Besides, if she's taken pills with vodka, she might vomit. Red could choke to death if her mouth is taped."

"You're right. She's going to be in enough trouble with Vulture and Spike. Let's get out of here before anyone else shows up."

Penny Sue was still dressed in shorts and a skimpy halter top. "You want my jacket? Aren't you cold?" I asked.

"Are you kidding, I've finally cooled off."

We carefully sat Rich up, then lifted him to his feet. With Penny Sue on one side and me on the other, we put our shoulders under his armpits and clasped our hands around his back. Concerned with speed and not stealth, Fran led the way with the halogen lamp while Ruthie covered the rear with the Taser.

Although the total distance we had to travel was only a few hundred feet, it might as well have been fifty miles. Rich was a dead weight, and Penny Sue and I had to walk sideways to get him down the narrow path. We stopped several times to catch our breath, but eventually made it. Fran stepped out of the brush and into ankle deep water.

"Oh no, the tide's come in!"

Maybe there's something to the bumper sticker slogan that menopausal women don't have hot flashes, they have power surges. The mere sight of the water gave Penny Sue and me a spurt of energy so strong, we literally picked Rich up and carried him to the front buggy. We slid him into the passenger side, while Penny Sue crouched in the small space behind the seat and held him up. I put the key in the ignition, turned on the headlights, and took off with Fran and Ruthie close behind.

I drove north, as close to the scrub line as I could manage, and we were making good time when an outcropping of rock showed in the headlights directly ahead. We'd skirted it easily before when the tide was lower, but now we'd have to drive into the surf. I stopped and watched the waves hit the rock for several beats. With luck, I could probably time it when the tide pulled back. I watched, waited, then floored the accelerator. The buggy lurched down the slope into about six inches of water. No problem—the tires were big. I hung a left to head back up the hill, but the right tires dug into the soft sand and stopped. The cart teetered as the right side sank. A wave crashed, finishing the job. The buggy rolled over, spilling the three of us into the water. Penny Sue cracked her head on the roll bar, knocking her out. Rich, already unconscious, landed face down in the water and floated out with the tide. Fran and Ruthie abandoned their cart and waded in to help. As I swam after Rich, they dragged Penny Sue up the bank toward their buggy. Before they got there, a wave smashed the cart from the side, sucked the sand out from under the tires, and drew it out to sea. They stood with slack jaws as Saul's cart, headlights still blazing, slowly went under.

I didn't have time to worry about them or the carts, because Rich was a handful. I rolled him on his back, hooked my arm under his chin, and crawled toward shore. If only I weren't so out of shape, I thought, puffing and blowing for all I was worth. Fortunately, my feet soon found purchase in the sand, and I could drag Rich up the incline. Ruthie rushed to help me, and we laid Rich out next to Penny Sue on the outcropping.

Drenched and exhausted, the three of us collapsed on the edge of the surf.

"I think it's time to call for help," Fran said, reaching into her pocket. Her phone wasn't there.

Ruthie moaned. "Mine was in the cart."

I unzipped my bike belt and pulled my cell out. I hit the button, nothing happened. I punched a few keys, then hit the power button again. Zip. "I guess it's not waterproof."

"Now what?" Ruthie asked.

"We wait. Carl knows our approximate location. As soon as he and the others are finished, they'll come looking for us."

I stood up to check on Penny Sue and Rich. Penny Sue had started to twitch as if she were coming around. Ruthie waded to the other side of the rock and began massaging Penny Sue's wrists. Rich's breathing was unusually shallow. Fearing he'd swallowed water, I rolled him to his stomach and smacked his back. He didn't cough anything up, so I sat down, turned him to his side and put his head on my lap. I could barely stand to look at his battered face. But, at least he was alive.

We sat in silence for a long time when, suddenly, Fran whispered. "I hear someone splashing through the surf."

I looked back toward the tunnels. "Where?"

"From the north. Listen."

I held my breath and strained to hear. There it was— splashing, footsteps in the surf. "It must be one of Vulture's goons, who else would be out here? What should we do? The Taser's gone."

"So is the derringer."

I reached into my pocket. I still had a flashlight.

"Give it to me," Fran said.

"Why, what are you going to do?"

"I'm the shortest. I'm going to crawl up the beach along the brush line. The guys will never see me. Then, I'm going to jump up, and knock 'em in the head with the flashlight."

I admired her guts, but ... "That's too dangerous."

She held her palms up. "What else can we do? We're sitting ducks with nowhere to hide. If we do nothing, the goon will probably shoot us on sight." She nodded at Rich. "A person who'd do that wouldn't hesitate to kill us."

I closed my eyes. Fran was right, of course. I let out a long breath. "Be careful."

Crouched low, Fran sloshed around the rock and started crawling on all fours. Ruthie and I locked eyes, barely daring to breathe. We could hear the splashing, it was getting closer. I thought of Zack, Jr. and Ann and wondered if I'd ever see them again. Had I told my children I loved them the last time we spoke? If I got out of this alive, I'd be sure to tell them every time we talked in the future.

Suddenly the sloshing stopped and a male voice mumbled, "What the—?"

To the south, lights flashed and a cacophonous cry tore through the darkness. The Klingons must have landed. Then, to our left, a shrill scream from Frannie, a dull thump, and a big splash. As we strained to make out Frannie May, a shrill whine—like Fourth of July fireworks—streaked across the ocean. A moment later, there was a burst of light that lit up the sky—the Atlas V.

With the light from the rocket, I searched for Fran. She was hanging on the back of a very tall man. As the rocket rose higher, I made out a wild hairdo—dreadlocks—on the man's head. Gawd, it was Sidney and Frannie was hanging from his neck, kicking his butt for all she was worth.

Chapter 19

"Ruthie, that's Sidney," I shrieked. "Get Fran off his back!"

Ruthie disentangled herself from Penny Sue and took off down the beach. Penny Sue's head hit the rock with a good thump, jarring her awake. She looked at me, trying to focus. "Leigh? Where are we?"

"Don't move. You've hit your head, you may have a concussion."

"Rich?"

"He's alive. Don't worry, Rich'll be fine." I wished my confidence matched my words.

By this time, Ruthie, Fran, and Sidney arrived at the rock. Sidney, rubbing his backside, kept a safe distance from Fran.

Fran raised her hands. "How was I to know he was FBI?"

Sidney rolled his eyes. "Do you really think Vulture has blacks in his gang?"

"I didn't know what color you were—it was dark, and I only saw your back." Fran looked at me. "I did what any patriot would do."

Sidney waved off her comment, kneeling beside Rich. "Don't worry, I'm not pressing assault charges. I know you meant well. How is Rich?" Sidney asked me, pulling out a flashlight and shining it on Rich's face. "Whoa! They did a number on him, didn't they?" Sidney reached in his pocket and pulled out a radio. "This is Shorty. I've found the Fox and we have a serious medical situation." He glanced at Penny Sue. "Make that two. We need a chopper with a medical team at these coordinates."

Literally a moment later, I heard choppers coming from the south.

Sidney saw my expression. "That's not for us. That's the Cape's security. Something big went on down there."

"Yes, and we know what it was," I said. "Fran's son and his friends stopped Vulture from shooting down the Atlas with a Stinger missile. We found an email on Rich's computer, indicating Vulture was planning to do it."

Fran pulled Sidney's sleeve, and pointed at his radio. "Call someone now, and tell them not to hurt my son. He saved the country. That rocket had a nuclear-powered satellite. If it weren't for them, we'd all be glowing." She tugged his sleeve harder, and gave Sidney the *look*. "Call, tell them not to hurt the Klingons and Navy Seals."

Sidney's eyes narrowed doubtfully, but he pushed the button on the device and spoke. "Shorty here. There may be civilian vigilantes—"

Fran poked his arm. "Patriots!"

Sidney gave her a look. "Cancel that. Civilian *patriots* may be on site. I don't think you'll have any trouble identifying them." He snickered. "Some are Klingons."

"Come back, Shorty. I missed the last part," the voice on the other end said.

"You got it right. The Klingons and some Navy Seals supposedly thwarted the gang's attempt to shoot down the Atlas rocket. Use discretion. Over."

The guy on the other end laughed hysterically, but finally gasped, "Copy that. Will do."

A few minutes later a helicopter with a big spotlight on the front rumbled up from the south. "That would be ours," Sidney said. He stood up and waved his arms. His radio chirped.

"Patrick Rescue Wing responding to a general call for aid. What's your status?"

"Two severely injured. We need backboards, neck braces, and a quick trip to a trauma center."

The helicopter pinpointed us in its spotlight and hovered overhead. "Roger that. We're sending down two paramedics." An arm swung from an open door on the side of the helicopter with a basket attached. Within minutes, two men were lowered to our location. They scrambled out of the basket, gave a hand signal, and the basket rose. A few minutes later a stretcher-type contraption was lowered in its place.

The medics quickly examined Rich and Penny Sue. By then, Penny Sue was fairly lucid, though they insisted she stay still and threatened to sedate her if she didn't. Sidney positioned himself beside her and kept his large hands on her shoulders, as the medics fastened a neck brace on Rich, lifted him slightly, and slid a backboard beneath. They strapped him to the board, then secured the board to the stretcher. A moment later, Rich rose into the air.

Penny Sue watched this with a mixture of relief and horror. "I'm afraid of heights; besides, I feel fine."

A paramedic hovered over Penny Sue with a flashlight. He turned her head to the side and took note of a massive bruise on her jaw. Whether that was the result of Red's slug at the Cabbage Patch or something that happened later, I didn't know. I also noticed, for the first time, that she had a beaut of a shiner. Gawd, what had she been through?

The medic flashed the light in her eyes several times and shook his head. By then, the stretcher had descended with another backboard, neck brace, and blankets. "Bring me a blanket, I think she's going into shock." Seconds later they had her on the backboard, covered in the blanket and on the stretcher.

"I hate heights," Penny Sue wailed.

Ruthie rushed to her side and stroked her forehead. "Say the mantra *OM-M, OM-M,* over and over. That's the highest vibration of all the mantras, it will protect you."

Penny Sue looked up, a tear sliding from the corner of her eye. "Okay, I'll say it for me and Rich."

The medic gave the signal, and Penny Sue started to rise. The higher she went the louder the *OM-M's* became until she was safely in the helicopter.

The basket came down, and the medics prepared to leave. "Wait, where are you taking them? I need to call Penny Sue's father," I said, catching the arm of one of the medics.

"Halifax Trauma Center in Daytona Beach."

The basket rose, and we stared at Sidney. "Now what?"

As the chopper plop-plopped into the distance, Sidney's tall pal, Frank, and a slew of park rangers swooped in on All Terrain Vehicles. We quickly filled them in on our rescue operation and the fact that we'd left Red and Spike in the palmetto scrub.

"Tunnels in the scrub?" a burly ranger scoffed. "Impossible, we'd have seen them."

"They're virtually invisible. We had a hard time finding the entrance with GPS," Ruthie said.

"If they're so well hidden, how did you find them in the first place?"

"Infrared," Fran replied tersely.

The ranger shook his head, but motioned for three others to follow him down the beach to search for Red.

We headed north in the ATVs. A half-hour later, we were standing next to Saul's truck, which was surrounded by a bunch of cars and jeeps.

"How did you find us?" I asked Sidney as he held out his hand for the key to Saul's truck.

Fran relinquished it sheepishly. "I have good insurance," was all she said.

Sidney smiled at Fran. "I'll bet you do." Then to me, "I put a GPS transponder on the truck bumper." He pointed at a black disc on the back of the truck.

"When?"

"When you stalled at the light on Peninsula."

"That was you?" Frannie May said. "I thought it was the kid who lives next door."

"I've been keeping an eye on you since Vulture killed my partner, Sammy."

"The guy behind Penny Sue's car?" I asked.

He nodded.

"I'm sorry. But, why were you following us?"

"Rich asked me to. He knew Penny Sue might come looking for him and feared for her safety. He'd also found out you," he looked at Ruthie and me, "were responsible for Vulture's brother being jailed on your last visit."

Ruthie and I stared at each other. My gawd, it was— we didn't have to say the name.

"All Vulture knew was that the snitch was a rich bitch from Georgia who drove a yellow Mercedes. With Penny Sue's car, it didn't take much to put two and two together."

"Vulture was the person taking shots at Penny Sue's license plate?"

"Yeah, he noticed the car when he nailed Sammy. Pure coincidence—same with Penny Sue's weird encounter with Red. We were watching both you and Red at the Pub that night. We couldn't believe it when you ran into each other."

"Penny Sue thought you were Sidney Poitier's son."

Sidney chuckled. "I wish." He handed the truck key to Frank.

"Are we going to jail?" Ruthie asked, her voice shaky.

"You trespassed and destroyed government property, among other things. I doubt you'll do hard time if you make restitution," he said blithely.

"What does that mean?" Fran snapped anxiously.

"Pay for the damage."

Our Italian friend held up her hands. "No problem, I have good insurance."

"We're taking you to the Ranger Station for questioning. That's the closest Federal facility."

"What about my son? Do you know anything about him? Are the boys all right?"

Sidney stepped away and spoke into his radio. After several minutes, he came back. "Agents on site think they have everyone sorted out. Your Klingon and Seal buddies will be brought to the station, too."

"Is everyone all right?" I asked anxiously.

"A couple of minor injuries were treated on the scene. Medics will check them out en route. If anyone needs additional treatment, they'll be taken to the hospital."

"Did your contact mention Carl Annina?"

"Your son?" Sidney asked Fran.

She nodded solemnly.

"Only that he and his friends were smart and gutsy."

Fran beamed.

* * *

It was a little after four in the afternoon when we got back to Fran's place. To say we were exhausted is an understatement. But, it could have been worse, we could be sitting in jail. Actually, at that point, I was so tired, I didn't much care.

Sidney took the lead in the interrogations, which weren't so bad, even with all the snickers and grunts from the park rangers. Fortunately, the tale was so outrageous, the Feds agreed we couldn't be making it up. And Sidney said he sure as hell didn't want to go before a judge and explain how a bunch of Klingons with lasers and paintball guns had accomplished what they should have done—stop the attack. And, the rangers didn't want to admit that a bunch of geeks, as they put it, discovered tunnels that were built right under their nose.

Roger, Saul, and Bobby got the worst of the tongue-lashing. "You should have known better," Sidney yelled. "You're grown men, trained professionals. You could have gotten these kids," he motioned to the Klingons, "killed."

There was also the issue that Bobby and his friends were carrying real weapons, such as assault rifles. Thankfully, they'd had the good sense to ditch it all when the security forces arrived, making it impossible to prove what belonged to whom, considering the huge arsenal Vulture had stashed at the site. Finally, there was the problem of the pontoon boat and whether Bobby had stolen it from the Marine Center. Joseph, the director, was an ex-Marine who loved trading war stories with Bobby. So, when Joseph heard what had happened and that the boat had not been damaged, he stated forcefully that he'd given Bobby permission to use the pontoon.

Case dwindling, Sidney and the park rangers conferred, eventually coming to the conclusion that charges would not be pressed against Bobby or any of us—provided, Rich's computer was returned and all the damage was paid for.

"No problem, she has good insurance," Ruthie and I said in unison, thumbs cocked at Frannie May. Everyone laughed.

In fact, Sidney obviously had real admiration for Bobby, Saul, and especially Roger, who'd gotten nasty cuts on his cheek and arm from Vulture's switchblade. In spite of his injuries, the big guy tackled the missile launcher in time to divert the Stinger from a direct path, giving the Atlas added seconds to get out of range. The Stinger fell harmlessly into the ocean.

Our interrogation finished, Frank insisted on taking Roger to a hospital to confer with a plastic surgeon about the slash on his cheek. Several of the park rangers slapped the Klingons on the back and asked if they could join in the games. Bobby and Saul headed out to check on his truck.

"Don't worry, Saul. I'll pay for the buggies and all the damage," Frannie May called.

Sidney offered to drive us home, which we gratefully accepted. We rode in silence until we turned into Fran's driveway. He stopped the car and got out to open our doors. He had on a serious FBI face. We thanked him profusely for his help and understanding, and his face cracked into a wide grin. "You ladies are a real piece of work. Try to stay out of trouble from now on."

We waved as he pulled out of the driveway. As soon as he turned onto Peninsula, Ruthie poked Fran on the arm. "Open the door, I have to go to the bathroom."

Ruthie flew into the half bath off the foyer, Fran went straight to her suite for a shower, and I poured a glass of wine and prepared to check our messages at the condo. I'd contacted the judge from the ranger station and suspected he was already in Daytona Beach at Penny Sue's side. I'd also called Zack, but couldn't get him, so left a message. I'd debated calling Ted from the ranger station, but didn't. It was a call from him that I feared might be on the machine.

I took a big gulp of the wine and hoped he hadn't heard about our little escapade. It would definitely be better if he heard it from me, so I could gloss over the details.

I dialed the number of the condo, punched in the remote code, and waited with bated breath. Instead of a peeved Ted, Ann's voice sounded. "Mom, I called Dad about the frequent flyer miles, and he told me what happened. Are you all right? What about Penny Sue? I've called your cell phone a hundred times.

"I talked to Patrick and he agrees our meeting can wait, that I should fly home to be with you. He called the Ambassador, who gave special permission for me to take some time off. Daddy will pay for the ticket. His secretary checked, and I can fly straight from London to Sanford, Florida. His secretary said that's close to New Smyrna Beach.

"Mom, call as soon as you get this. I'm frantic to hear from you!"

Eyes brimming, I clicked off. If there were other messages, they could wait. This was the most important one. I wiped my eyes. Geez, maybe I needed some of that black cohosh, too. I took another sip of wine and went to the doorway of Fran's suite. "Do you mind if I call Ann in London?"

The shower door clicked. "Hell, no. Be my guest."

My eyes went round. A profane word passed through Fran's lips!

Since I was talking on Frannie's nickel, I gave Ann the abbreviated version of the story. She didn't need to know the details—it would only worry her. I did make a point of mentioning how brilliant and rich Fran's son, Carl, was several times. How he'd almost single-handedly saved the

East Coast. Slight exaggeration, but hey, I was stressed myself. Besides, the important thing was that Ann was coming to visit me next weekend! Zack (or his secretary) had gotten her a seat on a plane to Sanford and she could stay for four days.

What do you know? Zack did have a kind streak left, after all.

"Baby, I'm fine and can't wait to see you." I struggled to hold back tears. "I'll call you tomorrow. We need to check on Penny Sue."

Ruthie emerged from the bathroom at the same time Fran appeared from her bedroom, clean, dressed, with full make-up. She winked at my juice glass of wine, snagged a new bottle from the wine rack over her sink, and took stemmed glasses from the china cabinet in the dining room. "I think we should toast ourselves in style."

We clicked the glasses together, which emitted the unmistakable ping of expensive crystal. I quickly filled them in on Ann and we toasted again.

"We should go see Penny Sue," Fran said. "After what she's been through, we don't want her sitting in a cold hospital alone."

"You're right. I suspect the judge is there, but if he's not ... I need to shower and change." Ruthie nodded agreement and stood up.

"You take a quick shower. I'll call the hospital and florist," Fran said.

In thirty minutes, Ruthie and I were clean, dressed and waiting downstairs. Ruthie, sweetheart that she was, had even packed a small bag of a gown, underwear, and make-up for Penny Sue. "You know she's fit to be tied if she doesn't have her lipstick."

Fran entered the foyer with her purse hooked over her arm. "They're holding Penny Sue overnight for observation. Rich is in stable condition. Apparently, they're sharing the same room at Penny Sue's request."

"You're kidding?"

"That's what the hospital said."

Ready to go, there was a moment of indecision about whose car to take. Fran's was at the Marine Center. Mine was available, but small. So was Penny Sue's, which had remained parked because of Vulture's potshots. With Vulture in the slammer somewhere—hopefully, far away—we decided to take Penny Sue's Mercedes.

An hour later we stood outside Penny Sue's room where Frank, Sidney's tall sidekick, sat on a bench next to Ted.

"Ted," I said sheepishly. "I guess you heard."

He stood and pulled me close. "Yep, you ladies are the talk of the town again."

I buried my face on his shoulder, feeling teary-eyed, as the fear and trauma of the last twenty-four hours washed through me. Ted must have sensed it, because he brushed his lips through my hair, then held me at arms length and grinned. "What am I going to do with you?" He released his hold and turned to face Ruthie and Fran. "What am I going to do with all of you? You're magnets for trouble. You're like Lucille Ball and Ethel Mertz times two. I wasn't trained for this at the academy." He turned to Frank. "Were you?"

The big guy stretched his legs and lounged lei-surely. "Nope. A course on wacky women wasn't part of the curriculum."

"Wacky?" Fran repeated with a frown. "Try gutsy, kick-ass patriots."

Chuckling, Frank did a palms up. "Whatever you say. Your tactics were *unusual,* but you got the job done."

"How's Roger?" Ruthie asked.

"Downstairs waiting for a plastic surgeon." Frank chuckled. "You know, Roger thinks he's a Klingon."

"We had an inkling of that."

"He wanted to keep the battle scar. I finally convinced him that the one on his arm was enough. No sense ruining his sweet baby face for womankind." Frank laughed again. "That guy's a trip. I'll bet Vulture messed in his pants when Roger came after him ... I might have. Vulture got in a lick or two, but Roger only needed one punch. Word is, Vulture has a bad concussion."

I nodded at the door. "What's the deal?"

"Judge Parker's in there with Penny Sue. She's not seriously hurt. Bruises, slight concussion, maybe. They're going to keep her for observation."

"Rich?"

"In there, too. That's why I'm here," Frank said. "He was working undercover for us, and we don't intend to let anything else happen to him."

"How bad is he?"

"You saw him—beat to a pulp by those maniacs. No serious internal damage, it seems. Believe it or not, the shot Red gave him was a painkiller. I guess she really cared for him."

My eyebrows shot up. Who would have guessed?

"Can we go in?" Ruthie asked.

Frank waved toward the door. "Be my guest."

"Did the flowers arrive?" Fran said.

"Not yet."

There was a commotion at the end of the hall as a large cart filled with floral arrangements was wheeled our way.

"That must be them. The florist promised to have them here in an hour."

Frank gave Frannie May a look. "Nothing goes into that room until I check it. We almost lost Rich once, and we're not taking any more chances. In fact, I should frisk you and search that bag." He pointed to the satchel Ruthie'd brought for Penny Sue.

Fran held up her hand. "Be my guest, check the flowers," then rushed through the door.

I turned to Ted. "Will you be here for a while?"

He brushed my hair off my forehead. "Yeah, I'll be here. Don't have to go back on duty for another few hours."

I stroked his arm. "That's great. I don't think we'll be long." I waved as I followed Ruthie into the room.

The judge held Penny Sue's hand and stroked her forehead lovingly. It was such a sweet scene, I almost teared up. Heavens, I'd better get some of that black cohosh, fast.

Ruthie went to the judge and rubbed his back. "How are you, sir? How's Penny Sue?"

"I'm fine!" Penny Sue struggled to a sitting position, took her father's hand and kissed it. "Daddy, you really don't have to stroke my forehead."

"Sweetpea—"

Sweetpea? That was a new one.

"—you loved it as a child."

"I did, Daddy, but it messes up my make-up."

I shook my head. No make-up left to mess up.

Penny Sue scowled. Ruthie handed her a compact and lipstick.

"Oh, shit," Penny Sue exclaimed, catching her image in the mirror. She smeared on some lipstick and handed back the mirror.

"Rich?" I asked.

"The doctor's in with him now." She nodded at the curtain separating their beds. Her eyes welled with tears and she lowered her voice. "He's going into the witness protection program. I may never see him again." The judge stroked her forehead. "His wife had cancer, you know that. Anyway, she was in a lot of pain and hospice doctors prescribed some pretty powerful painkillers. After her death, Rich was so distraught, he used the remaining narcotics to dull his pain. He got hooked, which is how he got caught up with Vulture's bunch. They were selling drugs to finance their arms deals.

"Rich was buying drugs from one of Vulture's branches in Georgia. Rich was busted in a raid, and rather than go to jail, agreed to work with the Feds undercover. He had previous police experience, which made him a natural. In the course of the drug investigation, he realized it was a lot bigger, and the drugs were funding arms purchases.

"Rich was working with Sammy—Sidney's partner— who'd infiltrated Vulture's gang. Somehow, Vulture became suspicious of Sammy and knocked him off. My car was in

the background and the rest is history." She paused. "Did
you hear why Vulture had it in for me?"

"Yes, the old two-headed coin. Who would have
guessed?"

The flowers were wheeled in at the same time as a gurney. Hospital volunteers put the bouquets on the windowsill,
as transporters lifted Rich onto the gurney.

"What's going on?" I demanded.

Sidney appeared in the doorway. He walked over to the
judge and Penny Sue. "The doctors say Rich is stable. We're
going to transfer him to a safer place. Vulture's locked up,
but he has ties to militant extremists and arms dealers. Rich
isn't safe here."

Penny Sue started to cry. I started to cry. Ruthie cried.
Only Fran and the judge didn't cry, and they looked close.

"Can I have a moment alone with him?" Penny Sue
sobbed.

Sidney nodded and herded us out of the room. We paced
in the hall, avoiding each other's eyes, trying to keep our
emotions in check. Ted came over and gave me a hug. Finally,
the gurney emerged from the room, and Rich gave us the
thumbs up.

I glanced up at Ted, my tears flowing uncontrollably.
He stroked my hair and nodded toward the door.

We all rushed in to Penny Sue.

She looked up at us and smiled. "He'll be back."

Read an excerpt from Book One
of the DAFFODILS Series

The
Turtle Mound
Murder

Chapter 1

"Damn, girl, you look like hell!"

I slid into the booth next to the window at the Admiral's Dinghy, a locals' hangout in the restored district of Roswell. Penelope Sue Parker, my long-time friend and sorority sister, was already finishing a glass of wine. From the gleam in Penny Sue's eye, it might have been her second.

"Thanks, that makes me feel real good," I said sarcastically.

Penny Sue studied me, sipping wine, sunlight bouncing off the two-carat diamond on her right hand. "You look like you haven't slept in a year. Heavens, you have dark circles under your eyes." She raised her glass, signaling the waiter. "What's wrong, honey? You still depressed?"

"I'm going to change my name," I said in a rush.

"I don't blame you. I'd get rid of that skunk Zack's name as soon as possible. I'm surprised you haven't done it sooner. As far as I'm concerned, you'll always be Becky Martin."

"Leigh," I corrected. The waiter arrived with two glasses of wine. I stared at the glass the waiter put in front of me. "What's this, Penny Sue? You know I shouldn't drink; I've been taking antidepressants off and on for months."

"Pooh, one little glass of wine won't kill you. It'll help you relax." Penny Sue pouted, fingering the substantial emerald hanging from her neck. "What's this stuff about Leigh?"

"My middle name. I'm sick of being Becky. Good old Becky; sweet, cute Becky; dumb shit, blind Becky."

"You were just too trusting," my friend assured me.

Stupid, trusting, the label made no difference; Zachary Stratton had played me for a fool. As soon as the kids were off to college, my loving husband took up woodworking. Each night when I went to bed, he'd retire to his shop in the garage for a couple of hours. A partner in Atlanta's most prestigious law firm, Zack claimed rubbing and sanding wood relieved the stress of his hectic day.

Wood, hell—it was silicon breasts!

While I snored blissfully, Zack sneaked out to meet a strip club dancer he'd set up in a house a few blocks away. The scam worked for over a year until Ann, our younger, was picked up for DUI late one night. I rushed to the garage to tell Zack. The tools were cold, and his car was gone.

A staunch believer in a person's right to privacy, I'd never intruded on Zack's domain. I made an exception that night. In a matter of minutes, I found a carton of wooden figurines identical to the ones he claimed to have made. In a sickening flash I realized the find's implications and gagged, recalling the times I'd ooed and awed over the silly statues. Rage suppressed the tears and gave me the strength to carry the box to the center of the garage. When Zack returned home, I was waiting, feet propped up on Exhibit A.

"I'm forty-six; Becky is a child's name." I took a drink of wine and glared. "Leigh, now there's a woman's name. Momma got it from *Gone With the Wind*. You know, Scarlett, Vivien Leigh. I deserve that name, don't you think?"

"Absolutely," Penny Sue said, raising her glass in salute, "Leigh it is. What in the world brought this on?"

"My therapist said it would help me release the past."

"Are you still seeing that squirrelly guy downtown?"

"No, I gave him up months ago. He was too strange."

Penny Sue threw back her head and laughed. "Of course, dear, he's a therapist. They're all weird. You teach what you need to learn." The New Age explanation for the purpose of life, the phrase was Penny Sue's pat answer to everything. "Why did you drop Dr. Nerd?"

I scanned the room to see who might be listening. "The jerk crossed the line when he suggested I attend a Sufi ceremony, saying a novel experience would help my depression. It was novel, all right. By the time I arrived, everyone was naked, lying in a pile. My therapist was on the bottom."

Penny Sue snorted with amusement. "Figures. I would have guessed as much. What about that other one? The attitude healer in Vinings? Did you ever try her?"

"Yes, lord, another dead end."

"What happened? Ruthie said she was good."

I sat back and folded my arms. "That's not saying much—Ruthie hasn't been right since she drove off the bridge and cracked her head. I signed up for the *Heal Your Mind, Heal Your Life* workshop, figuring it would give me a chance to see the therapist in action, before going for a private session. Am I glad I did; that lady's in dire need of analysis herself.

"Waltzes in the first meeting and announces she's a reincarnated priestess from ancient Egypt. Then, she starts in on visualizing the future we want." I waved expansively. "Nothing wrong with that; except we can't just imagine it, we've got to visualize her way. We have to cut out pictures from magazines and make paper dolls. She did it, too. All her pictures came from bridal magazines. Paper dolls? Bridal magazines? Does that tell you something? And I'm supposed to follow her advice? Yeah, right."

Penny Sue chuckled. "That explains why Ruthie liked her. Ruthie's always had a fetish for wedding gowns. Remember how she wore one to the Old South Ball at Kappa Alpha each year?"

"I'd forgotten about that. The gown wasn't so bad, it was the veil—"

"With sunglasses! Wasn't she a sight?"

"How's Ruthie doing anyway?" I asked.

"The same. Lives with her father; works on charities and an occasional political campaign. She's still into New Age stuff; you know, meditation and crystals. You should give her a call. She's always going to meetings and seances. I've been a few times, it's fun. Nothing else, it would get you out of the house."

I leaned forward. I could already feel the effects of the wine. "Maybe I will." Getting out with people was what I needed; I knew I'd become almost reclusive, dreading the thought of running into old friends and having to re-tell the story of The Big Split. Yet, the loneliness fed the depression, which made me more reclusive, and on and on until there was nothing except a dark emptiness. A great, gaping void in the center of my chest; a black hole which could not be filled by therapy or pills. "Does Ruthie ever date?"

Penny Sue said, "Heavens no, she'll never remarry, at least as long as her father's alive."

Ruthie's father was J.T. Edwards, a retired railroad executive who lived in a restored mansion in Buckhead. I blinked back tears. "Probably just as well."

"What's got you so down?"

I blotted my eyes with the back of my hand. "Zack moved out last week while I was visiting my folks."

"That's terrific news! Y'all living under the same roof while you fought over the property settlement was sick. I told Daddy so." Penny Sue's daddy was Judge Warren Parker, founder of Zachary's firm. "Daddy likes you and feels bad about the situation, but Zack's a valuable asset to the firm, because of his connections with the telephone people. They love him."

"Naturally," I said. "He takes them to strip joints whenever they come to town. That's how Zack met Ms. Thong."

"Who?"

"His little lap dancer. I found a picture of her in a silver thong bikini at the bottom of Zack's sock drawer."

Penny Sue shrugged. "Daddy promised to have a word with Zack, advise him to give you a fair shake. You know, fifty-fifty."

My cheeks flamed. "It worked," I said, trying hard to control my anger. "Mr. Fairness took half of everything in the house. Half of the pictures on the walls, half of each set of china, and half of the furniture, right down to one of Jack, Jr.'s twin beds."

"Half the Wedgwood?" Penny Sue asked. I nodded. "No wonder you're depressed."

"The Wedgwood's the least of my worries, he could have had it all. It was the spite that gets me. We're supposed to sign off on the property settlement tomorrow. I can't imagine what else he's got up his sleeve. A person who'd take half the sheets— I mean all the top sheets, no bottoms—is capable of anything."

"No doubt." Penny Sue drained her glass and clicked it down. "Girl, you need a vacation."

"Vacation? After tomorrow I may not be able to afford lunch. Besides, I have to sell the house."

"Hire a realtor; you need a change of scenery. New Smyrna Beach is beautiful in the fall, and Daddy hardly ever uses his condo anymore. Remember what a good time we had there in college? Come on, Beck—er, Leigh—it'll be relaxing, do you a world of good."

"I'll see how the settlement goes," I replied.

Thankfully, the waiter arrived to take our order, shutting Penny Sue down. I chose the Caesar salad, while she ordered quiche with a Dinghy Dong for dessert.

"A Dinghy Dong? Isn't that the extra large chocolate eclair?" Penny Sue cut me a look. "So?"

"Comfort food? What's wrong, did you breakup with the Atlanta Falcon?"

Penny Sue raked a hand through her meticulously streaked hair. "Honey, I'm dating a Falcon *and* a Brave, now. But, a

Dinghy Dong's something else; I always have room for one of them."

From Parker, Hanson, and Swindal's twenty-third floor conference room in downtown Atlanta, the people on the street looked like ants foraging for crumbs. I could sympathize, I had a bad feeling that's what I'd be doing at the end of the day.

I should never have quit my job, I thought ruefully. Until the fateful night when I found out about Zack, I'd been a part-time bookkeeper for a local car dealership. Money wasn't the issue, though I enjoyed having funds of my own. The job gave me a sense of purpose, something to think about other than bridge and local gossip. But I couldn't concentrate and started making mistakes after I discovered Zack's other life. Afraid I might do serious damage, like fouling up an IRS report, I decided to quit.

Although most of my sorority sisters were pampered Southern belles, my family was a hundred percent middle class. I was one of only two sorority pledges who had not "come out" at a debutante ball. That never bothered me, or them, for that matter. By my senior year I was president of the sorority and a regular at all the posh, hotsy-totsy balls.

Which was how I got hooked up with Zachary. A six-foot-one handsome blond from a poor, farming family, Zack was in his last year of law school when we met. He'd dated Penny Sue initially, but was dumped for her first husband, Andy Walters, the amiable, if dumb, captain of the football team.

I see now what a shameless social climber Zack was. I suppose he figured that if he couldn't have Penny Sue, I was an acceptable second, since I traveled in all the same circles. Second indeed. Considering Zack's lackluster grades and dirt farming roots, Parker, Hanson, and Swindal would never have given him a glance if it hadn't been for my friendship with Penny Sue.

Which was an ironic twist—I set Zack up in the firm that was about to squash me like an ant. I turned my back to the window angrily. Well, this was one bug that wasn't going to roll over and die.

I sat at the end of the conference table and fished a thick file of documents from my briefcase. Where was my attorney? Max Bennett promised to come early. He knew I didn't want to face Zack alone, especially on his own turf. How could Max be so insensitive? *Easy, he's male and a lawyer*, I answered my own question.

I had really wanted a female attorney, but decided a woman would be powerless against Zack's firm and the Atlanta good-ol'-boy network. Bradford Davis was handling Zack's case, a PH&S senior partner whose great-great-grandfather was a Confederate General who defended Atlanta in the War of Northern Aggression. I figured I needed a legal heavyweight of my own. I chose Max because his ancestors on his mother's side went back to Colonial times, and he'd handled several high profile divorces with good results. In any event, he'd seemed nice enough the few times we'd chatted at charity events and cocktail parties.

Appearances can sure be deceiving. However the day turned out, I would be happy to be rid of Max Bennett. I'd had a bellyful of his red, sweaty face; off-color jokes and patronizing remarks— not to mention the fact that he hadn't done one thing right.

The process had dragged on for nearly two years because Max couldn't or wouldn't stand up to Bradford Davis. The present meeting had been postponed four times at Bradford's request, once to accommodate a state bar golf tournament. In fact, Max was so openly solicitous of Bradford, I'd wondered if the two had something going on the side. I voiced the theory to Penny Sue, figuring she might have some insight since her second husband had turned out to be bisexual.

"Who can tell?" Penny Sue said. "Even straight men act like a pack of dogs, sniffing each other and posturing. All that butt slapping and carrying on, it's in their genes, goes back to ancient Greece where they played sports in the nude."

The idea of Max and Bradford romping around buck-naked was too much. I laughed out loud at the very moment Max, Bradford and Zack arrived. Clearly thinking I was snickering at them, each instinctively checked his fly. Even they noticed that synchronicity, which made me laugh even harder.

Scowling, Bradford and Zack took seats at the head of the table in front of an ornately framed painting of Judge Parker. Max sat next to me at the opposite end. He nodded coldly as way of greeting.

"I believe we can dispose of this matter quickly," Max said, passing a three page document to me. "Mr. Stratton provided a list of your joint assets and their market value. He wants to be fair and proposes to divide your belongings right down the middle. Since a quick sale could depress the value of your property, Mr. Stratton has offered to buy-out your share by making monthly installments over a five year period. In that way, he can dispose of the property in an orderly fashion."

I flipped to the last page of the document. The total was $1.1 million, including $550,000 for the house. "This can't be everything."

Max cleared his throat. "Uh, no, it does not include household furnishings, which have already been divided, or personal items such as your cars."

The total was far too low. My rough calculation put our assets at well over two million. I scanned the list. All the values were ridiculously low, and a number of investments were missing altogether. Zack was trying to cheat me, just as I'd feared. "These estimates are wrong," I said loudly, staring defiantly at Zack.

Bradford smirked. "You must remember, Becky dear, that the markets have been off the last few years."

"Leigh," I corrected.

"As you wish, *Leigh*," Bradford replied, putting particular emphasis on my name as if it had a bad taste. Zack snorted with amusement. "Names aside," Bradford continued pompously, "the property was evaluated by Walker & Hill, the most reputable *independent* appraiser in Atlanta. Surely, you cannot find fault with that."

Independent, hell! Zack played golf with Taylor Hill at least twice a month. I gave Max a pleading look. He patted my hand and flashed a thin, sleazy smile. I wanted to backhand him in the mouth. Luckily, Judge Parker entered the room at that moment and stood by the door, listening. I was too angry to meet his eyes.

"In our experience, it is difficult to get full value from the disposal of community property," Bradford continued. "Buyers expect bargain basement prices in the case of a divorce. It's very difficult to overcome that mind set."

"I've found the same thing in my practice," Max chimed in.

I glared at him. *Who's side are you on?* I wanted to scream. Of course, I knew the answer: he was a good-ol'-boy, a member of the *club*, and they were all going to stick together. "What about the stocks and bonds?" I demanded through tight lips.

Bradford consulted another list. "The securities were liquidated last November to take care of family debts."

November? Zack went to the Caribbean on business in November. Could he have sold the stocks and deposited the money in an off-shore bank? "What debts?" I demanded hotly. "I want to see proof."

"General household expenses." Bradford looked to Max. "We provided all of this to your attorney. There were several credit cards—"

Credit cards? "I haven't seen any proof!" Could Zack have spent that much money on his stripper? Then, it dawned on me. Zack had opened a bunch of accounts, taken-out cash advances and deposited the money in tropical banks. What a sneaky jerk ... all our savings gone and I didn't have a prayer of finding it.

Bradford continued, "Your attorney has reviewed these documents. We've also filed a copy with Judge Nugent. Of course, the judge would like a property settlement before he grants the final decree."

I pushed the paper away. "This is not fair; Zack has hidden our assets. I won't sign it." I caught Judge Parker from the corner of my eye; he winked and canted his head. I wasn't sure what that meant, and Bradford gave me no time to think about it.

He slammed his folder shut. "That is your prerogative, Mrs. Stratton," Bradford intoned snobbishly. "However, I caution you that a court battle could be *very* long and expensive."

The emphasis on *very* was crystal clear. While Bradford was probably handling Zack's case for free, I had to pay my own legal fees. Max's tab already topped $30,000. Holding out for a trial might double or triple the bill. And, what did I stand to gain? Nothing. The good-ol'-boys would protect each other to the end. I glanced at the Judge who nodded slightly. Damn, I hated giving in! But, the deck was stacked against me, it was time to throw-in my hand. My eyes stung with tears, from frustration more than anything. I blinked them back and raised my chin resolutely; I would not give those men the satisfaction of seeing me cry.

I jabbed Max with my elbow, hard. "Give me a pen," I spat the words. He rolled his chair back and handed me a Cross ballpoint. I signed the document with an angry flourish, pocketed the pen, and strode stiffly past Judge Parker and out of Zack's life.

* * *

I called my therapist as soon as I got home.

"How do you feel?"

"Angry, betrayed, hurt. Those men made me so mad." I

tugged my scarf off and wrapped it around my fist, wishing it was Zack's throat.

"No one can make you feel anything. You choose your feelings. If you're mad, you've chosen to feel that way."

Chosen to feel that way? Those scuzz balls ganged up on me. "It's the injustice that angers me. No one—not even my own lawyer—did a thing to help me. Bradford, Max, and Zack walked in *together*. Don't you see, it was a done deal before anything was said. I was set up!"

"So, you feel like a victim?"

"Yes, I'd like to cut off their private parts and hang them from their ears." I unraveled the scarf and pulled it tight, like a rope.

"Violence doesn't solve anything, does it?"

"For godssakes, I wouldn't really do it. It's a fantasy; a delicious fantasy at this moment." I balled the scarf up into a tight ball.

"Lashing out is a common reaction to situations like this. Let's talk about it. I can work you in tomorrow morning at eleven."

"I'll get back to you." I slammed down the receiver. *Lashing out is a common reaction.* I hurled the scarf against the wall. Damn! Then, I drew the blinds and went to bed feeling more depressed than I'd ever felt in my life.

But, sleep did not save me. My head had hardly hit the pillow when I was awakened by the sound of a siren ... no, the doorbell. And shouting.

"LEIGH. BECK-KKY LEEE-EIGH. We know you're in there."

It was Penny Sue. I had on my slip and didn't bother to find a robe. I looked through the peephole at the optically-widened images of Penny Sue and Ruthie, who was holding a gigantic bouquet of flowers. I cracked the door; Penny Sue barged through.

"Get dressed, girl. We're going to celebrate."

"Celebrate what?"

"The divorce, of course. Free at last, free at last. Praise the Lord, free at last! Besides, you're now qualified to be in the DAFFODILS."

Ruthie thrust a vase of daffodils into my face as Penny Sue fastened a silver and gold brooch to my slip strap. Both women were wearing the same pin, a circular swirl of graceful leaves, stems and daffodils in full bloom. Penny Sue's brooch served as the clasp for a wispy Chanel scarf; Ruthie's accented the square neckline of her black silk chemise.

"The what?" I asked testily, eyeing the daffodils and brooch that hung limply from my slip strap.

Penny Sue replied, "DAFF-O-DILS: Divorced And Finally Free Of Deceitful, Insensitive, Licentious Scum."

Deceitful, Insensitive, Licentious Scum. A smile tugged at my lips. I was definitely qualified, and so were Penny Sue and Ruthie.

I figured Penny Sue had probably founded the club. Her second husband, Sydney, was a television producer who'd had an affair with his male assistant. As painful as Zack's infidelity was, at least I hadn't been thrown over for a man. The huge settlement the Judge got for Penny Sue (Daddy took Sydney's escapades very personally) undoubtedly helped. Her third husband, Winston, wasn't much better; he had an eye for young secretaries.

Ruthie had also endured her share of heartache. Harold, her ex, was a cardiologist in Raleigh, North Carolina. A heartless cardiologist at that. (Maybe Penny Sue was right about teaching what you need to learn.) Ruthie worked as a librarian to put him through medical school, only to be ditched for a nurse the week after Harold finished his residency. Not one to mope, Ruthie Jo had packed up Jo Ruth, their only child, and taken a train back to Atlanta, where she'd lived with her father ever since.

I studied the bouquet of flowers. The symbol of Spring and new beginnings, there was something intrinsically happy about a daffodil. "Where in the world did you find daffodils at this time of year?"

Penny Sue responded, "My florist in Buckhead stocks them for me."

"A lot of members in the club, huh?"

"No, I just like daffodils." Penny Sue quick-stepped a jig. "Perk up, girl, it's party time."

I ignored her antics and headed for the kitchen with the flowers, my friends following close behind. "I appreciate the offer, but it's been a terrible day. I don't feel like celebrating." I put the vase on the sideboard and filled a glass from the kitchen tap. "Want something to drink?" I asked, holding up the glass of water.

"You didn't take any pills, did ya?" Penny Sue asked, eyeing me like a mother hen.

I sat down and buried my head in my hands, the brooch clanking heavily on the tabletop. "No, nothing like that."

"Good, 'cuz we've got champagne!" Penny Sue pulled a bottle of Dom Perignon from her oversized Louis Vuitton bag as Ruthie searched the cabinets for stemmed glasses.

"What are you doing here?" I asked, accepting a glass of the fizzing liquid.

"Daddy called me," Penny Sue replied.

My spine straightened reflexively. "*Daddy?* Why didn't Daddy help me today?" I said through gritted teeth. "I was rolled, raped ... swindled. Swindled! Lord, I can't believe it took me so long to make the connection—Parker, Hanson, & SWINDAL. I never stood a chance!"

I was shouting now and it felt good. Hell with my therapist. At that moment, I chose to be mad—foot-stomping, dish-throwing mad. Mad, furious, LIVID. I gulped the sparkling wine.

"Daddy wanted to help, but he couldn't interfere overtly. He called Judge Nugent after the meeting—they go back a long way, you know. Anyhow, he asked Albert to go ahead and grant the divorce, but to take a close look at the property settlement."

"What does that mean?" I asked wearily.

"Monday: the marriage is history. Tuesday: Zack will have some explainin' to do."

"Glory, there is a God." I stood and raised my glass. "To the DAFF-O-DILS."

"DAFFODILS." We clinked our glasses.

"Now, get some clothes on. We're going to have a fancy dinner and plan our trip to the beach."

Also From Inspirational Fiction ...

**FIRST RUNNER-UP, 2001 COVR AWARD FOR FICTION
FINALIST, 2002 IPPY PRIZE FOR VISIONARY FICTION**

Is today's freak weather caused by ocean currents and global warming? Are electricity blackouts really the result of inadequate supplies? Or is something momentous about to occur ...

Starpeople

Mankind Gets A Second Chance

The Sirian Redemption

a novel by

Linda Tuck-Jenkins

The X-Files meets *The Celestine Prophecy* in this fast-paced thriller centering on ordinary people who must come to grips with alien encounters and their destiny of helping humanity make a leap in consciousness.

ISBN 0-9710429-9-3   288 pages $15.50

Read an excerpt: www.starpeoplebooks.com